SEE ALSO PROOF

ALSO BY LARRY D. SWEAZY

SEE ALSO PROOF

A MARJORIE TRUMAINE MYSTERY

LARRY D. SWEAZY

SEVENTH STREET BOOKS®
AN IMPRINT OF PROMETHEUS BOOKS
59 JOHN GLENN DRIVE • AMHERST, NY 14228
www.seventhstreetbooks.com

Published 2018 by Seventh Street Books®, an imprint of Prometheus Books

Cover image © David Buzzard / Alamy Stock Photo
Cover design by Jacqueline Nasso Cooke
Cover design © Prometheus Books

This is a work of fiction. Characters, organizations, products, locales, and events portrayed in this novel are either products of the author's imagination or used fictitiously.

Inquiries should be addressed to
Seventh Street Books
59 John Glenn Drive
Amherst, New York 14228
VOICE: 716–691–0133 • FAX: 716–691–0137
WWW.SEVENTHSTREETBOOKS.COM

22 21 20 19 18   5 4 3 2 1

Library of Congress Cataloging-in-Publication Data

Names: Sweazy, Larry D., author.
Title: See also proof : a Marjorie Trumaine mystery / Larry D. Sweazy.
Description: Amherst, NY : Seventh Street Books, 2018. | Series: Marjorie Trumaine
Identifiers: LCCN 2017056060 (print) | LCCN 2017058489 (ebook) |
    ISBN 9781633882805 (ebook) | ISBN 9781633882799 (softcover)
Subjects: LCSH: Women detectives—Fiction. | Murder—Investigation—Fiction. |
    Missing persons—Investigation—Fiction. | BISAC: FICTION / Mystery &
    Detective / Women Sleuths. | FICTION / Mystery & Detective / Historical. |
    GSAFD: Mystery fiction.
Classification: LCC PS3619.W438 (ebook) | LCC PS3619.W438 S445 2018 (print)
    | DDC 813/.6—dc23
LC record available at https://lccn.loc.gov/2017056060

Printed in the United States of America

A proper index is an intricate network of interrelation-ships. The very nature of the hierarchical arrangement implies a graded series of relationships and results in an obvious structure for access to the information.

—Nancy C. Mulvany, from *Indexing Books*

And these few golden days I'd spend with you . . .

—Maxwell Anderson

We adore chaos because we love to produce order.

—M. C. Escher

CHAPTER 1

January 1965

The closet door stood wide open and an empty cardboard box sat at my feet. My eyes brimmed with the threat of tears at the sight of my husband's shirts, all lined up, waiting to be worn. I really didn't know how I could have any sadness left inside of me. I wasn't the type of woman normally prone to crying, but I'd shed my fair share of tears since Hank's death the previous October. Once I cleared the closet of his clothes and donated them to the Ladies Aid, the last of his personal possessions would be gone.

I knew, though, that Hank's presence in objects like the Western Auto .22 rifle would never leave the house. The reliable single-shot firearm, a Revelation Model 100 bought by his father in 1935 for $13.95, had sat behind the kitchen door since the day we'd married, and I was certain the rifle would remain there until the day I died. Seed catalogs piled up on our dinner table, addressed to him, as if he still held the hope of spring in his heart and the promise of a new crop in his gaze. Medical bills and the unpaid combine payment sat on top of the catalogs, waiting for a remittance that was sure to be late. I could never get rid of everything that belonged to Hank. Our lives were so intertwined that when he stopped breathing I thought I would too.

Hank had suffered life-altering injuries in a freak hunting accident two years before. Recovery was impossible from the start. He suffered more than any good man should have to, paralyzed from the neck down and blinded by buckshot. When Hank had succumbed at the hospital in Dickinson, I knew his only regret in death was leaving me. But he'd told me over and over again that he would have rather died instantly instead of living as an invalid. I missed caring for him, as selfish as that was.

Most nights since the funeral I'd slept on the davenport with our trusted border collie, Shep, at my feet. I couldn't bear to sleep in an empty bed any more than I could part with Hank's clothes. His flannel shirts and gray Dickie work pants still held a faint smell of him; sweat, worry, and love. How could I get rid of such things?

It's too soon, I thought. *It will always be too soon.*

Shep rustled behind me, stood up from his guard post, and stalked to the bedroom door, drawing my attention away from my broken heart with a subtle growl.

The dog was always nearby, keeping an eye on me. The frigid cold demanded that Shep be inside the house by the Franklin stove, instead of sleeping out in the barn. I couldn't stand the thought of Shep freezing to death. One more loss would be too much to take. Hank, of course, had no use for an inside dog. Most farm people didn't. I took pleasure in allowing a dog to live in the house. In a time of little comfort, he gave me as much company as he could.

"What's the matter, Shep?" I said, as I shut the closet door.

Shep's pointed ears flared alert, and his haunches drew tight. He looked like a statue cut from black and white marble when he switched from best friend to loyal protector. I recognized the stance right away and expected a bark to follow his growl. Someone, or something, had come onto our land.

I glanced over at the alarm clock on the nightstand and sighed again. I had lost track of time. There was no intruder. The women from the Ladies Aid had arrived.

"Relax, Shep," I said. "Our visitors are here." I wiped my face with a damp handkerchief, hoping to clear the roadmap of grief from my eyes.

A few weeks after Hank's funeral, the pastor at our Lutheran church, John Mark Llewellyn, had encouraged me to join the Ladies Aid. I've never been much of a joiner, so I declined. My attendance at church remained sporadic, almost nonexistent in the last few years.

Pastor insisted that I needed more social interaction than his casual visits, so I'd agreed to a weekly meeting with the Ladies Aid—with reluctance—and told him if I liked the idea of belonging, then I would join. I was still in the deciding phase.

The women of the Ladies Aid arrived every Thursday at three o'clock in the afternoon. They were as prompt and reliable as the mail carrier, come rain, sleet, snow, or subzero temperatures. I had promised them the box of Hank's clothes for weeks on end but had failed to deliver. This week would be no exception.

The director, Darlys Oddsdatter, drove a 1963 Fury, red as a ripe cherry. The bright color made her car easy to find alongside the road in a snowstorm; sliding off in a ditch was a common occurrence for us all. Darlys's husband, the local dentist, Dr. Henrik Oddsdatter, tried to persuade Darlys every winter to give up her gallivanting and social duties, but she wouldn't hear of sacrificing anything because of the weather. That woman was committed to her causes with unquestioned conviction. My sanity and entrance back into society was her latest effort. I liked Darlys's dedication. Shep did, too. I think he saw a kindred spirit in Darlys. They both were happier when they had a job to do. She was my favorite of the bunch, if I had to admit such a thing.

Darlys didn't seem to mind an inside dog. The other two women of the Ladies Aid, Anna Jacobsen and Lene Harstaad, held Hank's view of animals in the house. Such a thing was an abomination, but they were too polite to say so. At least so far. Lene was uncomfortable in Shep's presence. Her judgmental gray eyes were easy to read. Anna ignored Shep. As far as I could tell, that was her way of dealing with things she didn't like.

As I opened the front door to welcome the women into my house, a strong gust of wind pushed in right along with them. Darlys led the women inside, wrapped up in a blue parka heavy enough to keep any Eskimo warm. Her snow boots could endure an Arctic expedition, and I envied the comfort of her feet. A plaid scarf protected her face, and her hands were jammed inside creamy lamb's-wool mittens bought at the A. W. Lucas department store, over in Bismarck. Darlys looked like a tall, blonde-haired Swedish fashion model no matter the time of day or the reason. Anna and Lene were dressed for a January day, too, only their hats, gloves, and scarves were all homemade, like mine.

Darlys took off her mittens and fussed over Shep. He barked and wagged his tail with so much happiness I feared it would fall off. Lene and Anna stood back at a safe distance with twin frowns on their faces.

After our hellos, I swept the intruding snowflakes back outside where they belonged, closed the door, and took the coats and hats from my visitors. Once my arms were fully loaded, I motioned for Shep to follow me. I put the coats on my unused bed and closed the dog inside the bedroom. He didn't howl or whine in my absence, thank goodness.

"Oh, your house feels nice and warm, Marjorie," Darlys said with a bright smile, heading straight to the kitchen. She had managed to freshen up her red lipstick while I was away.

The women brought food every time they visited me. They wanted to make sure that I was eating. I'd gone down a dress size since Hank had died, and I was on my way to losing two. I wasn't hungry most days, even though I knew I needed to keep my strength up. Food didn't taste good, and eating alone was something I didn't think I'd ever become fond of. I'd loved to cook for Hank.

Darlys brought cold summer sausage and Ritz crackers. Anna brought Jell-O salad, a church pitch-in staple made with canned fruit, marshmallows, and a healthy dollop of whipped cream. Lene, the oldest of the trio, nearing sixty, brought sandkakes, a delightful Norwegian shortbread cookie filled with some of her famous homemade strawberry jam. My mother had baked sandkakes, and I couldn't resist them—or strawberry jam. Lene knew that.

"Oh, that wind's gonna pick up later, don't ya know?" Anna said. She was near my age, in her mid-thirties, dressed in flannel-lined denim pants and an oversized pink sweater that was a Christmas gift knitted by her mother. Anna had three children old enough to leave with her next-door neighbor for short stretches of time. She made herself clear that volunteering for the Ladies Aid was time for herself, so her kids didn't drive her crazy. They were all out of diapers, under ten years old, and full of energy. She always said things like that with a smile, but I thought she really meant what she said.

"You'll be wantin' to get home before the snow picks up, then," I said.

Even with the sweater on, I noticed a little pooch in Anna's belly that hadn't been there before. I wondered if she was pregnant, but I didn't say anything. I'd wait for her to bring the topic up. Pregnancy was something I was never in a hurry to talk about anyway. Hank and I had tried to have children over the years, but that never came to be. As it turned out, not being able to conceive had been a blessing. I didn't have a child to raise on my own.

Lene chimed in, "More snow comin' tomorrow, too."

I knew that, of course, had heard the forecast on the radio. No matter the season, every conversation in North Dakota started with the weather. Lene was a wheat farmer's wife, like me. She and her husband, Ollie, owned a little over three thousand acres east of town, halfway to Gladstone. They had reason for the weather to be on their minds as much as anyone did.

"That time of year," I said, eyeing Darlys in the kitchen. She'd made herself at home and put the percolator on. The welcome smell of strong, fresh-brewed coffee filled the house. "Be a surprise if there was no snow and wind, now wouldn't it?" I wanted to say that wet weather was good for the winter wheat crops, but there was no need to say that any more than there was a need for Lene to give me a snow report.

"Oh, ya betcha," Lene said.

I smiled, and turned to Anna. She'd snatched up a piece of sausage like a hungry little bird, then made her way to the front window. Anna was always tense when she arrived. Her husband, Nils, was the manager at the Red Owl grocery store and put in long hours; he worked from open to close six days a week. Raising the family fell on Anna's shoulders. They'd been married a little over ten years, and as far as I could tell the union was one that looked like it was going to last.

Nils Jacobsen had worked at the grocery store for as long as I could remember. I think he started working as a sack boy before he graduated high school. Everybody knew the Jell-O and marshmallows in Anna's salad were items that didn't sell. Her Jell-O was always lime flavored, and the marshmallows were always stale.

"Is something the matter, Anna?" I said.

Anna stared out the window with a worried look on her face. She glanced over at me, away from the window for a second, and said, "The *new sheriff* was out at the Rinkermans' when we drove by."

"*Him* and the ambulance," Lene added.

"Oh my," I said. I ignored the unsaid comments about the new sheriff, or the curious fact that they had driven by the Rinkermans' in the first place.

Guy Reinhardt had won the recent special election in Stark County, replacing Duke Parsons as acting sheriff. The election had been a squeaker. Guy had only won by a hundred votes or so, demonstrating the split opinion in the county. The new sheriff carried a checkered past, at least for an elected official. He was going through his second divorce, and there were rumors that he liked the taste of whiskey a little too much. I had known Guy for a long time, but I'd never seen him drunk or act out of line. Gossip was hard to avoid in a small town like ours.

Anna answered my question. "We stopped in at the Red Owl before coming your way. Darlys needed to pick up some cigarettes, you know. Nils heard that the Rinkerman girl had wandered off, and said we should keep an eye out for her."

I gasped at the thought of a young girl out in this weather, especially a girl like her. "Did they find her, then?"

"Can't say for sure," Anna said. "We didn't stop to find out, and we didn't see anything on the way here, either."

I knew of the Rinkerman girl, but I didn't know her or her parents well at all. Toren Rinkerman was a welder by trade. He'd sharpened some blades and installed some gates for Hank over the years. I'd never had reason to have any direct dealings with Toren, at least while Hank was alive. The time might come in the future when I'd need use of his services, though. Most folks said Toren was the best welder within a hundred miles, and I know Hank liked his work. That was a good enough endorsement of the man's abilities and character for me.

The Rinkermans had three sons and one daughter. The boys were grown and didn't live at home, as far as I knew. I'd seen his girl, Tina, in town from time to time. She was hard to miss; short, a little heavy, about fourteen or fifteen, the youngest of the brood. People whispered when she walked by, or ignored her, said she was retarded, or worse, a mongoloid. I never liked such words, but that was the only way I knew how to describe the girl. Her condition was rare in these parts, so she stood out.

"Going by the Rinkermans' place was a bit out of your way, wasn't it?" I said.

Anna pulled away from the window but held the curtain open. "Darlys is a curious cat. Besides, I told you, Nils said to keep an eye out. We were doing what he said."

I joined Anna at the window and stared out across the drive. I couldn't see anything but cold white snow everywhere I looked. I felt like I was standing in front of the Frigidaire with the freezer door open. "That's awful. I thought she was up in Grafton," I said.

Anna agreed with a flinch. "She was, at that state hospital for the feebleminded. Nils said she came into the store about a week ago, heard they had to bring her home for some reason or another. No one knows for sure. Those Rinkermans keep to themselves, don't ya know."

I heard a tone in Anna's voice that I didn't like. I was about to press more when I considered Grafton was a six-hour drive to the northeast, but Darlys walked into the room with the percolator and a tray full of mugs.

"Well, come on ladies, let's get this show on the road," Darlys said.

I knew she'd heard every word we'd said, but she didn't act like she had. Time was ticking. The weather outside was getting worse by the second, and for some reason the air inside the house was getting warmer by the second.

Maybe I wasn't in the mood for company. I was sure that was why I was uncomfortable. That and the thought of that girl lost, left to wander outside on her own. I couldn't imagine such a thing. There was a scent of tragedy in the air, a smell that I knew all too well and never wanted to experience again. I hoped I was wrong. I hoped I was only upset about hanging onto Hank's clothes for a little bit longer.

CHAPTER 2

There really wasn't anything formal about the Ladies Aid this time of year. Gathering at my house was an excuse to get together and visit. Though there were times when duties needed to be exercised: calling on a sick church member, gathering blankets and used clothing for the holiday bazaar, distributing fruit baskets between Thanksgiving and Christmas, that kind of thing. January was a slow season for everyone. There was little to do but while away the time and hope for an early spring.

"I don't understand this book thing you do," Lene said, after finishing her second sandkake. "Ollie said I should talk to you and see if I could take one of them correspondence courses. That way, I could come up with a money-makin' scheme for the winter, too."

"What I do is not a scheme," I snapped. "Indexing is hard work, Lene." I was quick to anger lately. Small things that never made me mad before, like misplacing my glasses, infuriated me. Poor Shep knew the best thing to do was ignore me. I was angry at Hank for dying, for leaving me, but the thought of such a thing was too much to consider.

Lene recoiled and twisted her lip. "I didn't mean nothin' bad, Marjorie. I'm only sayin' a job like yours would give me something to do in the winter. I've mended quilts and linens for a month. At this rate, I'll be twiddlin' my thumbs by Valentine's Day."

I took an exasperated breath and raised the coffee mug to my lips. I looked inside the mug and caught my reflection in the black liquid mirror. I didn't like what I saw. "I'm sorry, Lene," I said, forgoing a drink. "I don't seem to be myself today."

"How could you be, Marjorie?" Darlys said, casting a side-glance to Lene that I interpreted as *what were you thinking?* "When was the last time you were out of the house?"

"I went out to get the paper this morning," I said.

Darlys rolled her eyes. They were cornflower blue, like Hank's. She was warm and summery no matter the season. "You know what I mean."

"I don't know, maybe a week ago. I ran into the grocery store, dropped off a library book, and mailed off an index to New York. There's no cause to go out in weather like this."

Darlys leaned down and started to dig for something in her purse. "You need to get out more."

"I'm sure I'll have plenty to keep me busy, come spring."

Darlys raised a pack of cigarettes—Winstons—into the air. "You mind?"

"Ashtray's in the drawer next to the stove," I said.

Darlys smiled and headed into the kitchen. The small glass dish was an advertisement trinket for the Kaander's Tractor Supply store over in Taylor. The ashtray was another one of Hank's things I wouldn't dare part with, even though when he was alive I never smoked in the house. I tried to hide my smoking from him, to be honest, but there was no hiding anything from Hank Trumaine.

"I don't understand this job you have, either," Anna said.

"The indexing?" I said.

"Yes, that." Anna squirmed in her seat as if she were about to take a test.

I got up and headed to the spare bedroom that was once reserved for children. I kept my desk, typewriter, and bookshelf in there now. I retrieved a book, *Common Plants of the Western Plains: North Dakota*, off the shelf. I'd written the index just before Hank died.

I rejoined the group and handed the book to Lene.

She looked at the cover, then turned the book over in her hands as if it were a loaf of bread, checking to see if the bottom had burned. "What's this?"

"If you had to find something, say a weed on your land, and you wanted to know if your livestock would be poisoned, what would you do?"

"I'd burn that weed, is what I'd do. If the darn thing came back, I'd look for a picture of the stubborn thing in a book like this, or I'd call the extension agent out to see if he could tell me what I was lookin' at," Lene said.

Her answer wasn't what I was hoping for, but I understood. I was still standing up. All eyes were on me. "Okay, let's say there's no picture, but you know the weed's a thistle of some kind. What would you do?"

"I'd look in the back of the book and see where the word thistle was at in the book."

"At the index?"

"Yes, Marjorie, at the index." Lene opened the book and looked at the last few pages.

"That's what I do. I write the index," I said.

"Doesn't the author do that?" she said.

"Sometimes, but a lot of publishers hire people like me to write indexes. We're called indexers. Indexing's a different skill than writing the book. I read each page of the book and decide what the most important concepts or words are on that page. Usually I make note of people, places, or events; things I think a reader will want to look up. Then I type each of those entries on an index card. When I've read the whole book, I type up all of the entries on the index cards into one document and mail the completed index off to the publisher. A few months later they send me a copy of the book." *And hopefully a check*, I thought, but didn't say.

Darlys took a long drag off her Winston and exhaled as she stared up at the ceiling. Anna seemed confused. Lene looked like she was trying to decide if indexing was something she could do.

"You have to like to read, don't you?" Lene finally said, handing me the book.

"I don't think you could be an indexer if you didn't love to read." I sat back down in my spot. "I get to read so many interesting books this way. Sometimes, I know a little about the topic or theme, and other times I don't know anything about what I'm reading at all. I'm always amazed that I get paid to do something that I would normally do for free, like reading a book."

"You always did read a lot, Marjorie," Anna said. She flashed a smile. Her cheeks were fuller than I remembered. I was sure she'd put on a little weight since I'd seen her last, but she still hadn't said a word about being pregnant. I was probably wrong. Everyone put on a little weight over the holidays, eating all sorts of sweets and foods they normally left alone. Everyone but me.

"I was going to be a teacher, you know?" I said. "I married Hank instead of finishing college. I decided that I knew more about being a farmer's wife than teaching. That nearly broke my father's heart, but he never held a grudge against Hank. He finally had the son he'd wanted but could never have. When Lloyd Gustaffson was our extension agent he brought me a catalog from the USDA loaded with correspondence courses. I looked through the catalog, not interested at first, until it dawned on me that there were things in there I could do, things that would replace my yearning to teach and learn. To be honest, I'd never heard of indexing before I saw the skill described in that catalog, either. I didn't know you could make money doing something like that. The only way I knew how to make money was to plant seeds and worry. Anyway, I took the correspondence course for indexing, then sent out some letters to publishers, and to my surprise, I got an offer to do some work. I've been indexing steadily ever since. The money sure has helped with the bills, but more than that the job's given me something to occupy my mind ever since . . . well, you know."

All three women nodded in unison.

"I sure miss Lloyd," Lene said. "Don't get me wrong, that new extension agent, Curtis Henderson, is a fine young man, but he comes up short in a lot of ways. He probably wouldn't know thistle from milkweed if he stepped on the darn thing."

I agreed, but wouldn't say so. "Lloyd's family's been working this land for as long as any of us can remember. His nephew, Lester, is working over at the Knudsen place with Jaeger these days. The Gustaffsons know the weeds, the birds, and the clouds better'n anybody around. Lloyd had to retire, but this Curtis Henderson fella is fresh out of college. He has some new ideas."

"I don't like new ideas," Lene said.

"Lloyd's a cousin," Darlys interjected, as she ground out her cigarette.

"I forget that," I said. There were more Gustaffsons in Stark County than Smiths or Jones. I smiled, and saw that Darlys and Lloyd shared a good height and happy eyes.

Darlys shrugged, and continued. "So sad to lose your parents so tragically and so unnecessarily."

She was talking about Erik and Lida Knudsen, Jaeger's parents. They'd died less than a year ago—murdered in their bed. Jaeger's brother, Peter, had joined the Air Force afterward, leaving Jaeger to run the Knudsen farm alone. That was a real dark time for us all. The reverberations of that crime still rippled through our little town of ten thousand people. Folks locked their doors these days, and they didn't used to. Throwing the deadbolt was still an act I resented.

"Jaeger's doing fine," I said. "He calls every few days. We check on each other."

"Jaeger *has* been through a lot," Darlys said. She didn't need to say anything else.

Quiet filled the room, and it wasn't long before the women got up to leave. Darkness came on fast, and the wind screamed steadily now that the sun had gone down. Of course, the women left without the box of clothes. They were all nice enough not to mention Hank on their way out the door.

With the weather being so bad, I made Darlys promise to call me once she'd got home. Even so, I jumped when the phone rang. We were on a party line, so I didn't answer right away. I waited until I knew the call was for me. My ring was two longs and two shorts. I answered the phone on the third ring.

"Trumaine residence," I said into the black plastic receiver, then strained my ear to hear if anyone else was listening in. My neighbor, Burlene Standish, was notorious for eavesdropping on other peoples' conversations, but I'd had my say with her recently, so I wasn't too worried that she was hiding on the line. I was still suspicious of my other neighbors, though. My distrust wasn't something I was proud of, but I couldn't help myself.

"It's Darlys, Marjorie."

"Oh, you got home all right, then?"

"Yes, I got home fine, thanks." Darlys paused. I heard her light up a cigarette. "I hope you weren't put off by Lene today, Marjorie. We like to visit with you, and I hope you'll join the Ladies Aid."

"Well, we'll see. I do keep busy." I had started indexing a new project for my publisher, H. P. Howard and Sons, in New York. The index was for a book about birds and their migration patterns west of the Mississippi. It was good to have something that I could look out my window and see, instead of a subject like ancient Chinese war strategies that I didn't know anything about.

"You have a big job to do, Marjorie. I'd go bonkers out there all alone, I really would," Darlys said. "To be honest, I don't understand what you do, either. Henrik thinks you're a dream. He loves books, don't you know?"

I blushed and didn't know what to say. "He had a lot of schooling. I guess he had to read a lot."

"I would imagine that he did."

I was going to change the subject and ask Darlys if Anna Jacobsen was pregnant, or if my suspicion was merely my imagination at work. I wasn't envious of Anna. I was worried about her. But Darlys exhaled a puff off her cigarette and continued talking without missing a beat. "We went by the Rinkermans' on the way home. I stopped to say hello to Duke Parsons, the only deputy there. Duke's sister, Theda, is in the Ladies Aid, too, so I thought I'd pay my respects. The sheriff was gone."

"I think I knew that Theda was a member. Any word on the girl?"

"They still haven't found her. Toren, his boys, a group from South

Heart, and the Sheriff's department are going to continue the search in the morning, weather permitting. They looked until past dark but quit when the snow kicked up. I nearly ended up in the ditch three times. Lene's knuckles were white as a newborn lamb the whole way home. We're not in the middle of a blizzard, but the temperature might as well be fifty below if you're Tina Rinkerman wanderin' around without a coat or gloves on."

"Seriously? No coat and gloves?"

"That's what Duke said. Doesn't sound right to me. He said her coat and gloves were in the closet where they belonged. She up and disappeared this morning. Walked out of the house when no one was lookin'. I don't know about you, but I've seen that girl make a fuss at the Rexall, throw a real temper tantrum, and stalk off from her mother. Who knows what really happened. Duke wouldn't say anything more than that."

"Even a girl like her knows better than to go out in this weather unprepared," I said.

"That's what I said to Duke," Darlys went on, "but he shrugged and said maybe she didn't know any better. He didn't look none too happy to be there."

"He needs some time to get over his sour grapes from losing the election."

"That's not going to happen anytime soon."

"Well, this is awful," I said. "That girl's parents must be bereft. I can't imagine such a thing. I mean, I worried about Hank out on the prairie by himself when he went off hunting, and I was right to be concerned. I don't like the sound of this, Darlys. That poor girl. What must she have been thinking?"

"I don't know, but I'm going to put a hot dish in the oven tonight, then go over there tomorrow."

"That's a good idea. I have some blackberries in the freezer that I didn't use at Christmas. I'll put together some pies this evening and take them over, too."

"There you go," Darlys said, "You'll make a fine addition to the Aid, you wait and see. I'll meet you at the Rinkermans' at ten, how's that?"

I forced a smile, agreed on the time, then rang off. I glanced over at the Frigidaire and considered all of the ingredients I'd need for the pies. Instead of preparing the pies, I made my way to the window.

I peered hopefully outside.

The snow and wind had picked up like the weatherman had promised. Night had fallen a little before five o'clock. The days were so short you'd miss sight of the January sun if you blinked. The world was wrapped in a deep white blanket that wouldn't be pulled off the ground until early May.

A security light burned over the garage door, about twenty-five yards away from the house. Hank had put the light up so he'd have something to guide him home if he had to go out into a blizzard. The light looked like a distant star, cold and untouchable.

A shriek of wind caused me to shiver. With Hank on my mind, I was forced to acknowledge how much colder the house was without him. In years past, he'd banked snow three or four feet high around the foundation to beat back the wind and provide some extra insulation. I'd failed to do that chore this winter. No wonder my toes felt like they were about to fall off.

I looked past the light, longing to see a young girl looking for her way home, looking for somewhere to find warmth and comfort. But I didn't see anything moving, nothing alive, not even a hungry coyote lurking about. Anything that had an ounce of sense had already hunkered down to ride out the storm. I hoped Tina Rinkerman had, too.

CHAPTER 3

The next morning, the house smelled of lard, sugar, flour, and blackberries.

I had to decide whether there was a need to deliver the three pies at all. I imagined Tina Rinkerman safe and sound in her warm house, even though I had plenty of reason to doubt that the comforting image was true. My gut told me there would be no happy ending for the Rinkermans and their daughter. January weather was an unforgiving devil, unconcerned about love, pride, or disability.

My indexing project sat waiting for me at my desk, but any real work was going to have to sit a little longer. The new book I was working on, *The Central Flyway: Audubon's Journey Revisited*, had a reasonable deadline, one month out. Page proofs had arrived a few days ago, and I hadn't even started breaking down the structure of the book so I could plot out the index. Starting was the hardest part, but I couldn't seem to find my way to my desk. I'd been sleeping a lot and staring out the window at the blank landscape that surrounded me. The work would take all month, but instead of searching for terms and concepts I'd dressed to be outside, readying myself to deliver pies to a family in need.

There was no way to know whether the girl had made her way back to her family other than to call. I saw no need to disturb anyone. I was going to deliver the pies anyway. According to Darlys, I needed to get out more, and meeting her at the Rinkermans wasn't something I could say no to. When Hank had gone missing, half the county showed up to search for him. The other half brought food once word got out about the tragedy that had befallen us. This was my turn to give back, no matter the state of my own grief, the severity of the weather, or the certainty of Tina Rinkerman's fate.

I collected one of the pies and walked stiffly to the door. Layering clothes was the only way to stay warm and ward off frostbite this time of year. By virtue of putting on two pairs of long johns, two pairs of work pants, a heavy sweater, and Hank's quilt-lined Carhartt coveralls, I'd gained back the weight I'd lost since he'd died. I was sweating bullets with all the clothes on.

A cold, hard wind slapped my face as soon as I stepped out the door, but I was ready for the assault. I had rushed out a half hour earlier to start the truck, an old Studebaker that we'd owned for longer than I cared to admit. The pickup needed time to warm up. Driving a cold vehicle could crack the engine block, and then I'd have bigger problems than I already had. I would have no transportation and little money to replace the durable truck. I needed to take care of the Studebaker so it would take care of me. That was why I, like most folks around here, had a block heater or kept a burning light bulb anchored to the engine in sub-zero temperatures. Warming up the truck and scraping the ice off the windshield used to be one of Hank's chores, but that was no more. He'd taught me everything I needed to know to keep the Studebaker operating in the winter.

Shep happily followed me to the truck. I'd considered leaving him behind, but I decided that I didn't want to be on the road by myself. I didn't think the dog could help find Tina Rinkerman. He wasn't a bloodhound, but he was the smartest dog I'd ever known. Shep loved to ride in the truck no matter the reason, with his head stuck out the window. That wasn't going to happen today. The windows were froze in place.

"Wait," I said, as I held the pie with one hand and opened the passenger door with the other. I slid the pie onto the floor then closed the door. "You stay here, Shep. I'm going to go get the other two pies."

He did exactly what I told him. I was sure he wouldn't move until I released him. Shep was good at commands—unless something wandered by. Then all bets were off. His instinct to herd anything that moved was almost impossible to overcome.

I looked like the abominable snowman when I stepped inside the house. I brushed off the snow, quickly gathered up the other two pies, hurried back to the Studebaker, and lodged them on the floor next to the other one. Then I ordered Shep up onto the passenger seat. "Don't even think about taking a nip of that crust, buster," I said, as he settled in and eyed the pies.

The dog looked at me, back at the pies, then stared out the closed passenger window, sullen and rejected. His bushy tail trembled with restraint.

"Good dog," I said, putting the truck in gear. "Let's go."

The bed of the truck was loaded with snow. The weight gave me plenty of traction so I wouldn't fishtail or lose control on the icy, snow-packed roads. Thankfully, the Studebaker was good on winter roads—like any heavy-duty farm truck would be—but I still had to drive cautiously and slowly. Oncoming traffic would be hard to see, and the fact that my defroster only worked half the time made things worse. I had to wipe the windshield clear with my sleeve.

The Rinkermans lived a good clip away, almost to South Heart, which was why I was surprised when Darlys had driven so far out of the way to get to my house for the Ladies Aid meeting. South Heart was west of Dickinson. She and Anna had driven from Dickinson, east, almost to Gladstone, to pick up Lene. From there, they drove back west, stopped at the Red Owl for cigarettes, then drove a good twenty miles farther west to drive by the Rinkermans. I still scratched my head at the thought of Darlys's reasoning. Nils had told the women to keep an eye out for Tina. I guess that's what they were doing.

The sky was clear, but there was the promise of more snow on the puffy, gray horizon. Flakes that had already fallen raced across the flat, open fields, gathering speed and conspirators with no obvious destination. Spirals of snow danced across the road ahead of me, obscuring my vision. I felt like I was driving though a ghost tornado.

The way finally cleared and the road forked. I knew I was getting close. "Almost there," I said to Shep.

The border collie sat in the passenger seat quietly, happy to be with me. He flicked his tail and looked back out the window. I followed Shep's gaze, hoping to see something moving, something alive, but there was nothing but a field of white, an unmarked sheet of paper, for miles on end, to greet my eyes. I hadn't spotted a single hawk, human, or jackrabbit since I'd left the house. I'd had nothing to keep track of, to categorize, or sort. My brain craved organization, a trait that contributed to my indexing skills. There was absolutely nothing to file in my memory other than loneliness. Shep and I might as well've been the only living creatures on the planet.

That Rinkerman girl couldn't survive twenty-four hours in this weather. It would be a miracle if she was still alive.

There were fewer trucks parked in front of the Rinkermans' house than I had expected. Nine to be exact, and that included two Sheriff's Department vehicles and the volunteer ambulance from South Heart.

The trucks sat alongside the road, most with their engines idling. Exhaust spiraled upward into thin vapor clouds that smelled of burnt oil and antifreeze fluid. There was no sign of Darlys Oddsdatter's red Plymouth Fury, and there wasn't anyone milling about. The air was too cold for that.

I left Shep in the Studebaker and made my way to the house, juggling all three pies.

The Rinkermans' house was similar to mine; a small wood-frame box with a covered porch, two or three bedrooms, and a living room that most likely melded into the kitchen. Paint hadn't touched the wind-worn clapboard siding in a decade. Snowdrifts skirted the buckling foundation. The door to the storm cellar stood open, free of snow, and I assumed that someone had recently gone down looking for Tina. An occasional puff of smoke choked out of the lone chimney, and the woodpile looked incapable of heating the house through the winter.

Three work trucks sat in the drive, and a garage, in similar repair to everything else in sight, sat on the north side of the house. Toren

Rinkerman kept his welding shop in the garage. There were no other buildings on the property, no barns, no sheds, not even a chicken coop. As far as I knew, the Rinkermans didn't farm any of the land that surrounded them.

I heard loud voices inside the house as I made my way up the stoop. I hesitated, then knocked on the door with my elbow. My hands were full, balancing the pies. I feared dropping them. I wasn't going to leave a single pie in the truck or bring Shep with me. I didn't know if the Rinkermans had any dogs of their own. Farm dogs could be territorial, and I wasn't about to risk starting a fight.

Heavy footsteps approached, the door swung open, and Toren Rinkerman glared at me. I stepped back and looked up. He was a towering man, dressed in thick, grease-stained overalls, along with a long frazzled gray beard that hung halfway down his chest. His face was hard and wrinkled. I had almost forgotten that Toren was older, probably in his early sixties, not my age or Hank's.

"Mrs. Trumaine," he said, recognizing me immediately. "What are you doin' out on a day like this?"

"I brought you some of my blackberry pies."

Any anger or frustration in Toren Rinkerman's dark gray eyes quickly faded away. "So you did. I expect you heard about our Tina?"

I wasn't sure what Toren thought I had heard. That Tina was dead? I only knew she had wandered off.

"Come on in, then," he said, opening the door. "You're gonna freeze to death just standin' there."

I forced a smile, gripped the pies tighter, sucked in a deep breath of frigid air, and made my way inside the small house, not sure what I was walking into.

CHAPTER 4

The interior of the Rinkermans' house was as sparse and worn as the exterior. The family lived and breathed a utilitarian existence. That wasn't so unusual. Money was hard to come by in the best of times.

I couldn't see one expression of happiness or pride. No pictures, trophies, or knickknacks cluttered the room. Rickety furniture sat haphazardly about the front room along with tattered rugs that looked like they'd been woven in the last century. Nervous perspiration beaded on my upper lip.

I immediately searched for Tina but didn't see her. There were no children in the house at all. The room was packed with men; three of them, I assumed, were Toren's sons. All of them were dressed in overalls, thermals, and heavy boots, to endure long stretches of frigid weather.

Most of the men were unfamiliar to me, though I spied Duke Parsons and Guy Reinhardt right away, huddled in a corner talking quietly to each other. Guy was hard to miss, standing almost a head taller than everyone else in the room. Both men, like everyone else, glanced my way when Toren ushered me inside the house.

The house smelled of cigarette smoke, coffee, and dread. I could tell by the long faces and distant eyes that Tina Rinkerman had not returned home.

"This way, Mrs. Trumaine," Toren said, cutting a path to the kitchen.

The collection of searchers stepped out of the way, allowing us to pass. I followed Toren, not directly acknowledging any of the men. I ignored Guy and Duke after my initial sighting, and they did the same. This wasn't a social call for any of us.

Toren led me into the kitchen, where I found two women, one standing at a double sink and one sitting at the dining table, her face buried in a pair of wrinkled and drawn hands. She had recently finished crying or praying, I couldn't tell which.

"Mother," Toren said. His head nearly scraped the ceiling as he stepped up into the kitchen. The small room was a late addition to the original house; the floor was six inches higher than the front room. I had to peer around the side of him to see the women clearly. "Mrs. Trumaine brought some pies for us," he said.

The woman at the table looked up at him. She couldn't have been his mother but was most likely his wife. "She's dead then?"

"No, Mother. We don't know where Tina is. The neighbor lady here brought us some pies. Tell her thank you."

I lived nearly twenty-five miles away and I was still a neighbor.

The other woman stopped what she was doing, washing and drying dishes, and stared at me. I recognized her. She was Theda Parsons. Duke's sister, another member of the Ladies Aid. She had never visited my house. I wondered if Darlys had called and told her I was coming. I wondered if Darlys had already been there. There was no sign of her typical hot dish made with tater tots and Vienna sausages. I was really starting to worry.

I eased by Toren, bobbling the pies as I did, and sat them down safely on the dinner table.

Theda Parsons, tall and brittle as an October cornstalk, dried her hands on a dingy dishtowel, and said, "Adaline, you remember Marjorie Trumaine. Her husband, Hank, would come by to have Toren sharpen his mower blades from time to time. Their place is south of Dickinson off Duncan Road, you know?"

The woman, Adaline, looked at Theda, then at me. "The one that stepped in the gopher hole and broke his neck?"

"Yes," I whispered.

"Well, I was sorry to hear he passed away." Adaline Rinkerman looked to be in her early sixties, near the age of her husband. Her face was as wrinkled as her hands, and her hair was the color of the gray dishtowel. A hint of blue still held in her eyes, but any vibrancy of the color had faded long ago. She must've had Tina late in life after bearing the three boys; a surprise baby that had brought heartache and joy. I was speculating on the joy part.

"Thank you," I said. "I hope you can use the pies."

Adaline forced a smile and looked past me to Toren. "You go find her, Father. You go find our Tina now. If I have to live another minute not knowin' where she is, I'm gonna go mad. Do you understand? I'm gonna go mad."

"I understand, Mother." Toren's words were soft, but they were heavy with fear.

What was he going to tell her when he found her? I wondered silently.

Toren sighed, then lumbered out of the room taking care not to knock his head on the ceiling.

"All right, fellas, let's go back out there," Toren announced, drawing my attention away from the kitchen. His voice boomed inside the small house so loudly that the walls seemed to shake. My guess was that they'd already been out searching once, starting at sun up.

The group of men rustled into action with soft grumbles. I glanced over my shoulder to see Guy Reinhardt, the sheriff, all decked out in his brown and tan winter gear, lead the way out the front door.

A cold gust of wind entered the house as the men marched out dutifully. I was in no mood for visiting, either. I said my goodbyes, then fell into the line of men and headed toward the door. I wanted to get as far away from the sadness inside that house as I could. I had indexing work to do, a reason to leave, but I had something else on my mind. I wasn't going home yet.

The wind hadn't let up, and I tightened my scarf across my face, leaving my vision clear. My eyes watered as they adjusted to the cold. I almost couldn't bear Adaline's heartbreak.

The revving of an engine caught my attention. I looked up, relieved to see Darlys in her red Fury. She parked carefully on the berm, making sure to give the dispersing searchers plenty of leeway. Most of the long-faced men headed back to their trucks, while a few others broke out toward the field across from the Rinkermans' house, their heads down, searching for a clue or fending off the wind, I wasn't sure which.

Guy Reinhardt held back from the group. I quickly realized that he was waiting to speak to me. I wanted to talk to him, too.

"I was surprised to see you here, Marjorie," he said, as I walked over to him.

"I figured the Rinkermans had more mouths to feed than usual and could use some comfort and support," I said.

Guy flicked a half smile of approval. "Your blackberry pies are top-notch, Marjorie. Everybody in the county says so."

I had to look up to meet Guy's familiar brown eyes. We had known each other most of our lives. Guy had grown up nearby, in South Heart, which meant he'd attended a different high school than I had. Our sports events overlapped and our rivalries were fierce. He was an athlete in his younger days, had a good talent for basketball. There was talk of him going pro early on. After high school, Guy went on to play ball at the university and found success there, too. The sheriff was a golden boy back in those days, had everything going for him, but a week before the pro draft a bad car accident left him lame. The wreck killed any chance he had of playing basketball ever again. He walked with a Gary Cooper limp, and carried the burden of living with what might have been etched across his disappointed face. After the wreck, Guy slipped into obscurity as a deputy for the Stark County Sheriff's Department. Recently, though, he'd found enough confidence in himself to run for sheriff. The win looked to have done him some good. I was sure that he stood an inch or two taller, and his shoulders were squarer than I'd seen them in a long time.

"Sad thing, that girl wanderin' off like that," Guy continued. "It's hard waitin' for an answer when you know it's going to be bad news knockin' at the door." The color drained from his face as soon as the words left his mouth. "Oh, sorry about that, Marjorie, I didn't mean to bring up bad memories for you."

"I know you meant no harm, Guy." I lowered my head. Guy knew my troubles and I knew some of his. "I want to help," I said, looking him in the eye. Instead of going home and finding a reason not to start indexing the *Flyway* book, I needed to ward off my own sadness. I needed to contribute something to help ease Adaline Rinkerman's suffering. I knew the look in her fading eyes, how she felt: helpless, lost, her world crumbling around her with nothing to do but wait for the other shoe to drop.

"What do you mean, help?" Guy said.

"I mean go out and search with the rest of you. I'm dressed for the weather. I know this land as well as any of those fellas. Maybe better'n some. I'd rather do that than head home."

"You brought your pies."

"That's not enough," I said. "I want to help find that little girl."

Guy watched Darlys get out of the Fury and walk toward the Rinkermans' front door. She carried a hot dish and looked stunning in a red coat that I'd never seen before. "I don't think we're gonna find anything good, Marjorie. Wouldn't it be better if you . . ."

"Better than what?" I interrupted. "Stay here with the Ladies Aid now that Darlys Oddsdatter showed up? You know me better than that, Guy Reinhardt. Besides, are you going to be the one to break the news to that grieving mother in there? I think she'd take the worst thing imaginable a little better if another woman told her. No offense, but I'm a bit gentler with such things."

"Geez, Marjorie, I don't know. That'd be police business."

"This is neighbor business," I said. "The day that Hilo came walking up to me to give me the news about Hank was the worst day of my life. He gave me the details as gently as he could, but what he had to say was still hard to hear, hard to bear. They probably heard me wail all the way up to Saskatchewan. I can help, Guy. I can ease Adaline Rinkerman's pain. That is, if there's bad news to tell at all."

"That girl can't survive in weather like this, Marjorie, you know that. My toes are about to fall off, and I'm prepared to be out in the snow. She's not."

"You don't know what happened to her. All you know is that she's missing. She could be anywhere. She could be warm and safe somewhere for all you know. Besides, if Hank Trumaine were alive he'd be halfway across that field by now, looking for that girl. You wouldn't tell Hank no, now would you?"

Guy put his hat back on and sighed heavily. "Well, I guess you're right, Marjorie. If you're comin', I want you to stay with me. That's the only way I'll agree to such a thing."

"Shep's coming with me," I said.

He didn't say anything else, didn't wait for me to argue or agree. He turned and walked toward his truck. I followed without objecting.

I waved to Darlys as she knocked on the Rinkermans' front door. She waved back with a smile on her face. If anybody could bring some sunshine to that house, Darlys Oddsdatter could.

I kept my eyes focused on Guy, relieved that I didn't have to go home to an empty house, left to wonder and worry about things that on the surface had nothing to do with me. But, like Toren said, we were neighbors, and no matter the distance or lack of relationship, what happened to one of us, happened to us all.

CHAPTER 5

Guy pulled his truck, an International Harvester Scout, off the road about two miles west of the Rinkermans' house. A small flock of horned larks lit into the air. Larks often mingled alongside the road with snow buntings, foraging for any seed they could find. I wasn't sure of the birds' migration patterns, which encouraged me about indexing the new book. At least I was curious about the topic.

Guy shifted his weight behind the steering wheel, and said, "Toren said him and one of the boys found some footprints over by that fence post late last night. He was sure they were Tina's tracks. The prints headed north, then disappeared, so he gave up. Snow covered 'em, most likely. He came back here this morning at first light but didn't see a thing. There was no sign of any human presence at all. Toren's starting to doubt himself, hoping they belonged to Tina, not knowing for sure. I told him I'd have a look, to double check."

I followed Guy's gaze north across the open, snow-covered field. "There's nothing there. No reason that I can see for her to go that way. Or is there?" I said. I wasn't as familiar with this part of Stark County as Guy was.

"Interstate 94's a good ten mile walk, as the crow flies. She'd end up in South Heart before that, though, and come across a few farmhouses on the way. Everybody's keeping an eye out for her, on alert. I think she would have looked for warmth. I think somebody would have seen her if she would have come this way."

"You don't think she could walk that far, do you?" We both knew we could be looking right at her, frozen, buried under the pristine snow. I was betting Tina Rinkerman's body wouldn't be found until the spring thaw.

"No, not unless someone picked her up."

"They would have taken her home," I said.

"We would hope so, wouldn't we?" Guy exhaled heavily, then tapped his gloved fingers on the steering wheel. The inside of the cab of the truck was warm. I wondered if he was telling me everything that he knew.

"You're uncomfortable," I said.

He looked at me stoically, with concern. "People talk, Marjorie."

I studied his face and took in his tone. "Oh, you're uncomfortable that *I'm* here?"

"Yes." His admittance was weak, as if he wasn't proud of what he'd said.

"I don't care what people think, Guy. We're friends. I'm helping you look for Tina Rinkerman is all. What's wrong with that?"

"Word'll get out that you came out on the search with me. You're a widow, and I'm, well, I'm a divorced man. I was lucky to win the election with all of the family troubles I've had. You know how folks are. They see your home life as a reflection of your stability and trustworthiness. I've had my share of public failures, Marjorie. You know that. If I mess up bein' the sheriff, I have nothing left."

I flinched. I didn't like the word widow any more than Lene Harstaad liked new ideas. Beyond that, I didn't want to admit that Guy was right. People gossiped. He was on thin ice until he proved himself, and maybe even then. "That's silly," I said. "I'm another set of eyes looking for that little girl. How can that be wrong?"

Guy sighed again. "You have to realize things have changed for both of us, Marjorie. I have to care about how things look to people. You should, too."

"Why are we here then?"

Guy hesitated, looked away, then back at me. "I didn't want you out in these fields on your own."

"Do you want to take me back to the Rinkermans, back to my truck so I can go home?" I said.

"No, I want you to help if that's what you want to do, but I want you to see how other people might react."

"I think I'm starting to."

Shep's coat looked like a blot of black ink spilled on a clean white sheet of paper. A crisp wind pushed at our back as we followed the dog into the field. Snow snaked around our feet, wiping out any sign of the dog's tracks.

Guy carried a Motorola walkie-talkie with him, at the ready to call for help. The radio screeched with occasional voices, offering a startling presence in the vacant fields. The noise carried on the wind, and I could only hope that Tina would hear us and scream for help. I really wanted to find her alive.

Shep kept moving, sniffing one second, then running full out the next. We kept walking, putting one foot in front of the other. Moving was the only way to keep warm.

A shelterbelt rose in the distance like an oasis in a desert. The gangly cottonwoods were planted as a windbreak years ago by an early pioneer. The trees offered no shade or cover like they did in summer. Come June and July the stand of trees became a draw for all kinds of life. I stopped and looked over my shoulder. We'd covered at least three-quarters of a mile.

The sheriff's truck sat idling distantly on the road. The light ball on top of the all-wheel drive vehicle spun steadily, sending streams of red and blue light across the white fields. A thin, continuous cloud rose up into the air from the Scout's exhaust pipe, encasing the vehicle in a shimmering mirage that looked out of place.

Falling snow and all of its clouds had pushed east, but now there was another worry as the sky cleared and the sun reflected off the white ground. Snow blindness—photokeratitis—was a real concern. Without saying a word, Guy and I both reached into our pockets and put our sunglasses on. His were Ray-Bans. Mine were the fifty-cent variety that I'd picked up at the Walgreens. They worked. That's all that mattered. I wasn't worried about looking like a movie star in my Carhartt overalls and snow boots. The last thing I needed was a sunburned cornea.

A flock of snow buntings jumped into the air at our intrusion. The little white birds looked like snowflakes with wings, rising into the air instead of falling. The world seemed upside down, all wrong. I was rarely out in the fields this time of year. There was no reason to be— unless there was an emergency of some kind.

I started to breathe heavily, could feel the cold invading every cell of my body. Walking faster helped a little bit, but my lungs protested, and I coughed.

Guy stopped, and so did I. "You all right?" he said.

"I'm fine." I had kept my focus on the shelterbelt. A streak of light caught my eye. "There's something there," I said.

"Where?"

When I blinked, and looked again, the light was gone. "I don't see anything now. I saw a burst of light, like the sun hitting a mirror. My eyes could be playing tricks on me because of the angle of the sun." I pointed to the clump of cottonwoods, and Guy followed my lead.

"Let's go take a look," he said.

We headed for the tree line with a renewed sense of purpose. The cold melted away as I pushed the limitations of my body. Shep noticed the change in our determination. He circled us and barked as I pointed to the trees. "Go, Shep," I said. "Go see if anything's there."

Before I could bring my hands together to clap, the border collie took off running.

"He's a good one, that Shep," Guy said.

I kept an eye on the dog, hoping to see the light again.

I didn't see anything until we got closer.

Shep stopped about twenty-five yards from the first cottonwood, drew back into a crouch, and froze in position. He started growling, then barking. Something was amiss, something was wrong. I shivered and tried not to think the worst, but I knew deep down in my soul that I had no choice. Guy was right. We weren't going to find anything good. My heart started to beat faster. My first layer of long johns was soaked with sweat, and I knew I had to catch my breath before moving on. I had to prepare myself to see Tina Rinkerman frozen to death.

Guy hurried past me, raising his radio to his mouth. Shep waited for the sheriff, then followed after him, still barking. Something told me to stay where I was, that I didn't want to see what he saw, but I couldn't stand there. My feet moved on their own accord. Just because I didn't have children of my own didn't mean I didn't have motherly instincts.

I followed Guy and Shep into the shelterbelt, crossing a pair of deep ruts as I went. A farm path wide enough to accommodate a good-sized tractor cut through the trees, providing access to a deer stand that sat nailed in the tallest tree. The oasis of trees was a hunting spot.

I saw the object of the reflection farther into the trees. A car sat at the back of the grove. The driver's side was hidden, obscured by a sculptured snowdrift. The car itself, an older model Ford, was white to begin with, and would have been difficult to see from the road. A chrome-plated mirror jutted out of the snow, looking oddly foreign, but perfectly situated to reflect the sun. No one had tried to hide the car. Nature herself had rendered the Ford invisible.

Guy ran to the car, stopped at the driver's door, then turned to me and said, "Stop, Marjorie. I don't want you to see this."

His warning came too late. I was already to the hood of the car. I couldn't look away.

The windshield was a spider web of cracks, not shattered, still whole, ready to collapse at the first touch. Three unusual holes penetrated the glass directly in front of where the driver sat. There was no mistaking that they were bullet holes. A body sat behind the steering wheel, slumped over, eyes closed, and blood, frozen bright red, covered a man's face. I gasped at the sight, at the recognition. The man in the car was Nils Jacobsen, dead as dead could be.

CHAPTER 6

The presence of death provoked Shep into an unrelenting barking fit. His panicked voice pierced the purity of the winter silence, sounding an alarm that echoed miles away. The good thing was that the border collie's agitated voice would keep the coyotes at bay, or at least keep them on a wide perimeter.

"Down, Shep! Down! Be quiet!" I couldn't hear myself think.

Shep's haunches quivered with disobedience. He had that pushy border collie look in his sparkling amber eyes, and he continued barking as if I hadn't said a word. Once Shep became fixated on an object, there was almost nothing I could do to break his focus. He was Hank's dog long before he was mine. Hank could stop the dog in his tracks with a stern look.

"Be quiet, Shep, that's enough!" I yelled, then I stomped my foot, sending a cloud of dry snow into the air.

The border collie's eyes widened at the eruption. He whimpered and ceased barking straight away. I rarely admonished Shep. I think my deep, demanding tone caught him off guard.

Shep circled around me, jittery and unsure, focusing on me instead of the body in the car. He finally came to rest next to my left ankle, relenting to an obedient stance. His bushy black and white tail swished nervously in the snow like a single angel's wing. I know he was waiting for me to tell him that he was a good boy, but I wasn't about to reward the dog. Praise was hard to fake standing there staring at Nils Jacobsen, dead, riddled with bullets.

"Don't touch anything, Marjorie," Guy said. He stood next to the driver's door. With his height, he could look down into the car and see clearly. The radio was still in his hand, up to his mouth. He hadn't called for help yet. He looked like he was still figuring out what he needed to do.

"Holy buckets, Guy, that's Nils Jacobsen," I said.

"Sure does look like him, Marjorie," Guy said. "His car, too."

I didn't say anything else. I wasn't sure what kind of car the Jacobsens drove. Anna rode with Darlys when they had Ladies Aid business, and I never paid attention to the cars in the parking lot at the Red Owl. There was no reason to.

I was shocked to see Nils dead. I was expecting to find Tina Rinkerman stiff as a board, collapsed in the snow, not the manager of the Red Owl grocery store shot in the head. There was no sign of the girl. I was numb from the cold, grief, and confusion.

Instead of mourning a disabled girl, I would have to watch a friend enter into an early widowhood. There was no way to defer membership to that group like there was the Ladies Aid. *Anna. Poor Anna, left with three children. What was she going to do now?*

Guy looked at the ground and searched for something unknown, then turned his attention back to Nils. "Looks like he drove in here for some reason, then someone shot him from the deer stand. The bullet holes came from a high angle. I'm guessing, but that's how this looks to me." A puzzled look had found its way to Guy's face and stayed there. He was a statue of curiosity. I liked that about him.

"He was ambushed?" I asked, wiping my eyes, taking in the empty deer stand.

Depending on the time of day and the state of the weather, it *was* possible that someone could have lain in wait for Nils, sitting in the deer stand. Why was Nils Jacobsen out in the middle of nowhere in the first place? Was he looking for Tina Rinkerman, or was something else going on? My indexer mind was at work, cataloging what I saw and thought. I couldn't help myself.

Guy shrugged off my ambush question then tried to open the car door. He pulled too hard and the frozen door handle snapped off in his hand. "Son-of-a-bitch! I should know better than to do something so goddamned stupid." He eyed me, then bit his lip, looking like a little boy, holding back any other colorful expletives that he might have been tempted to use. I appreciated his restraint, but Hank Trumaine had a foul mouth, too. I'd heard every bad word there was to hear. I was a farmer's wife, not a prude.

Guy dropped the door handle, then stomped to the other side of the Ford. I couldn't tell if his red face was from the cold or from embarrassment. This time he pulled up on the handle gently. The door opened, to his obvious relief.

I didn't move. Shep didn't budge, either. He hadn't barked once since he'd sat next to my ankle.

Guy climbed into the car, took his right glove off, and pressed against Nils's carotid artery, searching for any sign of life. He exited the car a few minutes later. "Come on, Marjorie. Let's get you back to the truck so you can warm up. I knew there was no saving him from the first look, but I had to check."

Nils Jacobsen was dead. Guy's pronouncement made the tragedy final. I had known the truth before he'd said a word. No one could have survived three bullets to the head.

I started to protest about going back to the truck, but a stern look crossed Guy's face. *This is police business.*

"Try and stay in the tracks you made comin' up here, Marjorie," Guy said. "I didn't see any other footprints, but we'll have to verify everything we find."

I understood. The soles of my boots were like fingerprints. "Okay," I said, plotting my path back to the Scout. Snow had covered most of our tracks. "Come on, Shep, let's go." I clapped my hands together, releasing the dog from his stay position. He barked once, then ran in a few circles, and took off toward the Scout.

As Guy escorted me back to the truck, he called for help on the radio. He gave directions to George Lardner, the dispatcher, and told the ambulance driver that there was no need to hurry, "the victim was 10-45D." I assumed that was police talk for dead.

I kept my eyes fixed on the ground, looking for any sign the killer might have left behind, or a prairie dog town. The underground communities were usually near rivers and streams. Gophers didn't really hibernate in the winter. They slept a lot during the cold days, went dormant, but they still had to eat, still had to move around. My fear of stepping in a gopher hole wasn't unfounded.

"What do you think Nils was doing all the way out here?" I asked.

"I don't know," Guy said, keeping his eyes forward. "I've got some investigating to do. I'll need to talk to his wife, and then to the people at the store. Frank Aberle might know something. Those two have worked together for as long as I can remember."

Frank was the assistant manager at the store. He and Nils were about the same age. They went to school together and were best friends as kids.

"Or Mills Standish," Guy added.

Mills was the butcher at the Red Owl and husband to my party-line eavesdropper neighbor, Burlene. Mills worked a lot of hours, too. Like Nils, he seemed to be at the store every time I went in to get something.

"I saw Anna yesterday," I said. "She came out to the house with Darlys Oddsdatter and Lene Harstaad. Pastor thought my joining the Ladies Aid would be a good idea. They've been coming once a week for a little while." I thought briefly about the box of Hank's clothes, that Anna would have to face the chore of packing away Nils's things, too. My whole body tightened and I suddenly felt sick to my stomach.

The snow crunched underneath Guy's feet, but beyond that silence had returned to the world. The wind had finally died down and there wasn't a house or barn in view. "Did she say anything about Nils?" he asked.

I was determined to maintain my composure, not show Guy that I was upset, even though I had every right to be. "No, not really," I said. "She said they stopped at the store to get Darlys a pack of Winstons, and Nils told them that Tina Rinkerman had gone missing. They left me around suppertime, then Darlys drove out past here and stopped at the Rinkermans and talked to Duke on the way home. If Nils was missing when Anna got home, she would have sounded an alarm, don't you think? Called the police if she thought something was wrong?"

"I would assume so. I'll talk to her."

"She's gonna be awfully upset."

"And Mrs. Jacobsen seemed all right when she was at your house?"

Guy's question prompted an image to flash through my mind: Anna standing at the window, peering out into the snowy void with a worried look on her face, her stomach a little rounder than I had previously remembered. "We were all worried about Tina Rinkerman, and Anna's always a little frazzled chasing after three kids on her own. Nils doesn't help much around the house." I caught the tail end of my words as they left my mouth. I felt bad for gossiping about the Jacobsens' home life, even though my answers to Guy's questions were police business.

"Well, that helps, Marjorie. At least I know Nils was alive yesterday. He was cold as a Popsicle. I think he's been sittin' in that car for a good while."

The radio crackled with voices, and I heard the first distant moan of a siren heading our way. Once we'd found Nils, we'd had little time to consider Tina Rinkerman and her whereabouts. I was relieved that Tina wasn't in the car, but seeing Nils Jacobsen dead like that was a worse shock. Now Guy had two big things to tackle. I worried whether he could handle both investigations. This was going to be his first big test as sheriff.

CHAPTER 7

Warm, crispy air greeted me when I opened the passenger door to Guy's Scout. "Get in, Shep," I said.

The dog jumped up onto the bench seat eagerly. I followed, settling in quickly, pulling the door closed with a slam, keeping as much warmth inside as possible. I expected Guy to do the same thing, get in and warm up while he could, but he remained outside. He stood next to the passenger door like a sentry guarding some unseen treasure.

I cranked the window open slowly. My face tingled from the cold, and I could feel the ice crystals on my eyelashes starting to thaw.

"Aren't you going to get warm?" I said.

Guy turned his gaze down the road. The first set of flashing lights came into view. A police car, ambulance, fire truck, and a couple of pickups headed toward us. Snow kicked up like a cloud of rocket smoke behind the squadron of helpers.

"Don't have time," Guy said. "Roll up the window, Marjorie, and stay here. I'll check on you in a little while."

"But . . ."

Guy walked away with a stern look on his face. "Roll up the window and get warm, Marjorie," he said over his shoulder. He didn't look back, didn't give me a chance to argue—unless I was going to follow, which I wasn't.

What about Tina? I wanted to ask, but didn't. I did what Guy asked me to do. I rolled up the window, and settled in to wait for him to return.

Shep looked at me and wagged his tail. Water dripped off his jowls, snow and ice melting, and he started licking himself clean, seemingly unaffected by the weather or the tragedy that we had witnessed. I wanted to trade places with the dog.

The first vehicle to show up was another county sheriff's truck, a similar, but older International Harvester Scout. Guy continued walking and raised his hand. The Scout slowed down, stopped, and picked him up. Duke Parsons was driving. Guy climbed in the truck, then they took off into the field, driving straight for Nils Jacobsen's dead body.

The rest of the vehicles followed with their sirens blaring. Shep started to bay and yelp. The noise inside the truck was loud enough to shatter my eardrums, but I knew there was no quieting the dog, no matter my tone. He would carry on until the last siren wafted away on the wind. I imagined a coyote doing the same thing, announcing to the rest of the world the truth that I already knew. A man was dead—and no one knew why.

Movement caught my attention. I looked out the windshield to see a small herd of antelope, two bucks and five does, wandering in the field across the road. The sirens didn't seem to matter to them. The antelope were hungry.

One of the smaller creatures stopped and pawed at the snow, trying to break the crust, trying to dig down into the snow for anything green, anything edible. The doe didn't linger long; she had found nothing.

I'd always thought that antelope looked exotic. They looked like something you'd see on the African savannahs instead of on the western plains. But they existed in the Dakotas, no matter how precariously. This herd, like most all antelope, had come back from near extinction at the turn of the century; survival was in their genes. I looked away from the animals, back up to the shelterbelt, and sighed deeply. All of the police vehicles in the middle of a winter field looked as out of place as the antelope, even though the trucks were equipped for off-road driving. I was surprised any of us could survive on the frozen prairie.

I wasn't sure how long I'd sat in the truck. I had dozed off. Shep sat snuggled up against me, and I turned the heat down to low. I was finally warm and comfortable, but, like the antelope, I was starting to feel the first pangs of hunger. I hadn't had anything to eat since breakfast, and that was only a piece of toast and a cup of coffee. A snack was out of the question. I hadn't brought any food for me, only the pies for the Rinkermans. I grabbed my purse off the floorboard and pulled out my pack of Salems. Smoking curbed my appetite. Lately, I smoked more than I ate.

I was about to light the cigarette when I looked up and saw one of the police vehicles heading my way. Duke Parsons was driving. I put away the cigarette and ignored the growl of hunger in my stomach.

The truck got the antelope's attention, too. They bounced off in the opposite direction, disappearing quickly over a roll in the land.

Duke pulled up alongside me and motioned for me to roll down the window. I did, turning my face away from a strong gust of frigid wind.

"The sheriff wants me to take you back to your truck. Says there's nothing for you to do here." The deputy didn't wait for a response. He rolled his window up and stared stone-faced across the field, waiting for me to comply.

I climbed out of Guy's truck, led Shep to Duke's Scout, put the dog in the backseat, then made myself as comfortable as I could in the passenger seat.

The deputy waited until I settled in, then gunned the all-wheel drive vehicle out of the field and onto the road. I'd never ridden with Duke Parsons before, so I was a little nervous.

"Thanks for taking me to my truck," I said, once we were a little ways down the road.

"Didn't have much choice," he said.

"I could have waited."

Duke exhaled deeply and kept his eyes on the road. Shep was sitting in the middle of the backseat so he could see me. He stayed quiet, thankfully.

"Is something the matter, Duke?" I finally said.

"You have to ask?"

"I do."

He hesitated, then said, "I wouldn't be here if you hadn't interfered."

"I beg your pardon?"

"You heard me."

The truck slid over a rut, jarring me, causing me to bounce like one of those fleeing antelope. "I have no idea what you're talking about," I said.

Duke Parsons's barrel chest heaved. He smelled of Aqua Velva and coffee. The aftershave was too strong, used to cover up something, like body odor or the lack of a recent bath. His parka was as wrinkled as a campground bedroll. Every time I saw Duke Parsons he looked like he'd just woken up.

"I lost the election because of you," Duke said.

The statement caught me by surprise. I didn't know what to say.

"I should be leadin' this investigation," Duke continued, staring straight ahead, keeping his beady eyes on the road. He wouldn't look at me. "Not Guy Reinhardt. If you hadn't led him around by the nose, the county would have treated him like the screw-up he is. You make him look smart is what you do, Marjorie Trumaine. But all I got to do is wait. People will realize their mistake. Especially now with Nils Jacobsen dead on his watch. People won't feel safe. He'll get an earful and won't be able to take the criticism. You wait and see."

I knew the implication. Guy would start drinking, get sloppy, and that would be that. The people would have enough of Guy Reinhardt and his problems. His greatest fear would come true, he would fail, and Duke would have a chance at being sheriff again.

I stared through the windshield out into the barren white world before me. I didn't need to worry about being cold. My blood was boiling. "I don't even know what to say to you, Duke Parsons."

"Sorry would be a good place to start."

I bit my lip. An apology of any kind wasn't going to happen—ever. Duke Parsons could blame me all he wanted for his demotion from acting sheriff to deputy, but come hell or high water, I wasn't going to take credit for how the election turned out.

Thankfully, my trusted green Studebaker truck came into view. I crossed my arms with a thud and stared silently out the windshield.

Duke pulled up behind my truck and looked at me expectantly. I think he was still waiting for that apology. "Sheriff said for me to tell you not to tell anyone what you saw. They have to verify the identity of the body. Doesn't matter that you think you know who the body belongs to, he wants to tell the family hisself."

Duke expected me to respond, most likely to say that I would comply with this order, too, but all I said was, "Thank you, deputy." Then I got out of the truck, collected Shep, slammed the door shut, and walked away. I didn't look back, didn't wave. I hurried to the Studebaker.

I climbed in and hoped that the truck would start after sitting for so long without a warming light on the engine.

Duke drove off in a huff, spinning his tires as he went.

My truck started right away, but the engine coughed and ran rough, so I knew I'd have to sit there for a few minutes. Keeping warm—machines and humans—was a constant struggle. Waiting out winter was my only survival strategy.

I looked at the Rinkermans' house in its dilapidated state. Weak smoke wafted from the chimney, and there was no sign of anyone at home. All of the blinds were drawn shut. Only two trucks sat in the drive, and there was no sign of Darlys's red Fury, either. She'd obviously dropped off her hot dish then went on to another one of her causes.

I didn't want to talk to any human beings at all. All I wanted was to go home, lock my door, and pretend the day I had experienced hadn't really happened. But there was no pretending. Nils Jacobsen was dead, and Tina Rinkerman was still missing. How could I pretend that I wasn't standing in the middle of a tragedy that would only get worse once everyone in Dickinson found out what was going on?

My heart sank at the thought of Anna. Whether crying was the best thing to do or not, I let go. I couldn't keep my emotions bottled up one second longer.

CHAPTER 8

Icould hear the phone ringing as soon as I got out of the Studebaker. My ear strained to count the rings. Snow pelted my back as I hurried toward the house. The phone kept ringing like a persistent alarm. When I was finally close enough to hear two longs and two shorts, I knew the call was for me.

"Come on, Shep, let's get inside," I said.

The border collie barked once, then took a wide arc around me instead of running to the front door like he usually did. Shep stopped solidly between the house and the barn, eyeing the barn nervously. He growled and slipped into his statue stance, waiting for something to move.

The phone continued to ring. I was afraid the caller was going to annoy everyone on the party line if I didn't hurry up and answer the phone. Funny, the things I worried about, but I did. Sharing a telephone line was a constant exercise in decency, diplomacy, and respect.

Shep got my full attention when he barked again. I stopped, too. "What's the matter, boy?" I said, following the dog's gaze to the barn. I didn't see anything wrong. No open doors. No footprints in the snow. But I trusted Shep to alert me. "Something out of place?"

He broke his trance on the unseen intrusion, looked at me, wagged his tail, then made his way to me submissively. His shoulders dropped and his head cocked to the side. Shep looked like he was afraid I would yell at him again. Tentativeness toward me was a new behavior, a wrinkle in our one-on-one relationship that we would have to iron out. The dog didn't like my angry outbursts any more than I did.

I sighed, patted Shep's head, and told him everything was all right. The dog's attention to the barn was probably nothing, but Tina Rinkerman was still missing. I really had no choice but to investigate.

"Stay," I said to Shep, then hurried into the house and grabbed Hank's .22 rifle from behind the kitchen door. If my conclusions were correct about what Guy and I had found, there was also a killer on the loose, one that had ambushed and murdered Nils Jacobsen. I wasn't taking any chances. There wasn't another soul within miles of the house. I was on my own.

The phone kept on ringing. I was starting to get annoyed. I ignored the clatter and hurried back outside. If the call was important, the caller would try again, simple as that. I'd make sure and apologize to my neighbors the first chance I got, but for now they were going to have to suffer through the constant ringing like I had to.

Shep hadn't budged from his spot, which was a good sign. If anything had moved he would've been gone in a spilt second, curious, and certain to charge whatever was lurking about with a tirade of barks.

"Come on, boy, let's make sure nobody's around." I tried to sound confident, but the slight tremble in my hand betrayed me. My gloves saved Shep from seeing the result of my nerves, but I know he heard uncertainty in my voice.

There were three barns and a garage on our property. The first barn sat on the opposite side of the house from the garage. That barn was the smallest of the three and was usually where I kept the animals that we raised to butcher. I'd already taken the winter pig for slaughter, and I wasn't expecting a new batch of chickens or a beef Hereford until early April. I had no livestock to care for this winter, which was unusual. I had enough meat in the freezer to last me until summer or longer. Besides, I could get something at the Red Owl—or smoke my Salems if I got really hungry.

To my relief, the phone finally stopped ringing.

Luckily, the full force of any blowing snow was still at my back, but the frigid cold didn't take long to infiltrate my coat and layers of clothes. I couldn't stop shivering as I made my way to the barn. If I were the praying kind, I would have broken into a pleading prayer aimed at the good Lord above. I'd lost any zeal for such things after watching Hank suffer like he had. I couldn't find any love in God's will at all—which was one of the reasons for Pastor John Mark's weekly visits. He'd tried to restore my faith, even though I thought his efforts were a lost cause.

Shep stayed next to me as I made my way around the first barn. There was no sign that anything had been disturbed. No animal tracks, no sign of any human beings at all. I looked at the border collie and said, "You didn't hear anything did you? You're happy to be home, aren't you."

I was overreacting. I was on alert. I needed things to be in their place, too. I didn't think Tina could make it this far, but I had to check.

I inspected the barn anyway, then went to the garage, searching the ground as closely as I had at the first barn. I clutched the .22 like the dear, trusted friend it was.

After tromping all over the place for nearly fifteen minutes, I was certain that the girl wasn't anywhere on the property. The third barn was on the back forty, and I'd have to get in the truck and drive over to make sure she wasn't there. That expedition was going to have to wait.

I finally made my way into the house, past ready to shed my four layers of clothes, get warm, settle down, and do some indexing work to take my mind off the day I'd had.

The phone started ringing again as soon as I walked in the door.

I took off my hat and hurried to the phone. "Trumaine residence," I said.

"Hey there, Marjorie, it's me, Darlys." I recognized her voice straight away. I did have to strain to hear her, though. Her voice was low. She sounded like she was sitting in a deep well somewhere.

"Hi, Darlys, how you doin'?" I unzipped my coat. A puddle formed under my boots as the caked snow on the soles started to thaw. The house was warm even with the waning fire in the stove. I strained to keep the receiver pressed between my ear and shoulder as I tried to listen to Darlys and take off my coat.

"Okay, all things considered," Darlys said. "Boy, this day's been a little bit of sunshine and a whole lot of gloom. They say more snow's comin' tomorrow. Gonna drop in spurts like today, too. Here one minute, gone the next."

Uff da, I thought, but didn't say. The expression was a utilitarian North Dakota response with a wide variety of meanings that ranged from dismay, bafflement, and sometimes, agreement.

Darlys kept on talking. "Where you been, Marjorie? I've been tryin' to call you for an hour. I was really startin' to get worried."

I pulled one arm out of my coat slowly. Undressing after a long excursion out into the cold was a slow, methodical operation with so many layers of clothes on. "I told the sheriff I wanted to help look for the Rinkerman girl, so I've been out in the fields for a while looking with the rest of them."

"Oh, I saw you talkin' to Guy Reinhardt. I wondered what you was doin'. I guess that explains that. Did you find her?"

I hesitated, and said, "Not a sign of her." I groaned as I pulled my other arm out of the sleeve.

"You all right, Marjorie?" Darlys said.

"Yes, I'm okay. I hurried inside to answer the phone. I'm trying to get this darned coat off without tangling myself up in the phone cord."

"Oh, well go ahead and get yourself comfortable. I'll wait."

"What?" I had to strain to hear Darlys speak, and I couldn't make out what she'd said.

"Go ahead," Darlys said, loud and clear.

"Oh, okay, thanks." I sat the receiver down and took off the remaining layers of clothes as quickly as I could. I could move a little easier, and I wasn't going to overheat anytime soon. The puddle under my boots had stopped growing. "I'm back," I said.

Darlys exhaled distantly. I knew she was blowing out a lungful of smoke. "Have you heard about Nils?"

I almost said yes, that I knew what had happened to him, but I gasped, bit my lip, and rethought my response. "What about him?" I didn't say yes or no. It felt like I was at the start of a lie, but in reality all I was doing was what Duke Parsons had said to do—*don't tell anyone what you saw.*

"He's missing." Darlys's voice went low again.

That wasn't what I was expecting her to say. I gasped again, not quite shocked. I wasn't any good at acting. "Are you sure?"

"As sure as I'm standing in Anna Jacobsen's bathroom. He's missing, Marjorie. This is terrible. We're all worried to death about Nils. Something awful is going on. That Rinkerman girl is missing, too, and now Nils."

Nils wasn't missing. He was dead. I couldn't tell Darlys what I knew.

"Goodness," I said. "How long's he been gone?"

"He didn't come home last night. That's not so unusual. At least, that's what Anna told me. Especially after an argument. He sleeps in the office at the Red Owl on those nights, don't ya know. He wasn't there this mornin' when Frank Aberle came in to open up the store. Frank felt like something was wrong when he discovered that Nils wasn't there, so he called Anna. There's no sign of Nils anywhere."

Normally I would have questioned whether Nils had reason to run off or not, but I didn't have to. He didn't run anywhere. "Well, that's awful," I said, not knowing what else to say.

"Nils and Anna have been having problems for a little while." Darlys dropped her voice to a whisper.

On one hand, I was in no mood to listen to gossip about the Jacobsens' marriage, but on the other, I knew that Nils was dead. Maybe what Darlys had to say was important. "I didn't know that. Anna seems like she's at her wit's end, but she never talks much about her life at home."

"Oh, Anna wouldn't say a cross word about Nils when we're out on Ladies Aid duty. She wouldn't inflict her personal troubles on anyone. You know that. None of us do that."

"I'm glad she has you to talk to."

I expected Darlys to keep on talking, but she didn't. The line went silent. I strained my ear and thought I could hear distant voices. I couldn't make out any words. "Are you still there, Darlys?"

"Yes," she whispered. "The sheriff is at the door. I have to go." The phone went dead. I knew why Guy was at the Jacobsens' house. He had the worst news for Anna Jacobsen that anyone could ever imagine.

CHAPTER 9

Night returned right on schedule. There was no such thing as a lingering evening in January. Darkness arrived abruptly, showing up before the clock struck five as if the color black had ownership rights to the world.

I had finally gotten warm after standing next to the stove for nearly an hour. The phone remained silent, and as tempted as I was to call Anna's house I knew there was nothing I could offer her other than my sad condolences.

Words held an unintended hollowness after death visited a house. My own widowhood had taught me that lesson. I knew I couldn't save Anna from drowning in grief or confusion. Some people never recovered from such a loss. Darlys was at the Jacobsens' house, and I was sure Anna's family would brave the weather and drive down from Stanley to provide her some much-needed comfort, because I could offer none. At least not on this night.

I had some time to arrange my words, to find some depth to them if I could, before I saw Anna again. *I'm sorry for your loss* wouldn't do.

At that thought, I moved from the stove to the window in the front room. There was nothing to see except blowing snow and Hank's security light burning brightly over the garage. The blanketed white land was monotonous; there were no distant lights, no stars in the sky, no sign of life at all. I was surrounded by nothingness.

I kept the Revelation .22 in sight wherever I went. Between the door lock, the rifle, the dog, and my own wits, I was determined to stay safe, to survive the darkness. I had work to do, a deadline to meet, bills to pay, and a friend who was in need of whatever comfort I could offer.

The tracks I'd made after I returned home had already vanished under four inches of snow. Another five inches waited in the forecast for tomorrow. Running into town to Anna's house was out of the question. The roads would be too treacherous to drive on in whiteout conditions. No matter how prepared I was, spending time stuck in a ditch wasn't something I yearned to do anytime soon.

I couldn't consider a world without Nils Jacobsen. I had known the man all of my life. Not that we were friends, but we knew each other, had gone to school together. We weren't in the same grade, though; Nils was two years younger than I was. In a town like Dickinson, everybody knew everybody, or at least knew of them. Now I knew Nils's story, beginning, middle, and end.

In the past, me and Hank would have talked the day's events through, shared our memories together, and poured out our grief at such a loss. He was my comforting voice of reason, even after the accident. I missed the calmness Hank brought to every situation, no matter how dire the situation seemed. I wasn't sure that he could have made sense out of Nils Jacobsen's death, but he would have tried.

I looked away from the barren view, then made my way into the kitchen. Hank couldn't help me now. I had to find my own strength to carry on. Collapsing into a puddle of tears wasn't going to make anything better. I'd need to cook something to take to Anna and her family.

The phone started to ring again, startling me. I jumped unconsciously and held my breath. Two shorts, one long. The pattern of rings announced that the call was for the Standishes. I imagined the news of Nils's demise traveling from one house to the next. Mills was most likely still at work at the Red Owl, calling Burlene to tell her what he knew. For a brief second, I was tempted to pick up the receiver and listen in on their conversation, like Burlene had on mine so many times before. Someone answered on the third ring, rescuing me from my temptation.

Relieved, I searched for something I could cook. I had plenty of cream and some broth I'd frozen the last time I'd boiled a chicken, so I decided to make knoephla soup. The soup was a staple in most North Dakotan kitchens. Pronounced "nefla," the soup's origin was German.

Knoephla meant little knob, or button, which is what the little pieces of dough added to the creamy potato soup looked like. Everyone, including my family, had their variation on the soup, which was really more like a thick Russian stew. I'd stood next to my mother in the kitchen as often as I could and committed the recipe to memory as a young girl. The comforting soup was simple enough to make and a viable meal option in deep winter when meat was sparse. The dough was tough, and the buttons took time to roll and snip, but the end result was worth the effort. Knoephla was my favorite soup. The soup had been Hank's favorite, too, and, like most good soups, it was more flavorful the next day. There was no question in my mind that the soup would be the perfect comfort food to take to the Jacobsens.

I set about thawing the broth in my mother's ceramic Dutch oven, then headed to the larder in the mudroom.

The larder was empty. The vegetables I needed were in the cellar. The thought nearly stopped me in my tracks. I stepped back from the larder and reconsidered my options. I really didn't want to go back out in the cold, but the knoephla soup would serve two purposes; the effort would provide my supper and food to take to Anna's house. I sighed, acknowledging that I had no choice, grabbed up the .22 and a flashlight, then headed for the door. Shep followed after me. I was tempted to make him stay in the house, but that thought only lasted a brief second. I needed the dog's ears and eyes as much as I needed my own. Besides, the root cellar was another place I hadn't searched. For all I knew, Tina Rinkerman could have sought refuge there, even though I didn't think it was possible.

My hand was on the doorknob when the phone started to ring again. I stopped, cocked my ear to the phone, and was almost relieved when the series of rings announced the call was for me. I set everything down and hurried to pick up the receiver.

"Trumaine residence," I said.

I heard nothing but static, and then a distant click—the same sound I'd heard when someone was eavesdropping on my conversations. I gritted my teeth, "Hello," I said, not doing anything to clear the annoyance from my voice.

"It's me, Marjorie. It's Darlys." She was loud and clear. I hesitated for a second after she said her name, trying to figure out if I needed to let the person listening in know that I knew they were there, but the distant click came again. I was sure they'd hung up. Honest mistakes happened all the time.

"Oh, Darlys, you sound awful," I said. "Are you all right?"

"No, Marjorie, I'm not. Nils is dead. Somebody shot him." Darlys sniffled, then broke into a sob.

I drew in a deep breath and looked away from the phone. Shep was waiting by the door, ready to go to the cellar. "No," I said as softly as I could. My hand trembled and my body went numb.

Darlys heard me. "You know what I'm saying is true, Marjorie," she whimpered. "You were there. You found Nils when you were out on the field with Guy Reinhardt."

Along with the numbness came fear. Something deep inside my stomach felt broken. "I'm sorry. I couldn't tell you," I whispered. "Guy requested that I not say anything to anyone."

"You could have told *me*," Darlys said.

No, I thought, *I couldn't have*. We didn't tell each other everything. No one did. I didn't know Darlys well enough to trust her with a secret so large, so critical. Our paths hadn't really ever crossed until Pastor John Mark had sent the Ladies Aid to my front door. And with her husband being a dentist, a professional, Darlys had a larger group of friends and memberships to organizations than I could have ever imagined. I liked her, but that didn't mean I trusted her.

"I hope you'll forgive my omission, Darlys," I said. "I was only doing what I thought was right, what the sheriff asked of me. This is such a horrible situation. I'm sorry. I really am. I don't know what to say other than that."

Darlys drew in a deep breath, and I heard the strike of a match, then that first long draw on a fresh cigarette. "I didn't tell anyone that you knew," she said, exhaling.

"How did you find out?" The words jumped out of my mouth before I could stop them. I had to know.

"You shouldn't be mad, Marjorie."

"I'm not mad. Curious is all."

"Theda told me Duke brought you back to the Rinkermans."

Guy was right to be worried. People talked. That was clear to me now. I shouldn't have gone searching for Tina Rinkerman with him. I should have paid my respects to her parents, left my pies with them, and returned home. The bad taste of regret started to grow in the back of my throat. I wanted to join Darlys and share a cigarette with her, but my purse was out of reach.

"How's Anna?" I said, hoping to change the subject.

"The doctor had to medicate her to calm her down."

"I understand."

"Her mother's coming down from Stanley to help look after the kids. Theda and Lene are staying at the house until she arrives."

Anna wasn't originally from Dickinson. She was an outsider, introduced to Nils by a friend of a friend at a high school basketball game in Stanley. Nils was older than Anna, but I wasn't sure by how much. Anna had no family in town. As far as I knew, all she had was the church and the Ladies Aid. She never spoke much about her life outside of taking care of Nils and her three kids.

"I'm relieved that Anna's mother will be there for her," I said. My mother had already passed away by the time Hank had his accident. The only family I had to lean on were the lessons my dead parents had taught me: Keep your head up, carry on, don't inflict your troubles on anyone else, wait your turn. My father had patience. My mother had backbone. Surviving on the prairie for as long as they did demanded strength and persistence, their gifts to me.

"I'm going to need your help, Marjorie," Darlys said.

"How so?"

"I'm hoping you'll fill in for Anna. Join the Ladies Aid officially. We have to help her now. She needs us, but there are more needs in our world that need tended to than hers. The Rinkermans have a tragedy all their own, and there's more to give to the congregation than most folks know. Some people have a tougher time getting through winter than others. Those folks would be mortified if the rest of the world knew their trials. I trust you, Marjorie. And I think you need us as much as we need you."

Darlys might have been right about that, but I was leery of joining anything, especially anything connected to the church. I still had my own crisis of faith to deal with.

I had to admit that I was lonely, and I was going to cook food to take to Anna's house anyway, so I was already halfway to joining. I worried whether Theda Parsons and the other women of the Aid would welcome me into their club. All of them had worked together for years.

Saying yes to Darlys would get me out of the house—away from indexing, which had gotten little attention in the past few days. I'd helped run the farm in the past, and I'd taken care of Hank at the same time. Helping Darlys wouldn't require me to juggle my duties like I'd had to when Hank was alive. I'd still met my deadlines and handled everything that came my way. Maybe I needed more on my plate than I thought I could handle. Maybe that was normal for me.

"Well," I said into the receiver, "I really don't see how I can tell you no, Darlys."

CHAPTER 10

The root cellar door was buried under a snowdrift that looked like a wave frozen in mid crash. One footstep would collapse the sculpture. I took no pity on the icy art, though I was relieved to see the snow was pristine, undisturbed by visitors of any sort, including Tina Rinkerman. I kicked the drift from the door, then eased down the steps with the bright beam of my flashlight leading the way. Even though I had no reason to hope, I held my breath as darkness vanished from the root cellar and light won a short-lived battle.

Shep stood next to the door. He didn't take his eyes off me. I grabbed up some potatoes and carrots for the knoephla soup and made my way back up the stairs, careful not to slip on the snow that had followed me in. I was a little sad that I was alone, that Tina Rinkerman *hadn't* taken up residence underneath my house. Her presence would have answered a host of prayers, and brought a conclusion to one tragedy, anyway.

Maybe she's still alive. I brushed away the thought like I had the snow. I really didn't believe a girl like Tina could survive ten minutes on her own in this kind of weather, much less two days. *She's dead. We haven't found her yet.* I was as sure of that as I was the darkness I left in my wake.

I rushed back into the house with Shep on my heels. I tried not to consider Tina Rinkerman's fate any longer—lost in a cold world—but I had to wonder if the search for her was going to continue. No one had said so. A murder investigation would take precedence over the search for a missing girl. Guy Reinhardt's top priority would be to find the person who had killed Nils Jacobsen. Then I wondered again if the

County Sheriff's Department had the resources to handle both situations; their budget seemed constantly strained.

I wondered about Guy, too. I wondered if he had the fortitude and skills to manage two major investigations. But I had faith in Guy. I knew he wouldn't give up, no matter the severity of the situation. He'd put himself in harm's way if necessary. Guy Reinhardt was good at his job, and I knew that he was going to be a respectable sheriff. If I were superstitious, I would have crossed my fingers.

With that thought, I headed for the place that gave me the most comfort: the kitchen. Now that I had everything I needed for the knoephla soup, I cut the vegetables and put them in the boiling chicken broth. From there, I set about making the dough, which was nothing more than flour, an egg, a little salt, and some water. I rolled the stiff dough into a long rope, then quickly pinched thumb-sized pieces that looked like buttons. Once the potatoes and carrots were cooked, I dropped the dough into the soup.

I stirred the pot to keep the knoephla from gumming up. Nils Jacobsen's face flashed in my memory. The dead Nils. The cold, pale Nils with his eyes open and fixed, his head slumped to the side, covered in blood. There was no sign of life anywhere in the shelterbelt. The trees had looked skeletal and dead.

The memory was the stuff of nightmares. I trembled and stirred the soup faster, hoping the dough would expand and finish so I could walk away and leave it to simmer.

Once I'd finished stirring, I cleaned up the mess I'd made, then grabbed up some saltine crackers to snack on and headed to my desk. I needed the distraction of work. If I did nothing but stare out the window waiting for my supper to cook, I'd obsess over Nils's death and Tina's disappearance even more than I already had.

Shep remained by the Franklin stove. He did that sometimes, preferring warmth to my immediate presence. I didn't mind. I knew he had one ear cocked toward the door, always listening for something to move.

My desk chair, a high-backed wood dining room chair cut from durable hickory with a comfortable pillow on the seat, seemed to wrap itself around me in a welcoming sigh as I sat down. I stared at the pile of page proofs that sat next to my manual Underwood typewriter. The little black machine was at least thirty-five years old. A few of the keys showed wear from overuse. The A and the S were almost invisible, but my fingers knew where to go even though the letters on the keys had eroded.

The page proofs were nothing more than unbound book pages laid out flat and printed on one side. There were actually two book pages per proof. I would have to rifle through the pages repeatedly, searching for a single word or concept, making sure to keep the proofs in order. Indexing a book was a tedious affair.

An empty shoebox sat on the other side of the typewriter. By the time I finished writing the index for the book, the shoebox would be full of index cards, divided by twenty-six spacers, one for each letter of the alphabet. The box stood empty, waiting to be filled. Thankfully, the deadline to send the index off to my publisher in New York City was almost a month away.

A month sounded like a long time, but I would need every minute of every working hour to get the index finished in time. *The Central Flyway: Audubon's Journey Revisited*, by Jacob T. Allsworth, was three hundred and fifty pages from beginning to end. Each book had a signature, a design feature so the printer could maximize the budget and determine the total number of pages in the book. The signature consisted of even numbers. Most designs were sixteen page signatures. The design affected my job as an indexer. I needed to know how many pages were allotted for the index before I started. That knowledge, which I learned from the USDA correspondence course, helped me select the terms that needed to be in the index. I had to make a lot of decisions at the start of an indexing project, but all I could do now was stare at the pile of pages.

I could only index a certain number of pages every day, usually between twenty and thirty if I spent eight hours at my desk. That kind of focus was possible in the winter, especially now, with only myself to take care of, but I was distracted. I had already lost a couple of days, and I would most likely lose more time to the Ladies Aid and Anna's tragedy in the coming days.

Each index entry had to be typed on an index card, after I checked for a previous entry. Indexers tended to have great memories, and I usually knew if I had typed a term before—but I still double-checked myself. I was also good at seeing patterns and understanding the structures that most nonfiction books were built on. The type of books I worked on had a heading, a sub-heading, and sometimes, a sub-sub-heading. Being able to see that structure helped me determine if a term was a main entry, how many pages a topic should range, and whether to include a sub-entry in the index. Some books were built better than others, the structure clear. That helped make my job easier—and faster.

I had yet to crack the structure of *The Central Flyway* book. I think I was avoiding the task. The topic of migration hit too close to home. Migration meant change, travel, and transformation. I was in the midst of migrating from wife to a widow. I was in a new place in my life, somewhere that I had never been and didn't want to be.

Along with the typewriter, I had other tools on my desk. I had books to help me understand books. I kept the USDA course book close by, though I rarely cracked that textbook open these days. The other books on my desk, however, gained more use. I was constantly dipping into *The Chicago Manual of Style*, the eleventh edition, published in 1949, and *Webster's Revised Unabridged Dictionary*, published in 1913. The *Webster's* had belonged to my father, and I was loathe to replace the dictionary with a newer edition. I loved the smell of the book, and the knowledge that my father's fingers had touched the pages gave me comfort. He loved words, loved that we shared a passion for them. I also kept a *Roget's Thesaurus* close by, and a pad of paper to keep notes on.

I had added a new addition to the desk since Hank had died. An

ashtray sat to the right of my typewriter. I smoked at my desk when
I was stuck, when I needed a break, or when I was hungry. I'd never
smoked at my desk when Hank was alive. That was a larger abomination than allowing the dog to sleep on the davenport.

My Salems were secure in my purse. I had no desire for a cigarette.
I needed to work.

I took up the first page proof to read. The opening chapter of the
book had nothing to do with birds, but it introduced the reader to John
J. Audubon's emigration to America and subsequent journey west. I
was immediately pulled into Audubon's young life in Missouri when
the New Madrid earthquake struck in 1811:

> I thought my horse was about to die, and would have sprung from
> his back had a minute more elapsed; but at that instant all the shrubs
> and trees began to move from their very roots, the ground rose
> and fell in successive furrows, like the ruffled water of a lake, and I
> became bewildered in my ideas, as I too plainly discovered, that all
> this awful commotion was the result of an earthquake.

The section was from *The Life of John James Audubon, The
Naturalist*, published in 1868 by G. P. Putnam's Sons, and edited by
"His Widow." There was no mention of Audubon's wife's name in the
text as the editor of the memoir. I stopped reading and searched the
page proofs, only to find Audubon's widow's name mentioned a few
pages later: Lucy Green Bakewell Audubon.

My mind swirled with index entries, but I was stuck on the notion
of Lucy Audubon's name omitted from the cover of a book she had
worked on. The work was, after all, her husband's legacy, as well as her
own. Surely she'd supported her husband's endeavors all the way up
until the time he'd died. Her effort was a connection between us. One
I wasn't sure that I liked. Maybe the title, "His Widow," was merely a
reflection of the times, being nearly a hundred years in the past.

In today's world, women were crossing new boundaries into
society. Betty Friedan had published *The Feminine Mystique* a year ago,

and Margaret Chase Smith, the first woman elected to both the House of Representatives and the Senate, became the first woman to run for a major political party's nomination for president in 1964. The world was changing, though I hadn't seen much of this so-called women's movement come to North Dakota. I only knew of such things because of my many visits to the library in Dickinson, the newspaper delivered to my door every day, and the reports I heard on the radio. I didn't own a television set. I guessed I wasn't that modern, but I was modern enough to see discrimination when the intent was clear. The first entry I made for the index was:

A

Audubon, Lucy Green Bakewell, 9

I knew there was nothing I could do to right a historical wrong. An indexer's opinion on any matter found in a book was forbidden to be included. My job was to structure the information so a reader could find what they were looking for, and nothing more. Influence was out of the parameters of my contribution to the book.

I exhaled deeply, then went on to type other entries on separate index cards:

A   N

Audubon, John James, 1–5   New Madrid (Missouri, 1811)
                                            earthquake, 5
E

earthquake, New Madrid (Mis-
    souri, 1811), 5

The last two were examples of double posting, of putting the same information in two places. Readers didn't look up a term in the same

way, so having more than one access point into the text was helpful, and
a requirement of a good index—as long as there was enough room in
the pages allotted for the index.

I read on down the page, but I was more distracted than I thought I
was. My mind continued to drift back to the present, away from Audubon's journey.

I got up and checked on the knoephla soup and decided the con-
sistency wasn't quite right yet. Then I went to my purse and grabbed
my cigarettes. Shep raised his head and watched me make my way back
to my desk.

The wind continued to rage outside, and I imagined that the snow
had kept up like promised, obscuring any sign of the living or dead. My
mind turned back to Nils Jacobsen and Tina Rinkerman as I struck a
match to light my Salem, forgoing the saltines to stave off any hunger
I might have felt.

Indexing helped me focus my mind. I had to be completely engaged
in the text to decipher and organize the references properly. Focus
wasn't a problem on normal days. This was no normal day. Maybe a
cigarette would help me forget that a good man was dead and a young
retarded girl was still missing. There was nothing normal about that.

The first question that came to my mind was this: Was the murder
a random act?

I drew deeply on the cigarette, held the smoke in my lungs longer
than I should have as I pondered on the question.

I didn't have a clear answer to the question of motive for Nils's
murder. I didn't have enough information. Actually, I had only questions and no answers. Starting with: What was Nils doing in the shelterbelt in the first place? Was he lured there? Or did he go there of his
own accord?

I was confused and sad at the same time. I had tried everything I
knew to clear my mind, except one. When I was confused, I made an
index of my thoughts and the events that I couldn't see clearly. I did that
when I needed a fresh start, a better way of looking at things. I wrote
down my thoughts with the hope of deriving a conclusion of some kind.

J

Jacobsen, Anna (I hesi-
    tated to type widow)
Jacobsen, Nils (victim)

M

missing girl
    Tina Rinkerman
    who was the last person
        to see her?
motive
    who would want to kill
        Nils?
    why did Tina leave?

R

relationships
    did Nils know Tina?
    murder and disappear-
        ance related?
Rinkerman, Adaline
    (mother)
Rinkerman, Tina (missing
    girl)
Rinkerman, Toren (father)
Rinkermans (three sons,
    find out names)

S

suspects
    could be random, but
        doesn't make sense
    none right now

T

troubles
    did Nils have any
        problems?
    did the Rinkermans
        have any troubles?

V

victim, Nils Jacobsen

W

who saw Nils last? (I don't
    know)

CHAPTER 11

The wind, of course, still blew, but it was blunted in town by all of the buildings. Snow came and went, but much lighter than the day before. There was no blizzard or storm predicted for the day, only blowing snow, flurries, and subzero temperatures. In other words, a typical January day in North Dakota.

Jaeger Knudsen had opened our road with his tractor. The drive into town was easy, especially after I had turned onto the paved county road that led into town. I was only behind the steering wheel for an hour. Twice as long as the trip would take in summer. I was in no hurry to become an official member of the Ladies Aid, but there was no turning back.

The Jacobsens lived in a single-level brick house, three blocks from the Red Owl, on the corner of Sims and 3rd Street. The house sat directly across the street from the Stark County Courthouse, a four-story Art Deco–inspired building built in the mid-1930s. The government building was a durable artifact of the Great Depression and the Works Progress Administration and had stood the test of time. The snow-covered courthouse looked like a wedding cake.

Coming to town brought a clear realization of the sacrifices I made by living out on the farm. There were no businesses or services within walking distance of my house, only treeless fields, rolls in the fields— the wheat looked like ocean waves in the summer—and sloughs that reflected the constant changes in the sky. I loved the land, my house that had been built with my grandfather's bare hands, and every acre of our farm. Even now, as alone as I was, I couldn't consider selling the place and moving into town. I'd feel closed in, lost without the sight and sounds of the magpies and meadowlarks. I was sure Shep would go mad with nothing to herd but the mail carrier.

Nils Jacobsen walked to work on most days, and I did envy towns-folk who could pop in and out of the library. Getting information for an index or finding a book to read for pleasure was never going to be the same for me without Calla Eltmore as the librarian behind the reference desk. I'd avoided the library as much as possible since her death. Delia Finch, the new librarian, had big shoes to fill. I hadn't warmed up to her yet. I wasn't sure that I ever would.

There was nowhere to park in front of the Jacobsens' house. Cars lined the block, and all of the plug-posts for the block heaters on the courthouse-side of the street were already taken. I worried about the Studebaker in the cold. The temperatures were below zero. I had jumper cables with me, along with blankets, flares, and some candy bars, in case I got stranded. Survival gear was my lone passenger on this trip. Shep was at home, stowed away in the bathroom so he didn't spoil the rugs in case I was gone too long.

I found a spot to park half a block away. I heaved up the Dutch oven full of knoephla soup and made my way carefully to the Jacobsens' house. Thankfully, folks in town kept their sidewalks shoveled, but the cement was still slick. One wrong move and I'd fall flat on my behind, sending the soup flying.

I'd left my Carhartt overalls at home. Instead, I'd dressed in my best funeral clothes. I was covered in black from head to toe. I wore a knee-length wool coat I'd had since Hank and I had married, along with a dress that I'd made myself from a McCall's pattern and my trusted Montgomery Ward shoes. My toes were about to freeze off without thick wool socks to protect them, but I wanted to present myself as a full member of the Ladies Aid and an appropriate mourner. I knew more about one than I did the other.

I set the Dutch oven down on the stoop and knocked on the door.

I held my breath and squared my shoulders, waiting for what came next—a room full of sad, confused, grief-stricken people. I knew the mood of the gathering all too well, though I could never pretend to know the shock of murder as well as Anna Jacobsen did. My own troubles and grief were unimportant and best left behind, but I couldn't help but bring them with me. I had expected Hank to die at some point after the accident, but I'd had time to gird myself, as much as that was possible, for the loss. I didn't think Anna was expecting Nils to die anytime soon. They were still in the midst of raising a family. I'm sure they'd planned on growing old and gray together like Hank and I had.

The door opened, and I was relieved to see Darlys Oddsdatter's familiar face. "Oh, there you are, Marjorie," she said. "Me and Theda were just talkin' about you."

I forced a smile. "I hope the talk was all good." I wasn't real comfortable around Theda Parsons. I had expected Lene Harstaad to be there, too.

"How could you think otherwise, Marjorie? We're so happy you're joining us." Darlys smiled briefly, reached out and touched my shoulder, then looked down at the Dutch Oven. "Oh, that smells good. Well, come on, get in here out of the cold." She peered up at the sky, and said, "The snow's not too heavy today. Things could always be worse."

I agreed, then picked up the soup and walked inside the Jacobsens' house. The front room was small and packed with people from town and beyond. I spied a few familiar faces right away. Burlene Standish, who looked away as soon as I walked in the door, stood talking to her cousin, Olga Olafson. Olga worked the reception desk at St. Joseph's Hospital. I'd had plenty of interaction with her over the last two years. She looked away, too, when we made eye contact. My comfort level wasn't exactly on full tilt, but I wasn't going to show any discomfort to anyone in the room. I smiled as much as I thought was allowable for the situation.

I had expected to see Frank Aberle, the assistant manager at the Red Owl, but he was nowhere to be seen. He was probably manning the store. The weather had let up and they were probably busy with people restocking for the next wave of heavy snow. The grocery store never closed in January.

Duke Parsons stood inside the door. I almost didn't recognize him.

His brown uniform shirt was neatly ironed and tucked in, his black boots were polished, and his silver badge sparkled from the overhead light. He wore a stern face and looked me over in an official way. "Mrs. Trumaine," he said with a nod.

"Hello, Deputy Parsons." I forced another smile. I still couldn't believe Duke blamed me for losing the election. He had a lot of nerve telling me such a thing. "Good to see you," I said. We both knew that I didn't mean what I'd said, but there was no use allowing the tension to spread inside the Jacobsens' house. Doom and gloom sat heavily on every face I saw.

Six young children sat on the floor in the corner, parked in front of the television. Black and white images flickered, and the sound of a Saturday morning cartoon filled the room. The program was some kind of antics with a talking cat and mouse named Tom and Jerry. The children were lost in the make-believe world. None of them were laughing. Either the cartoon wasn't funny, or the children had been given instructions to be seen and not heard.

Three of the older children belonged to Anna and Nils. I didn't recognize two of the others, but I knew the youngest to be Pastor John Mark's son, Paul Mark. I looked around the room and saw Pastor standing in the corner talking to Henrik Oddsdatter, Darlys's husband.

"Come on," Darlys said. "Theda's in the kitchen with Pastor's wife. The neighbor lady, Helen Greggson, is helping out, too, but she had to run home for a second. Do you know her?"

The name didn't ring a bell. "No, I don't think I do. I should say hello to Pastor real quick, don't you think?"

Darlys glanced at Pastor, then at Henrik. Her faced changed, went blank, emotionless. "Yes, of course."

She cut through a crowd of fifteen people, and I followed. Both men saw us coming, stopped talking, stood, and waited. Pastor and I matched in our black attire, while Henrik Oddsdatter was dressed as stylishly as his wife was. He wore a tweed jacket, a brown pullover sweater, and a tie to match the flecks of gray in his sideburns. His smile was perfect, as one would imagine a dentist's smile should be.

I set the Dutch oven on the floor next to my ankle. I could still feel a bit of warmth radiating from the soup. My toes started to thaw.

Pastor took both my hands into his. "I can't tell you how pleased I am to see you, Marjorie," he said. His summer blue eyes sparkled with sincerity, and his perfect yellow straw-colored hair made him almost glow.

"Yes, well, I'm happy to help out."

Henrik stood and watched. He didn't have a smile on his face, and, with a hard-set jaw, he was easy to mistake for an angry man. That was how his face was made. Everyone knew him to be a gentle dentist and a kind, generous man. He spoiled Darlys to a fault, gave her everything she could want, including the finest wardrobe I had ever seen.

"Connie'll be so happy to see you," Pastor continued.

I forced a smile and withdrew my hand. I couldn't tell him that I didn't want to be at the Jacobsens' house. No one did. "Well, I hope to be of some service in the next few days."

"Your presence will be a comfort," Pastor said.

I smiled politely, then turned my attention to Henrik. "Hello, Doctor Oddsdatter. I rarely see you outside of your office."

Darlys stood beside me, still as an owl on a tree branch.

"The day demanded that I be here. You may call me Henrik, please." His Swedish accent was apparent and endearing. His face softened when he spoke.

"Of course," I said. "I'm sorry to see you here, though."

"Yes, so sad." Henrik looked down at the children watching the television. "Mrs. Jacobsen left to care for four children all on her own."

"Three," I said, before I could stop myself from correcting him. "They only have three children." It was an odd comment, and I wondered if Henrik and Darlys knew whether Anna was pregnant for sure.

"Yes, of course. Three. I see so many families in my office it is hard to keep up," Henrik said.

"I imagine it is."

"Have you read any good books lately?" Henrik said.

The question took me by surprise. "Only for work," I answered.

"Yes, this indexing thing you do. Darlys has filled me in. I am fascinated by a mind that can organize a book like you are able. We must speak of your skill sometime soon. We have something in common, I think."

"What is that?" I said curiously.

"Ah, well, a patient comes to see me because they are in pain, or they do not like what they see in the mirror and they want to change. I can give them a smile, as perfect a face as they could ask for. I make order out of what they were given. I make them beautiful. You make them smart by giving them the location of information. In the end, our pursuit is perfection. Everything has its place, no?"

"Yes, I guess it does." I didn't see how dentistry and indexing had anything in common, but I appreciated Henrik's effort to make it so. Most of the time I felt like an outsider as an indexer, an odd bird. Henrik didn't see me that way. I smiled consciously, knowing the health of my teeth were most likely being judged.

Darlys tugged on my arm. "We should get to the kitchen. I think the ladies are going to need our help soon. If you'll excuse us." She motioned for me to pick up the Dutch oven.

I smiled and did as I was instructed, then followed Darlys into the crowd, toward the kitchen. "That man," she said, under her breath, exasperated.

"I'm sorry, what?"

"Oh, nothing. Never mind."

We weaved in and out of people, heading slowly toward the kitchen, and I was left to wonder what her problem with Henrik was.

"Is that your knoephla soup?" Darlys said over her shoulder.

"Is that okay?" She wasn't going to expound, and I wasn't going to press.

"Oh, ya betcha. No one's brought knoephla. There's some lamb and cabbage stew, meatballs, some Fleischkuekle that Theda brought that I can't wait to try, and more pies and fruit salads on the table than you can shake a stick at."

I hadn't had a meat pie in a long time. Fleischkuekle was a German dish made with ground beef and onions that brought back warm memories for me. The first time I'd ever eaten it was at a little diner in Stanton, the county seat of Mercer County, to the northeast of us. Hank had taken me there on our first date.

The Jacobsens' eat-in kitchen was small, about ten feet by ten feet, enough room for a two-burner stove, a Kelvinator refrigerator, some cabinets, and a double sink. A heavy steel dinette set sat in the corner. All of the chairs were in the front room. The table was loaded with enough food to last a month. I resisted the temptation to start reorganizing the table in alphabetic order. Apple salad, banana pudding, crumb cake, kuchen, lefse, sour cream and raisin pie, and so on. All that food was nothing more than a smorgasbord of sadness that I had seen before.

Connie Llewellyn, Pastor's wife, turned from the sink and stopped washing dishes when I entered the room.

"Well, Mrs. Trumaine, how nice to see you. Darlys said you were going to join us." A big smile accompanied Connie's kind words.

"I'm happy to be here." That wasn't entirely true, considering the circumstances.

I carried the knoephla over to the table, found an empty spot between the lefse and the kuchen, then turned to face a grim Theda Parsons. The two of us had rarely spoken, our paths opposite and divergent. I could tell from the set of her jaw and the coldness in her dim blue eyes that she held the same grudge against me that her brother did.

"Good to see you, too, Theda," I added.

"Likewise," Theda Parsons said, then turned back around and resumed her chore of drying dishes.

"Where can I put this?" I said as I took off my coat. I was warm all over, except for my feet.

"I'll put your coat on the kids' bed," Darlys said. She extended her right hand. "You can put your purse over in the cupboard with ours."

I handed my coat to Darlys, then made my way to the cupboard.

The cupboard was stuffed full of crackers, canned soup, and at least fifty boxes of lime Jell-O. I set my purse on an empty shelf with the other purses. "What do you need?" I said, as I faced the two women. Darlys hadn't returned yet.

"You can make a round through the front room, collect any empty plates, and see if anybody needs anything," Theda said to me, more like she was talking to an employee than a friend. "Getting nigh onto dinnertime for most of these men, and we need to fix plates to take over to the sheriff's office, too."

Connie stepped in between us. "I think Pastor was hoping you would speak with Anna," she said in a low voice. "He knows you have a little experience at this sort of thing and might be able to offer some comfort that he can't." The look on her face wouldn't allow me to say no. "I'll take care of making the rounds. Go ahead and take a cup of tea to Anna. Something hot will do her good."

"Yes, of course," I answered. "I haven't a clue what to say to Anna, but I'm sure I'll come up with something."

"You have a gift for words, Marjorie. I know you'll have no trouble with an offering from the heart."

I stood there stiffly, surrounded by the smell of food created to ward off fear and shock, the sound of small talk, bordering on gossip at a low volume, all the while searching my mind for something more than clichés or greeting card sayings. I couldn't come up with anything on the spot. I was running a little low on hope and happiness myself.

CHAPTER 12

I knocked on the bedroom door, and said, "Hello . . . Anna, it's me, Marjorie." Then I waited, the teacup warm in my hand, Lipton orange pekoe aroma wavering upward in thin, familiar vapors. I was uncomfortable, certain that I was about to face a woman shattered by a cruelty no one deserved to experience. How did Guy tell her? *Your husband was murdered.* There was no easy way to say such a thing.

I heard a distant rustling and soft voices from inside the bedroom, then footsteps padded to the door. When the door opened, I stood facing a shorter, older version of Anna Jacobsen. I immediately assumed the tidy woman was Anna's mother. Her cotton-ball white hair was perfectly set, and she was dressed in a gray wool skirt, with a handmade sweater to match.

"Yes?" the woman said, eyeing me suspiciously.

"Pastor's wife sent me with a cup of tea," I whispered. "Do you think she's up to some company?"

The woman didn't let go of her suspicious frown. "And you are?"

"I'm Marjorie. Marjorie Trumaine. I have a farm south of town. Anna's been visiting me since my husband, Hank, passed away last fall."

Another voice, weak and distant, said, "Who's there mother?" I recognized Anna's voice. She sounded ill, next to death, shattered. I wasn't surprised.

"A Marjorie Trumaine with a cup of tea. Would you like that?" her mother said.

"Yes, please let her in. I'm sure you could use a break from me."

Anna's mother let her stiff shoulders fall. The tightness in her wind-worn face relaxed, too. Even in the light from where I stood, the woman looked ashen, drained of energy and emotion. "Yes, I think that's a good idea." She pulled open the door and stepped back to let me into the bedroom.

"Thank you," I said.

"I'm Abigail Olson, Anna's mother," the woman said, then closed the door, shutting out the low hum of chatter coming from the front room and kitchen.

"Nice to meet you." I balanced the saucer and teacup in my left hand, and extended my right hand. Abigail returned the gesture with a soft shake. "I'm sorry for your loss," I said.

Anna's mother sighed, and looked upward at nothing in particular. "This is quite a shock for us all. Anna has spoken of you, told me about your husband's accident."

"Yes. Hank fought a long, hard battle."

"He's in a better place now," she said.

I forced a blank look to stay on my face and stopped the words that were about to erupt from my mouth. I couldn't bring myself to accept the idea that the better place Hank was in wasn't with me. Most people took comfort in the idea that my husband was waiting for me in the afterlife, in heaven, but my broken faith wouldn't allow that kind of hope to take seed. My heart had suffered a severe break that had left lingering damage. Hank was the optimistic one. He'd had to be positive to make a living as a farmer. There was always a problem to confront and conquer: the weather, grasshoppers, rust on the barley, or a pigeon grass invasion. You name the challenge, Hank always had something to overcome, something to test his will, his faith. I wasn't sure that I would ever believe in anything again, though that in itself was like losing a part of myself.

I didn't say anything to Abigail. I wasn't about to share my feelings about a better place with her. Instead, I looked past her to Anna, who was sitting on the edge of an unmade double bed, staring at the dresser across from her. The small piece of furniture was loaded with perfume bottles and pictures, mostly of her kids but a few were of her and Nils when they were younger, at least ten years ago, before they'd gotten married and had kids. They looked good together, a perfect fit, with their whole life ahead of them.

"I think I will step out for a minute, Anna," Abigail said.

The room smelled of sickness. A sour, pungent odor met my nose as soon as I walked farther into the bedroom, replacing the soothing aroma of the tea. I spied the source of the smell as I looked back at Anna. A wastebasket sat at her feet. She was sick to her stomach, and the tiny house, like most houses I knew of, only had one inside bathroom. Anna had chosen to stay hidden in her bedroom for fear of running out and letting a room full of people see her in her current state. I didn't blame her.

"I'll be fine, Momma. I've told you, Marjorie is a friend," Anna said.

I waited until Abigail was gone before I took the tea to Anna. I restrained the temptation to ask, *How are you?* I knew how she was. Numb, lost, unable to say how she felt, because she had never felt this way in her whole life. I was certain Anna Jacobsen wanted more than anything was to lay down, go to sleep, and never wake up again.

Anna took the tea, stared into the cup, and didn't bother to take a sip. She wore a heavy pink robe, wrapped snugly around her body to keep herself as warm as possible. Her swollen feet were stuffed into a matching pair of fuzzy house-slippers. Her face was puffy, too, and I had the same fleeting thought cross my mind as the last time that I had seen her: *Are you pregnant?* I couldn't bring myself to ask the question. I could only continue to hope that I was wrong. Especially now.

I sat down next to Anna. "I'm sorry," I said. There was nothing else I could come up with to say. Then I shut up. If Anna wanted to talk, she would, and if she didn't, then I would sit quietly with her for a while. I couldn't change anything that had happened or anything that was going to happen. She had enough people telling her what to feel, what to think, what to do. She didn't need my two cents.

A little space heater hummed in the corner, the elements as red and hot as the inside of a toaster, and a small lamp on the opposite nightstand offered some dim light. Anna's face was pale. Her eyes were as red as the summer sun and dry as a drought—she looked all cried out.

"What do you think Nils was doing out there, Marjorie?" she finally said. "I haven't dared ask anyone because I can't make sense of any of this. He never went out to South Heart. I can't think of any reason he'd be near there. Mills Standish took care of any business with the Rinkermans." She let the name trail off. The girl was still missing, as far as we both knew.

I understood why a butcher would need Toren's services, either as a welder or as a blade sharpener, but that didn't explain why Nils was at the shelterbelt. That was a question for the sheriff to ask, but I was as confused as Anna was.

"I can't believe he's really dead," Anna went on. "I expect him to walk in the door any minute and ask what all of these people are doing in our house. What in the heck was he doing so far from town, so far from us?" she said.

"I don't know, Anna," I said softly. I wondered if she knew that I was with Guy when he'd found Nils. I wondered if Darlys had told her. "I'm sure the police will figure this out."

"You're sure of that?"

"I am. They're good, smart men. All of them." Anna had mentioned the new sheriff at my house in a negative way. I got the impression that she didn't think much of Guy Reinhardt but had restrained herself because she knew we were friends.

Anna trembled, pleaded with her eyes for me to tell her that this was nothing but a bad dream. I knew the look. The teacup and saucer clanked in her hand like the first notes of a sad song. "We argued the night before, Marjorie. We said terrible things to each other. He stormed out, and he never came back. I thought he'd go to the store and sleep in his office. That's what he always did, and then, the next day, I thought I'd find a box of chocolates on the kitchen table. But they weren't there. I'll never be able to tell him I'm sorry." A tear ran down Anna's cheek. She set the teacup on the floor, then dabbed the tear away. "How does a person live with something like that, Marjorie?"

I exhaled and looked up at the ceiling like Anna's mother had. I had no answers for her. None that I could form in my mind that would offer any comfort. I had told Hank all of my fears and regrets, and he had told me his. We'd had plenty of time to say what we had to tell each other before he died. Anna didn't get that time. I had no direct experience with the kind of loss she was experiencing.

Darlys had told me about the argument but not what it was about. I wasn't going to dare ask, but I couldn't help myself from being curious. *What in the world did Anna and Nils have to fight about?* Me and Hank had our disagreements, but they were never so severe that Hank went off and slept somewhere else. He'd refused to go to bed mad. I couldn't understand a marriage that wasn't like mine, but I knew everyone was different. Besides, what did I know about keeping house for a working husband and raising three kids in this day and age?

I leaned over and pulled Anna next to me. We sat in silence, glued in place, protected by the brick on the outside and the goodwill in the front room. Abigail eventually returned and relieved me from my spot. To be honest, I was glad to leave the sad and stuffy bedroom. I could hardly breathe in there.

CHAPTER 13

Helen Greggson, Anna's next-door neighbor, had returned to the kitchen. She didn't look familiar to me, and I was sure that I didn't look familiar to her, but I knew of her. She was the neighbor who watched Anna's children when she had Ladies Aid duties. Our paths hadn't crossed at church, and I had little contact with anyone at the university, where Helen worked.

Living a half hour out of town was isolating, to say the least, and Hank's accident had really kept me from circulating among people. Not that I socialized a whole lot, anyway. I've never been ambitious that way, not like Darlys Oddsdatter was, and I was sure I never would be.

"I remember your cousin," Helen said. The hard look on the woman's face said everything. She didn't seem to like Raymond too much. I couldn't blame her. Raymond had put on airs as a child and never took them off.

Helen Greggson was older than I was by at least thirty years. That put her in her mid-sixties, old enough to be my mother. She wore her age well. Her blue eyes were bright as a robin's egg, she stood up straight and tall, and she was dressed in a black wool dress that helped her look slender and fit. Her ring finger was bare and showed no sign that jewelry of any kind had ever touched her skin. I wondered if she was a widow like Anna and me or had chosen not to marry. I was curious how a woman survived life after the loss of a husband. There were no manuals for such things that I knew of.

"I have to say," Helen continued, "that I didn't see much of your cousin. I worked in the bursar's office for almost forty years. Professors of his ilk had little cause to visit us. I was a cashier and an accounting clerk, you know. His father, the dean, was another story. Mr. Hurtibese was a nice man when he was out of range of people who mattered."

I certainly wasn't going to gush on about Raymond or his father, but I wasn't going to speak ill of the dead, either. "Raymond rarely left his office, from what I understand."

"Well, he faced a sad end, didn't he?" Helen said. "But no one was really surprised."

The other women in the kitchen, Connie, Darlys, and Theda, went about their business, acting as if they weren't listening. Gossip was a type of currency in a small town, and not one that I liked to carry with me. There was no escaping peoples' fears and opinions. The stories we passed from one person to the other connected us in a way. I wasn't any more accustomed to sharing gossip than taking to off my wedding rings.

More food had arrived on the crowded table, and more dirty dishes had piled up next to the sink. A low hum of conversation wafted in from the front room. My mouth had dried up as I searched for some decency within myself. I didn't take the bait from Helen Greggson and speak poorly of Raymond.

Connie turned around from the sink, and said, "Marjorie, I was wondering if you'd like to run some food over to the sheriff's office with Darlys. I think the three of us can handle this crowd while you're away." She spoke to me, but stared at Helen Greggson with disapproval.

Rescued again. I was starting to like Connie Llewelyn even more than I thought I did.

Darlys and I shuffled across the street to the courthouse like penguins on a mission. The wind had picked up since I'd arrived at the Jacobsens', but the sky was void of any falling snow. Gray clouds marched eastward in as much of a hurry to flee the cold as we were. My plan was to be home before six more inches of promised snow started to fall in earnest. We didn't speak, didn't chatter on about anything. All of our focus was on staying upright and not dropping the plates of food Connie Llewellyn had sent over to the sheriff's office.

Once inside, we stopped to catch our breath in the building's small vestibule. A wall heater blew warm air out of a rusted grate, fighting a losing battle. Darlys was dressed in her blue parka and Arctic boots, and I was still in my long coat and dress shoes. I couldn't feel my feet.

"Goodness, Marjorie, you're gonna freeze to death if you don't watch yourself," Darlys said, pulling back her fur-lined hood. Somehow, she managed to keep every blonde hair perfectly in place. She must've practiced that move a hundred times.

"I'll be fine," I said. I set the plates down next to my ankle, then rubbed my gloves together and flexed my toes to warm them up.

Darlys smiled. "I appreciate your help."

"I haven't done much."

"More than you think."

"To be honest, I'm not used to being around so many people."

"You've done this before."

"Only when I had to."

Darlys smiled. "That's why I think you'll be good at this."

"I hope you're right."

"I am. You'll see. I'm always right about things like this. Well, let's get moving before this food gets too cold to be proud of."

I reached down to pick up the plates that I'd carried over. Darlys was through the door, heading for the dispatch desk before I was vertical. If I had half as much energy in my little finger as that woman did, I could index fifty books a year and run two farms. I hurried to catch up with her, making sure I didn't slosh the food off the plates.

George Lardner had worked as a dispatcher with the Stark County Sheriff's Department for as long as I could remember. He'd worked under the long-time sheriff Hilo Jenkins since he'd returned home from World War II, and he obviously had survived the recent upheaval in the department.

"We're over at the Jacobsens' house and thought you and the boys would appreciate some dinner," Darlys said to George. Dinner was the noon meal for all of us, and supper the evening meal. Lunch was for schoolkids.

"Oh, that's mighty nice of you, Darlys. Them skies out there are about to unload again. You be careful on your way home." George looked nearly as old as Helen Greggson but not as well preserved. His skin was mottled with age spots, and his hair was as gray and unruly as the clouds in the sky. "Watcha got there? Smells real good."

I stood back and let Darlys do the talking. There was no one else beyond the dispatcher's desk. All of the doors were closed. I figured all of the planning or investigating was going on in offices, hidden away from everyone's sight.

"Oh, some Fleischkuekle that Theda made, some salads, and a nice variety of pie for you all to share," Darlys said.

"Fleischkuekle sure does sound good about now. Theda only makes that dish for special occasions. I'll have me some of that," George said.

Somewhere in the back of my mind, I knew that George and Theda had dated on and off over the years, but for some reason marriage had never come for them. I didn't know why that was, and I wasn't real interested in finding out.

"You know Marjorie Trumaine," Darlys said, reaching back and pulling me forward to the desk.

"I know Marjorie," George said with a frown, then looked at me. "I heard you was helpin' out with the Ladies Aid, Marjorie. That's a good thing."

"I guess so." A cold draft pushed in from the door, running straight up my back. I didn't like George's tone, but I tried not to show my feelings.

Darlys glanced at me, then back to George. She leaned forward and said in a low voice, "Any word on who did this horrible thing to Nils Jacobsen?"

"Now, Darlys, you know I can't tell you anything like that," George answered.

"Well, what about that Rinkerman girl? Have they found her?" Darlys persisted.

"No, they haven't found her yet."

"Does one thing have to do with the other? Everybody's wonderin' that very thing, George."

"Can't tell you that, either, Darlys Oddsdatter. You got wax in your ears?" George said.

"Not even for an extra piece of sour cream and raisin pie?"

"Nope. Sheriff Reinhardt said we shouldn't talk about this investigation to no one. Not even our friends or families once we go home. He meant what he said, and I don't need no trouble, Darlys. None of us do these days, if you know what I mean."

"No, I don't think I do, George," Darlys said.

"People get nervous when someone new comes into office. We worked for Hilo for a long time. Most of us didn't work for no one else except for Duke that short period of time. Sheriff might be lookin' to make changes with his own people, that's all. I really like bein' a dispatcher."

"Oh, George, Guy Reinhardt isn't going to fire you. Nobody knows your job any better than you do," Darlys said.

"Well, I'm not gettin' any younger."

Darlys smiled again, then reached out and tapped George's wrinkled hand. "You tell the sheriff we brought him some dinner, George, and I put an extra piece of pie on your plate anyway."

"Thank you, Darlys. Always a pleasure to see you." George left his hand in place and looked Darlys up and down in a way that made me uncomfortable. There was no question that Darlys was a beautiful woman. She didn't seem offended by George's appreciation of her appearance. Maybe she was used to men looking at her like she was something to have and to hold. I sure wasn't.

Darlys pulled back and turned to go. I followed her lead.

"Oh, and you, too, Marjorie. Good to see you, too," George said as we walked away. He didn't sound like he meant it. That didn't surprise me, either.

CHAPTER 14

Instead of returning to the Jacobsens', Darlys pulled me around the corner of the courthouse. "I sure could use a cigarette before we go back in there. How about you?" she said.

I didn't see that I had much choice, but a cigarette sounded like a good idea to me. I wished I was dressed to be outside. We ducked into another vestibule to escape the bite of the cold wind. The temperature hadn't climbed above zero if I was to guess.

The vestibule was a three-by-eight-foot cube. Wind pushed through the cracks, bouncing off another set of double-glass doors that led into the courthouse. The doors were locked, and all of the lights in the foyer were off.

"George Lardner was in a mood," Darlys said, taking off her gloves. She stuffed them into a deep pocket, then produced a small, black purse. Hidden pockets were one of the many advantages of wearing a parka. I couldn't help but be a little envious.

"I think this last election soured some people," I said.

"Nobody likes change." Darlys pulled a pack of Winstons out of the clutch and offered me one. I took it. My purse was stowed away in the cupboard at Anna's house.

Darlys pulled a cigarette out for herself, then produced a Zippo lighter and flicked the little wheel with her thumb. Her fingernails were perfectly manicured, painted with an understated flesh tone nail polish. I wondered what else she had in that little purse.

She offered me the flame, and I drew in on the cigarette. I coughed like it was my first time inhaling. I didn't know what I was thinking. I smoked Salems—menthols. Winstons weren't flavored in any way;

they were harsh and strong and tasted like burnt straw, which was okay if you were used to smoking them. I wasn't.

"Are you all right?" Darlys said.

"Winstons." I coughed again, then took a gentler draw on the brown-tipped cigarette. This time I was successful.

"You might be right about the election," Darlys said, tucking the cigarettes back where they belonged. "But I think this murder really has everyone on edge. Who would have ever thought someone could kill Nils Jacobsen? There are some other fellas around this town that I could see something bad happening to, but not Nils. He was a decent, hard-working man. The Red Owl won't be the same without him being there."

"I can't imagine him not being there." I rarely spoke with Nils when I was in the store. I'd wave hello and hurry on about my business. I took his presence for granted. We all did.

"I'm baffled by all of this."

"Not everything is as simple as it looks." We both knew that I had some experience with murders.

"I think you might be right, Marjorie." Darlys took a long drag off the cigarette and stared out the door. "But I can't make sense of any kind of violence."

This vestibule had a heater in the wall like the one at the Sheriff's Department entrance. The warmth helped, but I was still cold. I let some silence settle between us, then said, "Can I ask you a question, Darlys?"

"Of course you can."

"I really don't know how to ask because what I want to know is really none of my business. I don't want to be a gossip, but maybe if I'm right about what I'm thinking, I can help."

Darlys let her hand with the cigarette drop to her side, and a concerned look fell over her normally cheery face. "Nobody will think you're a gossip, Marjorie."

I hesitated, then blurted out the question. I'd had my suspicions since the most recent Ladies Aid visit to my house, and I was hoping Darlys knew the answer. "Is Anna pregnant?"

Darlys studied my face closely. I wasn't sure what she was looking for, but she took a deep, shivering breath before she answered me. "That *would* be a tragedy, wouldn't it?"

"You don't know?"

Darlys took another draw off her cigarette, then blew the smoke out slowly, breaking my gaze. "I have my suspicions, but you've been around Anna enough to know that she doesn't talk much about her life outside of taking care of the kids and Nils. Anna and I are not the best of friends, you know. We work well together, but that's all."

"She seems to ignore the things she doesn't want to deal with."

"Exactly," Darlys said. "I've been trying for years to get her to open up to me, and she won't budge. I'm surprised she agreed to come out to your house on your regular visits with me and Lene. I've got a feeling that she doesn't like me much. I do know she had problems taking the pill. Made her sicker than a dog. Didn't work at all for her and Nils. I guess they had to resort to the old-fashioned way of doing things."

I felt my face flush a little bit. Me and Hank never worried about birth control. We figured out pretty quickly that a child wasn't going to come our way. The topic of birth control had become a hot and sensitive topic over the last few years, giving a woman the choice of having a baby or not. I guess I hadn't thought about the pill having a bad effect on some women. Small talk like that was one of the things I missed working at home as an indexer and taking care of the farm. I was around men and dogs more than I was women.

"Maybe she feels like an outsider being from Stanley," I said.

"She's been in Dickinson long enough to claim this town as her own."

"You know how people are."

"I guess I do."

The wind gusted a little harder, rattling the entrance door. I looked away from Darlys to the blank white world outside and wondered what I was doing standing there.

I had another question to ask that was none of my business. I was as concerned about Darlys's state of mind as much as I was about Anna's condition. "You've been busy with everything. Are you all right?"

"What do you mean?" Darlys said.

"You seemed annoyed at Henrik when I first arrived."

"Oh, that. He was engaged with you, but if that was me talking to another man, he would have had a fit once I got home. Sometimes I can't breathe around him is all."

"Oh," I said.

"Don't get me wrong, Henrik is very good man. He just needs to control everything around him, including me, and sometimes I don't like it. That's probably more than you wanted to know, right?"

Henrik was jealous. He knew how men looked at Darlys, how they treated her different from everyone else. He was a smart man, he would see that. I suppose I understood, but I was uncomfortable knowing what Darlys had told me. "I thought I saw a strain, that's all. This is hard on everyone."

"Can you come back tomorrow?" Darlys said.

I wasn't expecting her to change the subject. I hesitated with my answer. I had indexing work to do. "Yes, I can come back. Is Lene going to be here?"

Darlys shrugged. "I don't know. She called this morning and said she had to help Ollie clear the roads. It was their turn, or something. She didn't say much other than she was sorry she couldn't be there for Anna. I guess she'll be here tomorrow. I hope so. Anna could use her comfort."

"Are you going to church tomorrow? I almost forgot tomorrow is Sunday."

"Yes, but Anna's not."

"Why don't I come while everyone is at church? I can help around the house, get things ready."

"That's a good idea. I'll check with Abigail, but I think she'll welcome your company."

"I think Anna will really need us all after the funeral," I said.

"I hope we have some answers by then."

"Yes, I hope so, too."

People came and went from the Jacobsens' house all day. I stayed busy in the kitchen making sure plates were picked up and everyone was being served. The four of us had found a rhythm in our shared duties. Connie was in charge, even though Darlys was the director of the Ladies Aid. Me and Theda only dealt with each other when we had to. Helen Greggson stood sentry at the dish sink, wearing yellow plastic gloves that reached up to her elbows. She had eczema, and mentioned the irritable skin condition every five minutes, but wouldn't give up her spot at the sink once she had relieved Connie from that post.

The air in the crowded house smelled of rich, sugary food meant to ward off grief and fear, and mixed with cigarettes and sweat it only served as a reminder of the need to gather in the first place. Someone had brought a bouquet of carnations as a gesture of hope. The long-stemmed flowers were an unusual sight in winter, the promise of better days ahead consolidated in a bright pink bloom, offering a simple fragrance that was meant to be comforting—like the food—but instead it was the smell that I most often associated with funerals. There was no escaping the subject of death in the front room, in words, actions, or smells. The questions I heard most often were the same as Darlys's and mine:

Maybe it was a hunting accident?

Nils doesn't have any enemies that I know of. The person who did this must have been a stranger to this town. Right?

Should I be afraid?

Who do you think the killer is?

Who would do such a thing to such a nice man?

Why haven't they caught the killer yet?

Beyond that, there was talk of the weather, of politics—President Johnson's Great Society program was a thorn to most of the older anti-New Deal men in the room—the Vietnam War, hockey scores, and of course, grain prices and the predictions of the coming growing season.

One word blended into another, and before long all of the conversations meshed into a singsong of sadness and fear.

I started to get the itch to go home late in the afternoon. The front room had thinned, and Darlys and Connie had signaled that they would stay on through the evening, leaving me, Theda, and Helen Greggson to consider our own schedules for the rest of the day. I had already committed my service to Darlys for the next day. I wasn't sure of the other two women.

"Well, then," I said, peering out the kitchen window, "I think I'll get myself ready to go. I'd like to get home before the snow starts flying again."

I inserted the key into the ignition with baited breath. There was a good chance that the Studebaker wouldn't start. The truck had sat along the street for more hours than I cared to count, with the plug to the block heater dangling out of the grill unattended. I pumped the accelerator at the same time I turned the key. The engine whined, *I'm cold, I'm cold, I'm cold*, warning me to back off and try again before I ran down the battery. I exhaled, and my breath filled the cab with vapors that turned to crystal as soon they hit the windshield. I thought I was going to have to search for someone to give me a jump, but then the gas in the carburetor sparked and the engine coughed and chugged, then started to shake and run. I would have to sit there for ten minutes, babying the accelerator to keep the engine going while all of the oil, grease, and parts warmed up enough to drive home.

My mind wandered away from the Jacobsens and their troubles, but not too far. I thought of an old argument that I'd had with Hank, one of the few times I could remember that he was angry enough with me to consider going to bed mad.

Our life had been moving along at a normal pace a few years before the accident, with Hank working the farm and me learning to index books. Harvest season was coming on, a busy time for everyone. After that came readying for winter and all that entailed.

Hank came walking into the kitchen with greasy hands and bloody knuckles. He slammed the screen-door behind him. I about jumped out of my skin.

"I know you don't want to hear this, Marjorie, but now's the time for me to go buy that new combine," he said. "I don't care what you say, I'm going over there today and that's that."

I was standing at the sink, my hands deep in lukewarm dishwater, washing up a roasting pan that I had used for our noontime dinner. I didn't like the sound of an ultimatum before I had a chance to have my say. "You're sure Farley Kaander over at the implement store doesn't have a part that will work on the old one?"

We'd been having this talk for a couple of years. The old combine was on its last leg, but every year Hank had managed to repair whatever was the matter to survive the season. The economy was bad as the Eisenhower years ended, and the price per bushel had dropped to a dangerous low. And, of course, the weather had not cooperated. More like conspired against us, if I could say such a thing aloud. I didn't dare. Between the wind and dry weather, it was a wonder that any soil remained on top of the ground at all. There was never a good time to take a loan out on any kind of equipment, but I could tell by the look on Hank's face and the blood on his hands, that he'd had enough. He meant what he'd said.

He had his heart set on a new Allis-Chalmers Gleaner Model E, and there was no way we could buy the combine outright. We'd have to take on more debt, and I wasn't keen on that. Neither was he, but, without saying so, he thought my indexing money was a windfall for us to use to keep the farm going. I thought my winter earnings were a nest egg for a rainy day.

"I'm sure Farley doesn't have what I need, Marjorie. You know that." Hank stood in the middle of the kitchen, his hands at sides as if he were a gunfighter in a Western movie about to draw on three.

I dried my hands off with a damp towel and took in the stance, and the look on Hank's face. "Seems to me the more machinery you have the more land you have to work to pay for the machinery. You and Shep both'll be chasing your tails before long."

I wished I hadn't said it as soon as the words left my mouth. Hank's neck turned red, then exploded upward to his forehead until his entire face flushed with anger. "I might as well give up then. Talkin' to you about this is like talkin' to a brick wall."

"We can't lose this farm," I said. Another dumb thing to say, because that was all I ever had to say to remind Hank that this was *my family farm*, built with the sweat of my grandparents and parents. He never said a word out loud, but Hank felt like a renter on the farm for most all of his life.

"I might as well quit bein' a farmer right here and now then and go into town and become an insurance salesman like Hamish Martin."

I refrained from laughing. I knew that was never going to happen. Hank Trumaine wouldn't put a tie around his neck unless he had to go to church or a funeral. I could tell where this argument was heading, and I didn't like the feel in the air. A dangerous thunderstorm was brewing. I turned around and went back to scrubbing my roasting pan. Only this time I put a little more elbow into it.

"That's all you have to say, then? You're going to ignore me?" Hank had said.

"When you can talk to me rationally, we'll sit down again and look at the numbers. But until then, I'm going to get this pan clean."

I heard a big *humph!* Then Hank stomped out the door and didn't stop until he found Erik Knudsen sitting on his porch pondering one of his own problems. Hank didn't come home until well after dark, and I served supper, and my shoulder, to him cold. He worked his frustration out on some chores, then came to bed, kissed me, and promised to look at the numbers with a calm mind in the morning. Two days later, we had a new combine sitting in the barn, but I worried the whole time that this could be the argument that broke us apart. I knew what was at stake.

I couldn't help but wonder what Nils and Anna Jacobsen had

argued about the night before he was killed, and if their fight had anything to do with what had happened to him.

The Studebaker's engine coughed, then caught and started to run smooth. I could see part way out of the windshield, enough to pull out onto the street. I was ready to be home.

CHAPTER 15

Villard Street was the main thoroughfare in Dickinson. A wide assortment of businesses fronted the street, erected on an old pioneer trail that had matured year after year with the demand of a steadily growing population. Hardy and optimistic homesteaders had encouraged the Northern Pacific Railroad to post handbills across Europe, advertising free land in the Dakota Territory. Risk takers and dreamers gave up everything they had to come to the new world. We all carried determined, persistent traits in our blood, and no matter the tragedies or harsh conditions that confronted us, we drew on our durable inheritance to keep putting one foot in front of the other. The thriving business district stood up to the prairie in prideful defiance, mindful of the past but moving into the future—whether people were ready for the modern world or not.

The Walgreens store, stood next to Home Furniture. The Service Drug Store sat on the other side of Home Furniture, a door down from the Walgreens, at the corner of Sims and Villard. As I sat idling at the stop sign, I imagined Nils Jacobsen walking home from work on Sims Street, day after day, night after night, regardless of the weather. I admired a man dedicated to his work—no matter what that work was. I knew I would never see Nils again; smiling with his perfectly bleached white Red Owl shirt on, greeting customers in a store he treated like he owned the deed to—but didn't. He was a renter in the same way Hank was. That fond memory of Nils was replaced by a man slumped over the steering wheel, bloody and dead, never to smile again.

At the thought of Nils and the store, I considered what I might need to stock up on before heading home. Instinct and training

97

demanded that I didn't waste a trip into town. I decided to replace the chicken and potatoes I'd used for the knoephla soup and get a couple of packs of cigarettes. I didn't want to run out.

Evening had come on fast, bringing with it an overcast sky full of gray promise. Snow spit downward, the wind carrying the haphazard flakes quickly away as if they were tiny balloons set free from a child's hand. I could tell by the dark horizon that a steadier drop of snow was yet to come, and if I had any sense at all I'd head straight home instead of stopping at the Red Owl. The truth was, my cellar was full enough to survive two blizzards, and I could make a pack of Salems last a week if I had to. I could get by without that chicken, but something told me I needed to stop and go into the store.

I turned onto Villard Street and made my way toward the grocery store, creeping along the snowy street as slowly as the traffic would allow. My tires crunched on the hard snow and ice underneath me. I had the radio off, already assured of the weather and news.

The Dickinson Theater, where Hank had gotten his hand gently slapped for moving too fast, stood proudly down the block. The twenty-five-foot-tall oblong sign caught my attention. The rolling lights on the sign looked like lighting bugs caught in a bottle, trying to escape with every flicker. Movies were a treat I'd long forgotten. I hadn't stepped inside the theater in years. The marquee said a movie called *Goldfinger* was playing. I didn't know anything about the film. It sounded like a candy bar to me.

Even in January, with the prediction of snow and diving tempera-tures, Villard Street was vibrant and active. There was hardly a parking spot to be found, and since it was Saturday all of the lights in the store-fronts blazed brightly, doing their best to look warm and welcoming. Once five o'clock hit, though, most of the businesses would close. Beau-doin's Main Bar, opposite the Service Drug, was busy with customers. Televisions faced out of a tall plate glass window in the appliance store, stacked high, flickering with moving images in vibrant color. I couldn't spend the money on something that I knew I wouldn't use, but, like everyone else, I couldn't keep my eyes off the televisions. The F. W.

Woolworth store would soon go dark, along with Quinlan's Café. The St. Charles Hotel would remain open, and a few blocks away the Wild Pony Tavern would welcome customers late into the night. I was never comfortable in town. All of the coming and going made me nervous.

I found a parking spot a few doors down from the Red Owl and counted myself lucky to claim a plug-in for the block heater. I didn't think I would be long, but I had strained the battery by letting the truck sit along the street outside of Anna's unattended. I was sure the battery could use a charge. I was in no mood to find myself stranded in a ditch.

After checking my hair in the rearview mirror, making sure that I was presentable, I made my way out into the cold once again. The wind rumbled in my ears, pushing most of my thoughts away. I wanted to stay upright and get into the store as soon as I could. The electric stands in town reminded me of hitching posts. I plugged in the block heater, then shuffled to the store.

The Red Owl was a long, narrow room, with shelves stacked perfectly with canned goods on the right. Fresh vegetable bins ran down the center aisle, and the meat counter stood shining on the left, all white and stainless steel, gleaming under bright, overhead lights. The floors were hickory, the grain worn down over the years with steady traffic, and the ceiling was pressed tin in an alternating pattern of circles and triangles. The aroma was distinct to grocery stores, a mix of fresh-ground coffee, dried beans, a hint of decay, and the distant, metallic smell of raw meat.

Frank Aberle, a middle-aged man who looked like Chef Boyardee, rotund, balding, with a thick mustache, looked up when I walked in the door. He wore a clean white grocer's apron and a sad, droopy expression that had settled on his face a long time ago. I don't think I'd ever seen him smile. Frank was the assistant manager at the Red Owl, as well as the president of the German-Hungarian Club. He and Nils had remained friends since they were boys. There was reason for him to be sad.

"Oh, hey there, Mrs. Trumaine. What brings you out on a night like this? More snow comin' in, you know," Frank said, as he laid a pencil down on the counter.

"Little flakes are already starting to drop," I said, as I wiped my feet on the black mat inside the door. Snow and salt fell off my heels, and a briny puddle formed under my feet.

"You heard about Nils?" Frank said.

"I was at the house with the Ladies Aid."

Frank ran his big, meaty right hand over the top of his baldhead as if he was trying to warm his scalp up. "Everybody's heard. People been wanderin' in and out all day, not buying a darn thing, lookin' me in the eye and askin' if I know what in the heck is going on. Of course, I don't know a thing. Not a gall-durned thing. You don't have any questions like that, do you?"

"No, I need some potatoes and a fresh chicken if you have one."

I looked beyond Frank to see if Mills Standish was in the butcher's room. I didn't know what hours Mills worked, but the lights in the stainless steel room were off. Frank was the only person in the store.

"Well, sure, I can fix you right up with some chicken and potatoes, Mrs. Trumaine. You wait right there," Frank said, then loped off with a look of relief on his face.

Of course, I had more than a few questions that I wanted to ask Frank, but I restrained myself. I stood at the counter looking at everything a little closer. The only thing that I found related to Nils was a picture of him on the wall that I'd seen a thousand times. A thin plaque stating he was the manager sat underneath the picture. Other than that, there was no sign of Nils Jacobsen's former presence to be found in the store.

Frank came back with a chicken that looked freshly plucked and held the plump bird up for my inspection. "Will that do you?"

"Looks fine to me, Frank. Thank you." I looked over my shoulder to the potato bin. I wasn't so thrilled with the selection I saw offered. "You don't have any good potatoes in the back do you?"

Frank drew in his cheeks, puzzled, like he was trying to make a quick decision but got stuck halfway through the thought. "Well, I do, but they're not normally stocked until morning. I think I can make an exception for you, Mrs. Trumaine. I guess I'm in charge until someone says different."

"It still hasn't sunk in. I understand," I said.

"I'm sure you do. I'll wrap this up for you." Frank hurried off to the butcher's room, carrying the chicken with him. The smell of raw meat lingered closer to my nose than I would have liked. I wasn't the least bit hungry.

I had pieced on one thing or another in Anna's kitchen all day, and Darlys and I had sneaked off when we could to the empty garage for a cigarette when the visitors slowed. Helen Greggson had shown some disapproval concerning our smoking habit, but no one else seemed to mind.

Frank came back to the counter carrying a brown paper bag, and set it down. "You didn't say how many potatoes you needed," he said, "so I packed you up five pounds worth."

"That's fine, Frank."

"Anything else for you?"

The store didn't sell cigarettes. The Walgreens did. "Yes, that'll do."

I waited for Frank to ring up my order, but instead he cast a glance at the front door, then looked back at me. "You know that bad feeling when a doozy of a storm's comin'?"

"I do. Everything gets quiet. The wheat stands up tall. The pigs get pensive. The birds seem to sigh in retreat, waiting for what's next, eyeing the closest place to take cover from hail or wind." I studied Frank's face. His skin had tightened a bit, and his eyes had dimmed. "Won't be long before spring's here and we have those worries. Why do you ask, Frank?"

"It's been quiet here for about a week or so, the air real thick with Nils, all for no reason that I could figure," Frank said. He seemed nervous, his attention shifting to the door, then back to me, over and over again.

"You've talked to Guy about this?"

"Yes, but there wasn't much to tell. Only that I had a feelin' that something was off with Nils."

"Okay, then." I didn't know what else to say. I didn't want to press. "Are you all right, Frank?"

"Yes, yes, I am. I knew . . ." He hesitated, then went on with a little tremor in his voice. "I know you've faced bad times. The worst anyone can imagine. No one lives a long life and doesn't have some kind of loss to bear, but I sure wasn't expectin' this, like you wasn't expectin' to lose Hank like you did." Frank searched my face for a reaction to see if he'd said the wrong thing.

I reached out and touched his big, cold hand. "I'm sorry, Frank. You and Nils worked together for a long time. I know he was your friend, too. This is hard. I'm really sorry."

Frank's eyes went glassy, then he turned to the cash register. "I better ring you up. Snow's startin' to come down harder, and you've got a ways to go before you get home."

"I do. If something comes to mind, you'll call Guy won't you? Or me, if you need to talk."

"Thanks, Mrs. Trumaine, I really appreciate that. I will. I'll call the sheriff if I think of something."

His words sounded hollow. I wasn't sure that Frank would take me up on my offer, or call Guy. I hoped he would. If he knew something that could help catch the person who had killed Nils Jacobsen, then I sure did hope he wouldn't keep anything important to himself.

I had to scrape snow off the windshield twice before the engine was warm enough to drive. I didn't have anything to do but look out the window until the truck was ready to go.

The traffic slowed on Villard as the snow fell at a steadier pace. The wind kicked up, making the street harder to see. The rumble and groan of the Studebaker's engine was all I had to keep me company. I had the radio turned off. I'd had more than enough voices to sort in my mind for one day. I didn't need any more.

I'd heard a lot of questions, suffered silent glances that questioned my presence, and smelled enough fear and Old Spice to last me a lifetime. I knew I'd need some time to make sense of everything that I'd heard at Anna's throughout the day. At that thought, I turned on the windshield wipers, cleared off the fog on the inside glass, pushed in the clutch, and shifted the truck in gear. I needed to get myself home.

I backed out onto the street carefully and made my way down Villard, the businesses on one side, railroad tracks on the other. Wind buffeted against the truck, rocking the old Studebaker like it was made of paper instead of steel. The drive home was going to be long and slow. I couldn't see twenty feet in front of me as I inched down the street. The streetlights blazed like beacons, and about half of the businesses were still open for customers. Country driving was going to be even slower.

I pumped the brakes, preparing to stop at the intersection ahead. A pair of headlights appeared on the other side of the street, and I didn't know if the car was going to go straight, or turn at the stop sign.

The Studebaker slid a little bit, then came to a full stop. The car opposite me did the same. We both sat there waiting for the other one to move. I was going straight, and so were they. Without any further hesitation, I took my foot off the brake and inched forward, being as cautious as I could. Some people gunned a start so they wouldn't get stuck in the middle of the intersection. Depending on the driver's skill, and the type of car, fishtailing or losing control was a real possibility. Thankfully, this driver knew what he was doing. He'd inched out into the intersection slowly, too.

We passed each other crawling along, our safety assured. I glanced over at the car, a long, dark-colored four-door sedan that could have been a Chevrolet or a Ford. Car models weren't important to me, but Hank knew every one of them, and commented, hoping I would show some interest. Since he'd been gone, I couldn't have cared less whether a car was a Plymouth or a Cadillac.

I couldn't see the driver clearly at all. He wore a black toboggan, a ski cap that covered his hair and head, and a similar colored muffler around his neck that reached up to his cheeks, making his face hard to define. I really wasn't sure if it was a man or a woman that sat behind the wheel, but I assumed the driver was a man. There wasn't anything unusual about the driver that I saw in the snowy, gray, fleeting second that I had to see him. But there was something unusual about the passenger in the backseat staring out the window.

I saw a young girl with a moon face and tiny slits for eyes, staring out the window blankly as if she were on a ride to nowhere, not panicked or afraid. My heart skipped a beat and a breath got stuck in my throat. Before I could count to five, I was past the car, craning my head for another look. But I was too late; all I could see was a pair of red taillights disappearing into the snowy void.

I was almost certain the girl in the car was Tina Rinkerman. Almost certain. But not positive.

CHAPTER 16

*H*ad I imagined seeing Tina Rinkerman?

I had to go back and find out.

I slammed on the brakes. My impulsive reaction sent the Studebaker immediately into a bending slide. Cold South Bend steel protested, and the tires moaned against the icy street instead of squealing. I knew better than to do such a thing, but my foot reacted as if it had a mind of its own. Common sense had left every part of my being as soon as I saw that face.

I'm sure the girl in the car was Tina Rinkerman.

The rear end jerked to the right, giving the rest of the vehicle no choice but to follow. Gravity, fear, and black ice created a recipe for disaster. The heavy load of snow in the bed didn't matter. There was no stopping the truck's entrance into a swing dance. I yanked the steering wheel to the left, pulled my foot off the brake, then started pumping the pedal furiously. That's when the world really started to spin. The truck gained speed like a Tilt-a-Whirl ride at the summer carnival.

What were you thinking, Marjorie?

The Studebaker wasn't equipped with safety belts like the newer cars were. I doubt I would've worn a belt anyway. Wearing one of those things would be like binding yourself to a horse. Who would do that? Though, as I was rocketing down Villard Street, using a harness of some kind to keep myself from tumbling over to the passenger side of the bench seat would've been helpful. The truck didn't have power steering or power brakes, either. The truck was for work, not pleasure. This was no joyride. I was afraid and out of control.

I wrestled the truck, keeping an eye out for anything coming my way. With one more pump of the brakes, and a hard turn of the wheel with all of my might, I forced the Studebaker back under my control. Somehow, I'd managed to keep the truck in the middle of the street, though I now faced the opposite direction. I was looking back at the Red Owl. I had spun completely around—more than once. I was panting and my heart raced, but my vision was clear, on a mission.

Where are you, Tina?

There were three or four pairs of red taillights glowing in the distance. I couldn't tell which, if any of them, was the car that the girl was in. As soon as the truck had come to a complete stop, the windshield started to collect snow. My breath quickly fogged the glass, making things even worse. I turned the wipers on and cleared the condensation with the sleeve of my coat. No matter how hard I strained my eyes, no matter how hard I tried to see through the blowing snow with the help of streetlights, I couldn't make out any of the cars for sure. I was a hunting dog with too many rabbits to chase.

I'd lost her. *Damn it, I lost her.*

I found the closest phone booth and called the Sheriff's Department. I knew the number by heart. George Lardner, the dispatcher, answered on the second ring. I recognized his voice right away. "George, this Marjorie Trumaine. I need to speak to the sheriff," I said, talking as fast as my New York editor, Richard Rothstein, ever had.

"Oh, hey there, Mrs. Trumaine, what can I do for you?" George said casually, as if we were going to chat away the evening.

"I need to speak to the sheriff." I had to restrain myself. I wanted to scream that I needed to talk to Guy, but I knew better than to get personal. I had to respect the office Guy occupied as much as everyone else did. George had made himself clear earlier in the day that he didn't trust the shift in power from Duke to Guy, and I certainly didn't want to call in any special favors—or to appear like I was. Word would get around to Duke and his sister and anybody else who didn't like Guy, quicker than I could bat an eye.

"Oh, he doesn't take calls from folks. That's my job. Is this a personal call, Mrs. Trumaine?" George said, validating my concern.

"No, this is not a personal call."

"Is something the matter?"

Finally . . . I gripped the cold receiver so hard I thought I was going to break the plastic thing in half. "Yes, I think . . ." I stopped and caught my breath, then restarted. "I saw Tina Rinkerman, George. I'm sure I saw her."

"You're sure you saw that girl?" He sounded like he'd sat up straight in his chair, didn't miss a beat.

"That's what I said, George."

"No sense in gettin' snippy with me, Mrs. Trumaine. I gotta ask these things, you know? Where'd you see her?"

"At Second and Villard. I'm in the phone booth right down from there."

"And she was out walkin' in this weather? Why didn't you bring her here? Sure would have saved people a whole lot of trouble."

"No, no, she was in a car. In the backseat."

"Oh, well, that's different. Who was drivin'?"

"I don't know."

George cleared his throat. "What do you mean you don't know?"

"It's dark and snowing out. I didn't get a good look."

"More snow comin' tonight, too. I sure do hope the roads are clear for church in the mornin.'"

I rolled my eyes. All I had to do was look out of the phone booth to see that the snow wasn't going to let up anytime soon. "I didn't get a good look at the driver," I said. "I'm not even sure it was a man that was driving."

"You're sure you saw a man driving, you say?"

"No, maybe, yes, I think I saw a man."

"You don't sound so certain, Mrs. Trumaine."

I sighed, frustrated. "Can I talk to the sheriff?"

"I told you, he's not taking calls. Got his hands full. You know that. He's tryin' to figure out what happened to poor Nils Jacobsen. That's all I can say. I'm the one that takes phone calls, not the sheriff."

"Maybe a man was driving that car, George." I wasn't frustrated. I was exasperated. Even though I was freezing cold, I was sweating. "I'm certain that I saw Tina Rinkerman sitting in the backseat of that car."

"If you say so."

"I do."

"What color was the car?"

"Black, I think."

I heard George groan. "You don't know the model and make of this possible black car, do you?"

"No, I, uh . . ."

"How about a license plate number?"

"No, of course not."

George cleared his throat again, then said, "I'm sorry, Mrs. Trumaine, but how can you be sure that the girl you saw was Tina Rinkerman? Nobody's seen hide nor hair of that girl since she walked out of her house. And then you see her joyridin' down Villard on a Saturday night like she doesn't have a care in the world, in a car that might be black, driven by a man or a woman?"

"I didn't say that she was joyriding, George. I know what I saw."

"You didn't answer my question. How do you know for sure that the girl you saw was Tina Rinkerman?"

"How many moon-faced teenage girls live in this town, George? I know what I saw. It was Tina Rinkerman in that car as sure as I'm standing here freezing to death talking to you. And the longer we talk, the farther away she gets, you hear me? We need to find that car, George."

"You're gettin' snippy again, Mrs. Trumaine."

He was right. My fuse was short. I exhaled deeply. "I'm sorry. I'm cold, tired, and upset."

"Tina Rinkerman's not the only retard who lives in Dickinson, Mrs. Trumaine. There's more than one. You want it to be that girl is all. Nothing the matter with that."

"That's not very nice, George."

"Well, that's the truth."

I didn't know what to say. George Lardner didn't believe me. I guess I would've had some questions, too, if I were on the other end of the line. I had no proof that the girl in the black car was Tina Rinkerman. I wanted all of this madness to end. Maybe I wanted to believe that she wasn't dead, that I could take her home to her mother where she belonged. All I wanted was a happy ending. I wanted Tina Rinkerman to be alive. That's all. I wanted her to be alive. I didn't even know if the car was really black.

"Can you tell the sheriff that I called," I finally said. "And have him call me if he's got any questions for me?"

"Do you want me to send a deputy over?" George said.

"No, I don't see the point. The car's long gone. You might tell everyone to be on the lookout for a black car with a girl in the backseat." Even that sounded crazy, but I couldn't help myself.

"Sure, Mrs. Trumaine, I'll do that."

I didn't believe him any more than he believed me. "All right, George. I'm sorry I bothered you."

"You be careful going home, Mrs. Trumaine."

"I will. Goodbye."

"Goodbye."

We both hung up. I felt like an idiot. I was sure of what I saw. When I closed my eyes, I could see Tina Rinkerman's face pressed against the window, looking out of it like she'd never seen the town all lit up at night. I didn't see fear. I saw wonder. Maybe George was right. Maybe I was seeing things that I wanted to see.

The drive home was slow and treacherous, although there was no traffic to deal with once I left town. Snow blew from one side of the road to the other, leaving me inching along in near whiteout conditions. Fluttering white sheets of snow made it almost impossible to see three feet in front of the truck. All I could do was keep moving forward and hope I didn't meet anyone fool enough to be out in this weather. I didn't see one living creature on the drive. I was alone in the world, left to relive my vision of Tina Rinkerman and encourage my doubt to grow. Maybe the girl I saw wasn't Tina. Maybe it was a father and a daughter out for a joyride on a snowy night.

Once I arrived at the house, I hurried inside to free Shep from his prison. I'd put him in the bathroom before I left. I hated to do such a thing, but with him being an outside dog, locking him up was the only thing I knew to do. There was nothing for him to destroy in the bathroom. Not that I thought that he would tear anything up. But he hadn't been able to contain himself. There was a mess in the corner. I wasn't angry. I knew right then and there that confining the dog in the bathroom while I was away wasn't going to work. I was going to have to ask Jaeger to look after Shep while I was away from the house for long stretches at a time. I'd call him first thing in the morning.

After calming Shep down—he was really happy to see me—I put him outside and cleaned up the bathroom. I couldn't get Tina Rinkerman and Anna Jacobsen off my mind. Both were lost in ways I couldn't imagine.

I'd settled in at my desk when the phone rang. Two shorts, one long. It wasn't for me. The call was for the Standishes, Mills and Burlene. The butcher and the eavesdropper. I listened closer as the phone continued to ring. I put both of my hands on the desk, tempting myself again to launch to the phone and do a bit of eavesdropping myself.

Thinking about listening in on the conversation was as far as I got. I hated it when Burlene hid on the line and listened in on my business, but that didn't stop me from wanting to do the same thing. What if Mills knew something that could help Guy find the killer? Would discovering a clue to what had happened be worth breaking my own vow not to ever eavesdrop? Maybe. Maybe not. The phone stopped ringing before I could move another muscle. Thankfully, I was relieved of any temptation I might have had.

I shrugged off any more notions of deceit and went back to what I was doing—trying to make up for being gone all day, doing some work. I had to work at indexing every day regardless of what other things I had gotten myself into or I was going to miss my deadline, simple as that. I couldn't afford to lose my job, no matter what.

I stared at the page proof before me, and all of the letters looked jumbled. I was tired and I couldn't focus, but I had to move forward. I didn't want to get behind on my daily page count, no matter what time of the night it was. I was beginning to regret telling Darlys that I would sit with Anna in the morning.

I looked at the page again. I was beyond the summary of John J. Audubon's life, and I was now working in a section of the book titled "What Is Migration?"

The heading seemed basic to me, but sometimes the simplest information was where the most important index entries were found. Those were the questions I could assure myself a reader would want to look up.

> Migration is the seasonal movement of animals or birds from one region to another. Primary reasons for migration are related to food resources and nesting opportunities.

I sat back and thought about what I'd read and found three or four index entries in two sentences. Food. Migration: reasons for. Nesting. Seasonal movement: *See* migration. I was about to reach for an index card but was stopped again by the intrusion of sound. The phone rang again. Two longs, two shorts. This time the call was for me.

I hurried to the phone, hoping Guy was finally calling me back.

"Trumaine residence," I said.

I expected a voice, but none came.

Silence. No words. No sound except the hum of the line.

"Hello," I said, then strained my ear, listening closer. No one else had picked up, but I could hear someone breathing on the other end of the line.

I waited a few seconds for a response. "Hello," I repeated.

The breathing got louder.

I was starting to get uncomfortable. "Hello, who's there?" I said, almost yelling.

The breathing got even louder, then whoever was on the line cleared their throat and slammed down the phone.

I almost threw the receiver back in the hook. I wanted to get the blasted thing out of my hand. As soon as I'd settled the phone on the hook, it rang again. One time. Then stopped. Was the caller mocking me, taunting me?

I stood there staring at the phone, hoping I was wrong, hoping that someone had dialed a wrong number. But I couldn't stop my mind that easily. Bad things had happened to me before. My thoughts wandered to dark places a lot faster than they used to.

What if the driver of the black car saw me looking at him?

He didn't know that I didn't recognize him.

He had to know that I saw Tina Rinkerman.

What if he knew who I was?

CHAPTER 17

The snow had subsided overnight, but the wind continued to roar dutifully from the west. I found no surprises in the morning view from my window. More of the same. A blank white world with no sign of life at all. Even a stray Hereford cow would have been a welcome sight. Brown to offset white, a sure sign that I had not become blind to color.

I had expected winter to be difficult after Hank's death, but not this difficult.

The phone had remained quiet, and any threat that I might have imagined stayed on the edge of my frayed mind. I flinched at every creak and moan of the house as the wood and nails protested against the unrelenting attack from the wind. Shep had laid unfazed at my feet as I worked deep into the night. I'd quit indexing when I couldn't keep my eyes open any longer. I was proud of myself. I'd indexed twenty pages of the *Central Flyway* book. I only had a few hundred pages more to go, but a start was a start, and I knew I would have to remain persistent with my work schedule if I was going to meet my deadline.

I pulled away from the window, assured that the roads were in worse shape than they had been the day before. The drive to the Knudsen farm would take more time than I'd counted on. I had to drop off Shep, then make my way into town to Anna's house.

I was more concerned about Tina Rinkerman. If there was any solace in the events of the last twenty-four hours, it was the sighting of that girl in the car. At least I knew she was warm. I didn't know if she was safe, but I did know that her body wasn't buried under the snow waiting to be discovered in the spring.

Last night I was sure the girl I saw was Tina, but after a bit of sleep I wasn't so sure. Maybe George was right. Maybe there *were* more girls like Tina in Dickinson. I had no idea. I'd never had reason to notice. Mongoloid was an overlooked index entry in the text of my personal life. My memory was as blank as the view out my front window. I couldn't recall ever seeing a girl like Tina except Tina, and she was as rare a sighting as an albino meadowlark.

First thing I did was call Jaeger, who, of course, said he'd be happy to watch Shep for the day. From there, all I had to do was eat some breakfast, bathe, dress, and head into town. I sat and decided to have a Salem with my cup of coffee instead of eating anything. There would be plenty of food at Anna's house. I really wasn't hungry and didn't expect to be anytime soon.

I stood back up, changed my mind about smoking a cigarette, and made my way back to the window. There was nothing to see, nothing different from the last time I'd looked outside. My reflection stared back at me in the cold glass, reminding me that I was alone, on my own. In the recent past, I would go into Hank's closet, pull out one of his shirts, smell the flannel cloth for reassurance and comfort, then burst into a round of angry tears. I wasn't going to do that this time. I was afraid and lonely, but I had things to do and ways to protect myself. There was nothing for me to do but get on with my life.

The lane up to the Knudsen farm was freshly plowed, and Jaeger stood waiting for me on the porch. Shep sat up straight in the seat. He knew where he was. I was glad to see a wag of the tail. I couldn't bear the thought of leaving the dog locked up in the bathroom two days in a row. I assumed my day would be filled with Ladies Aid duties.

I pulled the truck up to the house and let Shep out the door before he leapt through the window. He loved Jaeger. I think the oldest Knudsen boy reminded the dog of Hank. The two men were a lot alike—stubborn, hardworking, short on words, and long on love for the land and its creatures.

Shep barked and circled Jaeger, a tall stick of a young man, with unruly black hair and a permanent frown etched on his face from the unfortunate pull of the forceps when he was born. Jaeger had his own grieving to do, and I wasn't the one to tell him that he should be eating better than he was, but I would.

"Good to see you, boy. Good to see you." Jaeger bent over, ruffled Shep's black and white coat, then stood and faced me. "Good to see you, too, Mrs. Trumaine. Come on inside. Lester's put some coffee on. You don't look like you're dressed to be out in the cold."

"Going back to the Jacobsens' today," I said. I had on a dark blue Sunday dress, and the rest of the black accoutrements I could cobble together. None of my clothes were flashy. Most were homemade. And I didn't have a deep enough closet, like Darlys Oddsdatter, to wear a new outfit every day. There'd be wash to do soon.

"That's bad business, what happened to Nils Jacobsen," Jaeger said. "You'd think we'd had enough of that kind of thing around here to last us a lifetime."

There was nothing for me to add. Jaeger's shoulders slumped, and a heavy shadow crossed his eyes. Sadness had settled on the blank white slate of his face a long time ago. We both knew his mother would be visiting the Jacobsens if she were still alive. Lida had tried to get me to join the Ladies Aid for years. I'd neglected to consider her failed insistence. There was no way I was going to leave Hank any more than I had to. I knew from the time he stepped in that damn gopher hole that our time together was short.

I made my way up the steps and into the house. Jaeger followed. Shep stayed outside, happy to go inspect the chicken pen and farmyard to see if there was anything for him to herd. I was relieved of worry about the dog. He knew his way around the place, and Jaeger wasn't opposed to bringing Shep inside the house when the ice crystals formed on his face.

Jaeger had not changed a thing inside the house since the death of his parents. The only addition was Lester Gustaffson, the hand he had hired to get through the last harvest and the upcoming planting season.

Jaeger had let the young Gustaffson boy a room, and by all appearances their arrangement looked to be working out well.

"Hey, there, Mrs. Trumaine," Lester said with a quick smile. He looked a lot like his Uncle Lloyd, our previous extension agent; tall, broad-shouldered, a shock of yellow hair on the top of his head that looked blessed by the touch of a sun god. Even deep in January, Lester had a touch of color on his skin. He was obviously one of those people who tanned when they were outside instead of burning red.

I didn't know Lester well, but we had seen each other enough over the winter to be on friendly terms. "Good to see you, too, Lester."

"Do you have time for a cup of coffee?" Lester held up Lida's blue porcelain coffee pot.

"No, thank you. I've got to get into town."

"My guess is your drive's going to be slow going." Jaeger made his way into the kitchen and pulled a coffee cup out of the cupboard. "I was out this mornin' with the plow. You should be fine over to the county highway. Take that curve by the Standishes as slow as you can. Snow's as tall as the truck, and with the wind blowing you'll be drivin' through a tunnel you can't see out of."

"That curve's always bad," I said. "Probably will be until April."

"I hope not." Lester poured Jaeger a cup of coffee, then made one for himself.

"You boys heard about that Rinkerman girl didn't you?" I said. I hadn't moved from my spot in the front room.

"Did they find her?" Jaeger said.

"No." I hesitated to say anything else.

"I was hoping they would," Lester said, then took a sip of his coffee. "I sure don't see how a girl like that can survive out in this weather."

I flinched. I wasn't sure why. Then I took a deep breath and stared at Jaeger. I trusted him. I wasn't so sure about Lester, but I respected Jaeger's judge of character. "I think I might have seen her last night on the way home."

Jaeger set his coffee cup on the counter and returned my stare, covering every inch of my face. He knew me well enough to know that I was concerned, exposing myself. "Where'd you see her, Mrs. Trumaine?"

"In town. On Villard in the backseat of a car, a couple blocks down from the Red Owl. I stopped in to see Frank Aberle and picked up some staples for the larder."

"No sense in wastin' a trip into town," Lester said.

"Exactly," I answered, not taking my eyes off Jaeger. I wasn't convinced that he believed me any more than George Lardner did.

"You're sure it was her you saw?" Jaeger said.

"I thought it was, but I couldn't be sure. I slammed on the brakes and sent the truck into a spin. By the time I got myself oriented, the car was gone."

Jaeger stiffened. "You called the police, right?"

"Yes. George Lardner said there was more than one moon-faced girl in Dickinson, and there's probably more black cars than you can shake a stick at. I couldn't tell him the make or the model, so he was probably right."

"I have a black car," Lester said. "A '52 Chevy sedan parked out in the barn. No use drivin' a car in this weather. If I go anywhere, I take Jaeger's old Harvester truck. That thing's a brute."

"There *are* a lot of black cars in the county," Jaeger said. "But I don't know about girls like Tina Rinkerman."

"Me, either," I said. "George was supposed to tell the sheriff, but I never heard back from him. Guy has his hands full. I wish I could say for sure that I saw her, but I can't. Weather was bad, and I only got a quick glimpse of the girl in the backseat. I can't be positive. I'm not sure George believed a word I said. I'm not sure I would have, either."

"I believe you, Mrs. Trumaine," Jaeger said.

"Me, too," Lester offered.

"All right," I said. "You boys keep an eye out for a black car if you're out and about today. If you see something suspicious, call Guy Reinhardt as soon as you can."

"We will," Jaeger said.

I left the Knudsen farm feeling a little better than I had when I'd arrived. I appreciated not having to worry about Shep all day, and I was relieved to tell someone who believed me what I had seen. The more sets of eyes looking for that girl the better as far as I was concerned.

CHAPTER 18

I was tempted to head toward South Heart instead of going into Dickinson. Anna needed me, but so did the Rinkermans. Or so I thought. But I knew I had little to offer the Rinkermans except my company. I felt bad that the tragedy of their missing daughter seemed to be overtaken by the murder of Nils Jacobsen. Maybe Darlys or Connie had already thought of sending someone else to see to their needs. The Ladies Aid had more members than the three of us, but I wasn't quite sure how many members there were. I hadn't been to a meeting yet.

Going to the Rinkermans' house didn't really seem like a good idea. I wasn't convinced that I'd be able to contain myself and not tell them about my experience driving down Villard. There was no use giving the family false hope or adding to their worry by telling them that I *might* have seen Tina. I knew my presence would be more hurtful than helpful. No point in that. I drove on toward Dickinson with a small amount of guilt simmering in the pit of my stomach.

Jaeger had done a fine job plowing the road and informing me about the snow tunnel on the Standishes' curve. It was like driving through a snow globe, all shaken up. I couldn't see an inch in front of me. I was surrounded by pure white, going as slow as I could, with nothing to rely on but my faith in an unknown driver coming from the opposite direction, using the same precautions I was. By the time I drove out of the tunnel, I was past Mills and Burlene's house, but I was still curious about who had called them the night before. Hard telling who the caller was. I wasn't about to break my rule against eavesdropping on the party line, even though I could almost convince myself that there would be a good reason to.

Once I was on the county road into town, I had an easy drive. I arrived at the Jacobsens', giving Abigail enough time to take the children to church. Unlike the day before, I was able to park in front of the house. There were almost no cars on the street or in the courthouse parking lot. If I'd had a little more time, I would have parked the Studebaker in the lot and plugged in the block heater, but I was worried about being late. I had jumper cables with me if I needed them.

I hurried up to the door, knocked, and was greeted by Lene Harstaad. She had missed the day before, and I was happy to see her. I secretly hoped she'd brought some of her sandkakes and homemade strawberry jam to add to the kitchen table.

"Well, there you are, Marjorie Trumaine. I was beginning to get a bit worried about you, out on the road by yourself and drivin' that contraption you call a truck." Lene ducked her head out the door and looked up to the sky. "Good thing that snow stopped or we'd be back to diggin' out again, don't ya know? Clear skies are comin' the next two days, so they say. I'll believe good weather when I see it. Come on, get in here before we let out all the heat."

I smiled, made my way past Lene, and stepped inside the Jacobsens' house. Lene was one of those women who minced no words. She said what she meant and meant what she said. I liked that about her, but I still wasn't used to her brusqueness. I could see that she had a caring heart and she didn't wear her emotions on her sleeve. I understood that. Life on the farm was hard, full of disappointments and bad luck. Spirits could be broken and never healed.

The television was off, no one was in the front room, and the house smelled clean, free of stale cigarettes and the presence of a crowd. Open curtains brought in some sorely needed daylight, allowing me to see that all of the furniture was back in its place. Any sign of yesterday's gathering of mourners was gone, erased with the sweep of a broom and the wipe of a dust rag. Someone had spent a fair amount of time straightening up around the house. There was a hint of pine scent in the air from the floor cleaner. I wondered when Lene had arrived. Probably at first light.

"If I'd known you were going to be here, I would have swung by to see the Rinkermans." I stopped in the middle of the front room and took off my coat. This time, I wore my boots and brought black pumps with me. I wasn't about to freeze my toes off two days in a row. I had been tempted to put my long johns on under my dress and take them off after I'd arrived, too, but that would have looked silly, especially if I'd been in an accident. Imagine what the ambulance driver would have thought.

"Darlys and Theda are out there today," Lene said. "Took them some of the bounty that was piled up on Anna's table at the end of the day. With Anna's blessings, of course. Even in her state, she couldn't stand to think of food goin' to waste or them people in South Heart bein' without somethin' she had."

I was relieved to hear that the Rinkermans were still in Darlys's thoughts. I shivered, though, as Tina's face flashed through my mind. "They haven't found the girl yet?"

"Not that I know of."

I hesitated a bit before I asked the question that George Lardner had planted the seed to. "Do you know if there are any other girls in town like Tina Rinkerman?"

Lene's face flushed red, and both hands immediately latched onto her hips, her elbows pointed like sharp arrows. "Why would you ask me such a thing, Marjorie?"

"I thought you might know. I can't think of anyone else."

Lene glared at me in a way she had never done before and didn't offer another word. I sat down in the nearest chair to change out of my boots and into my shoes. "How is she today?" I said, changing the subject. I dropped my voice to a whisper as the furnace kicked on.

Lene relaxed her arms and face, and said, "Still in shock, if you ask me. Doc came by to check on her last night and left her some of them sedatives. I'm not one for pills, but in this case I think their use is warranted. Can't say for sure if she has taken any, but I suspect so. Her eyes are glassy, and she hasn't said ten words this morning."

"She needs her rest," I said. I cocked my ear toward the bedroom but didn't hear a thing. "Any word from the sheriff?"

Lene stepped closer to me, squaring her shoulders and pursing her lips as if she was trying to hold something back. Her German heritage was in full view.

I wondered if Lene was a member of the German-Hungarian club along with Frank Aberle. I'd had little time previously to consider the relationships between the people in town and the farmers in the outlying fields as closely as I had in the last few days. In indexing, one entry was normally related to another in an apparent or obscure way, linked most often with a *See also* reference. I could link words like *season* and *migration* contextually in the index I was working on, but I had no idea if Lene knew Frank, if she was connected to him in any way. It didn't matter if they were connected, really. The consideration was nothing more than a realization that all of my years spent on the farm and tending to my own unending string of tragedies had left me without the relationships that most folk seemed to take for granted. I had lost Ardith Jenkins, Calla Eltmore, and Lida Knudsen, the pillars of my entire social foundation, all in a matter of months. The truth was I felt lonelier standing there talking to Lene than I did when I was home alone with Shep.

Lene did nothing to fight off the scowl that appeared at the mention of the sheriff. "From what I understand, he came by early this morning," she said. "I missed his visit, but Abigail was here. There's no change, no one to arrest, to no one's surprise."

What's that supposed to mean? bubbled on my tongue, but I swallowed hard, and the words disappeared. I knew what she meant. We both were at the limits of our restraint, and I wasn't sure why that was.

I made a mental note not to mention Tina Rinkerman or the sheriff to Lene again. "I'm sure everyone's working as hard as they can to find out what's going on, Lene."

She stood over me, on edge, her eyes narrowed, ready to tell me exactly what she thought of Guy Reinhardt, but I really didn't want to hear her opinions. I stood up, slipped on my pumps, and said, "Has Anna eaten this morning?"

I heard a rattling in the kitchen. A dish touching a dish with little regard to a chip or damage. I had assumed that Anna was in the bedroom, that me and Lene were the only ones in the house. I looked toward the kitchen in unison with Lene.

"That neighbor lady is fixing her a plate now," Lene said. "I took her some hot tea and toast after the children left, but she refused to eat or drink."

I was more accustomed to Lene's ways and attitudes than I was to Helen Greggson's, but I was tiring quickly of Lene's company. "I'll see what I can do."

I headed into the kitchen, leaving Lene to herself and whatever she was doing before I arrived.

Helen was standing at the stove stirring some familiar smelling knoephla soup. She didn't seem to notice my presence, so I stowed my purse in the cupboard. I was already starting to develop habits and patterns here, even though I had no idea how long I would be attending to Anna's needs as part of the Ladies Aid.

"Good morning," I said.

Helen flinched a little bit, stopped stirring, and looked to me. "Oh, I didn't hear you come in. Lost in thought, I guess. Good morning, Marjorie. How was your drive in?"

"Slow going, like usual."

"Yes, well, it is January."

I heard the tips of hard straw hit wood and I knew Lene had taken the broom to the floor. She seemed happy to work out her frustrations on whatever dirt remained.

Helen started stirring again but kept her eyes on me. "Thankfully, Abigail wanted to take the children on her own. I had no desire to step into that church. Last time was for a wedding, and that was years ago. I'm not much for churches, but I guess when bad times hit, there's a comfort to be had and people to keep you company. If you want such a thing."

I feigned a quick smile. I wasn't going to get into that conversation any more than I was willing to do any kind of battling with Lene. I'd already stepped into one hornet's nest. I wasn't anxious to step into another. "What can I do to help?"

I looked around the kitchen. The counters were clean and cleared. The kitchen table was half full of non-perishables, breads, cakes, cookies, and pies. Hot dishes and salads must have been in the Kelvinator. Leftovers would be warmed up, and enough food to feed an army would parade through the door after church services were over.

"I think some chicken broth would be easy on Anna's stomach. Do you want to be the one to take her something to eat?" Helen said.

"Yes, sure, I'd be happy to."

"I heard the Harstaad woman tell you that the sheriff stopped this morning." Helen lowered her voice and looked out to the front room suspiciously.

I stepped closer so we could talk without Lene hearing. Helen Greggson looked like she had something she wanted to tell me. "She said there was no change."

"That's true," Helen said, whispering. "They don't have any suspects, but they're bringing in Toren Rinkerman and his three boys for questioning."

"Why would they do that?" I said, surprised by what I heard.

"I don't know for sure," Helen said, "but I think it has something to do with where they found Nils. He wasn't killed that far from the Rinkermans' place from what I understand."

CHAPTER 19

Daylight stole in around the edges of closed blinds, a pale yellow glow that could not reach far enough to make any difference inside the gloomy bedroom. The light could not serve its purpose with the blinds closed. If only banishing grief and sadness was as easy as turning the slats on a blind.

"Anna," I said, easing the door closed behind me. "I've brought you some broth." I stopped to balance the bowl and allow my eyes to adjust to the shadows.

The room looked and smelled the same as the day before; disarray and sourness accosted all of my senses. A wastebasket sat at Anna's feet, and the bedsheets lay tangled up in a mess that reminded me of a dove's nest: haphazard, poorly constructed, with whatever sticks and leaves that could be found, offering no safety or security. Anna was sleeping in fits.

Anna looked up at me, pale and uninterested. "I would have thought you of all people would know that I'm not hungry and have no desire for food." She was sitting at the foot of the bed, hunched over as if she didn't have the strength to hold up her head. My guess was she'd used the wastebasket as a catchall for whatever bile remained in her stomach.

I made my way to the dresser and set the broth on a doily so the heat and moisture from the bowl wouldn't mar the wood. "I know you can't stay in here forever." I felt like a hypocrite. Who was I to offer Anna advice or encouragement? I couldn't even bear to part with Hank's clothes. I sat down on the bed next to Anna and took her cold, fragile hand into mine.

"Mother said that, too. She is frustrated with me, but that's nothing new, is it?"

There was no way for me to know. I had no idea what Anna's relationship with her mother was. All I knew was that Abigail was where she needed to be, in charge, looking after the children and house the best she could under terrible circumstances. I didn't answer the question. I sat there quietly trying to figure out how I was going to get Anna moving again. Or not. She would have to figure out how to live again on her own, for her own reasons. No one could goad her into living again. I knew that.

"The new sheriff was here," Anna said. Her eyes were blank, and her face was as white as the doily the soup sat on.

"Lene told me."

"He had a lot of questions."

"He's trying to help."

"You like him, don't you?"

"I respect him." I didn't hesitate. Maybe I should have.

"We all should," Anna said with a sigh. "He hasn't hid his problems from our view. I think it's a minor miracle that a twice-divorced man with a drinking problem got elected to anything in this county."

I felt the skin tighten across my entire body. I stared at Anna, surprised in a way by the direction she'd taken the conversation. I wasn't going to defend Guy to her. I didn't know if that's what she expected. She was entitled to her opinions just like Lene.

Anna continued, didn't wait for me to interject. "The sheriff knows things about people that no one else knows. Nils did, too. Did you know that?"

"I guess I never thought about what Nils might know about people," I said.

Anna looked at the glow around the closed blinds. The edges looked like they were about to burst into flames. The clouds must have parted and the sun beamed directly from the east, trying to push into the room. It was a losing battle.

"He knew when people were short of money," Anna continued.

"Who stole food, who he could trust in the store alone. Thefts were worse at the end of the month. A few people would run short on their widow's pensions, and they'd pocket an extra can of tuna to get them by until the check showed up in the mail. Nils turned a blind eye, paid for the tuna out of his wages. Frank isn't as generous as Nils. He'd call the police no matter who the thief was, or whatever the reason they had for taking a little extra." Her voice was weak, and every time she mentioned Nils's name her throat quivered.

"I didn't know that," I said, shifting uncomfortably on the bed. I couldn't imagine being so desperate that I would steal a can of tuna. Like I'd told Anna, I never thought about a grocery store manager knowing such things. I had to wonder if Nils knew something that had got him killed. It was a worthy question, but not one I was going to push on Anna. Not right now. Maybe not ever. "I'm sure the sheriff has talked to Frank."

Anna shrugged her shoulders. "I don't know. Right now, I don't care about that store or what's going on there. The Red Owl's been our whole life since the day we met, and now I won't have to hear about inventory or cash flow or Frank Aberle kicking someone else out of the store."

I looked away from Anna to the dresser. "Your broth's getting cold."

"I'm really not hungry, Marjorie."

"You'll need your strength the next few days. I hate to be one more person telling you that, but it's the truth. You can't turn away from things, Anna. The world hasn't stopped spinning. It's changed. It's broken your heart."

"My life will never be the same again," Anna said, as a single tear toppled from her right eye.

"You're right."

"Please don't say time heals all wounds. Please don't say that."

"I wouldn't tell you that, because I don't know if it's true. I do know that time changes things whether we want it to or not. I miss Hank Trumaine every day, and I long for his touch, his voice, his encouragement, every second. Sometimes, I can't breathe. You know that. But I have all of my memories in my heart. That will never be enough. We had hard times, too, Anna. But here I am, trying to find my way, thanks in large part to you showing me that there's things left for me to do in this life. I can't thank you enough for taking time away from your life to come out to my house, making time for me like you have."

Anna rolled her lips together, unsuccessfully fighting off more tears. I couldn't hold back my tears, either. I reached over and took her in my arms, where she was happy to stay. We both had a good cry together. I would like to think that the comfort I could offer was something she needed. I didn't fully understand her pain, but I knew her loss.

Time passed as we held each other, both of us lost on our own continent of grief but forever tethered together, allowing us to know that there was no reason to ever be alone again. "You really need to eat," I whispered.

"I know."

"I can have Helen warm up the broth."

"You know what I really want?" Anna said.

"What?"

"Ice cream."

"Ice cream?" I smiled. I hadn't expected Anna to say ice cream.

"Yes, ice cream. Snow ice cream. When Nils and me first got married, we didn't have a lot of money. He was still a sacker at the Red Owl, and he didn't want me to work. He'd bring home some fresh cream after a good snowfall. We'd snuggle in and eat ice cream in the middle of winter, keeping each other warm, planning our future, laughing and playing like the kids we were. We quit doing that a long time ago. Do you know the recipe?"

I hadn't thought of snow ice cream in years. People said you shouldn't eat snow ice cream these days with all of the radioactive elements in the sky, but the fear of something you couldn't see didn't stop them. The recipe was simple, not buried too deep in the snowdrifts of my memory: Get a pan of fluffy snow, add sugar, vanilla, and cream. The good kind of cream, yellow cream skimmed from the top of a farmer's crock. Then fold everything together gently—real gently—and eat the ice cream right away. Snow ice cream could be frozen, but the taste was never the same as fresh if you asked me.

"Yes," I said. "I remember my mother's recipe." I stood up and looked down at Anna, who was looking up at me like an expectant child. "The cream will be easy on your stomach."

Any glee that had returned to her eyes quickly faded away. A familiar shadow fell over Anna's face as she looked away from me and rubbed the small pouch of her belly unconsciously. "If you say so."

I made my way out of the bedroom on a mission, though I nearly stumbled on my own feet and my own words. If one of Anna Jacobsen's secrets was that she was pregnant, then she was the one who was going to have to tell me. I wasn't going to pry into that. Not on purpose, anyway.

CHAPTER 20

I stared into the Kelvinator, searching for a suitable substitute for yellow cream, ignoring the commotion around me. Church services had let out, and there was already a steady stream of mourners leaving their offerings of breads, desserts, and hot dishes on the kitchen table. My own memories of funeral food were still fresh, though this was different. The whole town of Dickinson had shown up on the Jacobsens' doorstep.

Helen and Lene handled the onslaught of people, but I caught a few frustrated glances directed my way as I ignored the newcomers and went about gathering all of the ingredients to make Anna's ice cream. I was doing my best to find something to give her some much needed comfort, all the while digesting everything that she'd said. I really needed time to organize my thoughts. I needed to index the patterns and terms that had settled in my mind so I could be free of them. But I didn't think that was going to happen anytime soon, at least not until I returned home. If then, if I had time. I had real indexing work to do. I felt detached from the *Central Flyway* book in a way that seemed lazy and dangerous. The Ladies Aid was overtaking my life, my schedule, and my energy.

I pushed aside a glass bottle of milk and found a carton of half-and-half. The thin cream wasn't exactly what I was hoping for, but store-bought cream would have to do. Sugar and vanilla were easier to find in the pantry. All I needed was fresh snow. There was plenty of that outside the backdoor.

I navigated my way through the steady stream of people, some I recognized and others I didn't, and retrieved my coat. Then I hurried back to the kitchen, pulled out a saucepan from the cabinet next to the stove, and headed toward the backdoor. Someone said, "Hello," behind me, but I wasn't sure if the salutation was for me, so I kept on going. I was focused on one thing: snow ice cream. Nothing was going to get in my way.

I closed the door behind me and stood on the stoop, adjusting to the outside. The cold air nearly took my breath away. Muffled conversations tapped at the walls from inside the house, and I was left to wonder how Anna could get any rest at all.

The sky was full of fragile gray clouds, and the wind was light. The temperature hung a few degrees above zero, its favorite spot in January. Without the roaring wind, the cold in North Dakota felt tolerable to those who were seasoned to frigid conditions. The air was dry. Once the sun came out, some men would walk around without a coat and hat, wearing their work shirts like they were strolling around in the middle of summer.

I searched for some fluffy snow, but my eyes were drawn to the garage at the back of the property. Darlys was standing at the corner, out of the wind, smoking a cigarette, staring away from me, her back to the house. She either hadn't heard me come out, or she didn't care that I was there.

A tall drift had come to rest against the side of the single-car garage, preserving a bank of fresh snow under the outer crust. That was my hope, anyway. As I made my way toward the bounty of icy goodness, Darlys turned and made eye contact with me. "Oh, Marjorie, I wasn't expecting to see you out here," she said, flipping her Winston into Helen Greggson's yard.

I watched the orange tip spiral away like a Fourth of July firecracker. I could tell by the look on Darlys's face that there was nothing to celebrate. She looked upset, angrier than I'd seen her since she'd been coming to the house.

"I didn't expect to see you, either," I said.

She was dressed in her thick blue parka and had the hood up, shielding her face from the wind. A thick shadow sheltered her eyes. "I was taking a minute before going inside," she said.

"You came from the Rinkermans' house?"

"Yes. Out of the fire and into the frying pan."

That seemed an odd thing for her to say; my forehead scrunched in confusion. "Is everything all right?" I meant with them *and* her.

"No, everything's not all right. The sheriff took Toren and the boys in for questioning."

"I heard that."

"Of course, you did."

"I think that's terrible," I said. And that was the truth. I wondered how Guy could put that family through more than they had already been through. I assumed that the questioning was simply routine, that none of the Rinkermans were murder suspects.

"They seemed resigned to the fact," Darlys said.

"Only the men, and not the mother?" I blurted out before thinking about the question.

Darlys turned her face so I could see her teary eyes. "I honestly don't know, Marjorie. I hadn't thought of that. I'm sure Toren and his sons had nothing to do with what happened to Nils. I can't think of one reason why any of them would do such a thing."

"That's all the sheriff's doing. He's making sure he talks to everyone. I'm sure he doesn't think the Rinkermans are suspects." I didn't know that for sure.

"Guy Reinhardt has a job to do."

"That's right. Everybody's watching."

"They are." Darlys looked down to the pan in my hand. "What are you doing out here, Marjorie?"

"Getting some snow. Anna said snow ice cream sounded good."

"Well, that's a start. Good for you. Nobody else has been able to get her to eat anything. I'm not surprised, you're a natural with people."

"I'm not sure I'm any good at this Ladies Aid thing at all. I don't seem to fit in, not even with Lene."

"She's here?"

"Yes, she was here when I showed up. The house is sparkling clean. I think she's been here since sun up."

"That'd be Lene," Darlys said. "You shouldn't worry about her. She's direct as a hammer, that's all. You know that."

Darlys looked like she wanted to say more, but she didn't.

I didn't give her much time. "I know you need me here, but I'm worried that I bit off more than I should have. I'm afraid my indexing work will suffer if I keep coming to town every day. I'm falling behind on my deadline."

Darlys stared at me in a way I didn't know how to interpret. "I can't imagine what a deadline really is. I keep busy, and I have to be on time at my meetings and the like, but I don't have to worry about not getting paid, or getting fired, if I'm late for something. I only have Henrik to answer to. I don't mean to open a wound, but you know how life is when someone passes away. There are days that are really busy, and then things calm down after the funeral. I thought you'd be a help to Anna, and I was right about that. Even her mother couldn't get her to agree to eat any food. Once we bury Nils and the police find out who did this horrible thing, everything will get back to normal. I'm sure of it. There are other women who can help out then. Can you give me a few more days?"

What Darlys said made sense. "Yes, okay, I can work around the deadline for a couple more days. I'll make up the time." I wasn't sure that I believed what I'd said, but I didn't really feel like I could say no.

"Good," Darlys said. "Anna's going to need us long after this is over with. I honestly don't know how she's going to manage, but I'm sure she will. She has to. She has children to raise." She flashed me a smile, stood up straight, pulled off her hood, and said, "Well, I better get in there before Lene starts to think she's been abandoned." And with that, Darlys marched off as if she didn't have a care in the world, determined to make a difference and bring some light to a dark world. No one but me would ever know that she was upset. I was really beginning to admire that woman.

Anna stared at the whole bowl of ice cream with vacant eyes. Not exactly the reaction I was hoping for. "I had to use half-and-half," I said. The snow was already starting to melt.

"This looks wonderful, Marjorie," Anna said.

"The cream will settle your stomach."

"Nothing can do that."

"I know." I my put hand on hers. She was trembling. I knew how she felt, like she could never eat again without remembering one memory or another. Food was a trigger for good and bad. Anna reminded me of Hank the last two years of his life, paralyzed from the neck down, unable to do even the most basic functions for himself. I didn't ask or hesitate to do what I did next. I took my hand away from Anna's, grabbed up the spoon, dug up a small dollop of ice cream, and offered her a bite. "You can do this," I whispered. Hank had tried to starve himself to death in the beginning, too.

Anna stared into my serious, loving eyes, and opened her mouth halfway. She reminded me of a little sick bird, drained of energy and will, but she took the bite, swallowed, and didn't refuse the next spoonful of ice cream. We sat there until the bowl was empty, and then I held her, humming a Norwegian lullaby my mother had sung to me as a child.

"What is that you're humming?" Anna asked.

"A lullaby my mother used to sing to me when I was girl. Her mother sang it to her on the boat over when she was afraid. The song is called a bånsull in Norway."

Anna smiled weakly. "Do you know the words?"

"I do. In English, the title is 'Cradle Me a Little.' In Norwegian, the song is called '*Sulla meg litt.*'"

"Can you sing it?"

I didn't want to. I couldn't remember the last time I had sung a song for anyone. I'd hummed around Hank, nothing more. But I didn't see how I could refuse Anna. "In Norwegian or English?"

"Both?"

"Yes, I can do that." I closed my eyes and tried to forget where I was and why I was there. My mother would have liked that I was comforting Anna with her bånsull.

"Sulla meg litt, du mamma mi,
Skal du få snor på skjorta di.
Vil du ha gule? Vil du ha blå?
Vil du ha blanke? Skal du det få,
På skjorta di,
Du mamma mi."

"That is beautiful," Anna said. She leaned in to me and closed her eyes. I waited until her breathing regulated, then sang the lullaby again, softer, gentler:

"Rock me a little, mama mine,
And you shall have ribbons on your shirt.
Do you want yellow? Do you want blue?
Do you want shiny ones? I'll give them to you,
On your shirt,
Mama mine."

The sun had already started to drop to the west before I was able to make my way out of the house and head toward home.

Darlys, Helen, and Lene remained in the house. Abigail and the children had returned long before and had settled in as the steady stream of visitors to the house continued throughout the day. I had stayed busy, but I begged off around four o'clock, anxious to get home before dark. With no clouds in the sky, the temperatures were going to drop deep below zero before the sun rose again.

I stopped at the sidewalk and looked up and down the street. Even in the dimming light, I could see the street was lined with all colors of cars. I wasn't surprised to see that the majority of them were black. Jaeger and Lester were right. There were a lot of black cars in Dickinson. I had to wonder if there were more girls like Tina Rinkerman than I knew about, too.

CHAPTER 21

The door to the Studebaker groaned open, and the frozen springs creaked reluctantly as I stepped up into the truck. I had to muscle the door closed. Whatever grease remained on the hinges had given way to the cold, forcing metal to rub against metal. I was amazed the entire truck didn't shatter like an icicle dropped to the ground.

I put the key in the ignition, pumped the accelerator, then turned the key. The engine moaned, the flywheel winding away as if it had purpose, but the spark refused to erupt and set the pistons in motion. I stopped and tried again. Same thing. More grinding—only the familiar sound grew weaker. I knew what that meant. The battery was getting ready to die. One more try. Like last time. Third time's a charm. But not this round. The engine sputtered, then started clicking. The death knell. I wasn't going anywhere soon. "Shit," I said aloud. I really wanted to go home.

I eased the back of my head against the empty gun rack, closed my eyes, exhaled again, releasing more vapor into the cab, then gathered myself to go back outside, back up to the Jacobsens' house to find someone to give me a jump. Dead batteries were as common as snowflakes in January. Finding help wasn't the issue. I was aggravated. I should have parked in the courthouse parking lot this morning, plugged in the block heater, and walked over to Anna's. But I was worried about being late. The curse of an indexer. Tardiness wasn't allowed. I'd always been on time, even before I was an indexer. But the habit of being on time was worse now. Being late meant losing a job, a publisher. My obsession with being late had consequences. I obviously needed a refresher on that lesson.

I got out of the truck, opened the hood, and left it open; the universal sign for *I need a jump*. Still frustrated, I looked down the street at Anna's. I was certain somebody would be willing to help me. But I had to wait for an oncoming car to pass before making my way back.

I recognized the driver, and he recognized me.

Guy Reinhardt tapped the brakes and signaled with his finger that he saw me, that he was coming back to my aid. I waited and watched the sheriff's brown and tan Scout turn around in the nearest driveway, then head back my way. I had mixed emotions about seeing Guy. I had plenty of questions that were none of my business waiting to be asked.

Guy pulled up alongside the truck and stopped, almost kissing the corner of my front bumper with his. All he had to do was pop open his hood, hook up the cables to his battery, and give the key a turn. He knew the drill, probably gave someone a jump ten times a day.

Guy stood up out of the car, instantly towering over the roof. "Hey, there, Marjorie. What's the matter? Truck won't start?"

I didn't have the energy to offer him a smile. At least he didn't give me a weather report.

"Well," Guy said, "go on, get in my truck and keep yourself warm. I've got this."

"The jumpers are under the passenger seat," I said.

Guy headed to the truck, and I headed to his Scout, more than willing to take up his offer to get out of the cold. I slid into the passenger seat and was greeted by a blast of air that was hot enough to melt the makeup off my face. My foundation and lipstick had probably worn off hours ago. I wasn't too fussy about refreshing my face; there'd been too many people to keep up with in the Jacobsens' front room for that. Not that a made-up face would have mattered. Being presentable wasn't something I had to put a lot of thought into during the day.

I watched Guy go through the motions as he hooked up the jumper cables. With both batteries connected, he headed to the cab of the truck. He had to turn the key a couple of times, but the engine finally fired.

Guy left the truck running and the cables connected, then returned to the Scout. "I'm gonna let the battery charge off mine a little while before I send you on your way, Marjorie. That all right?"

I looked up at the sky, calculating what bit of daylight was left. "Sure," I said. Even if I drove home in the dark, at least I wouldn't have to worry about the battery.

I hadn't seen Guy since we'd found Nils. I really didn't know what to say to him without asking questions that weren't any of my business. "Thanks for stopping," I finally said.

Guy reached over and turned down the heat. "I wasn't gonna leave you standing there on your own."

"I was going back to Anna's. Someone would have helped."

He looked down the street toward the house full of mourners. He looked tired. Any boyishness in his square-jawed face had vanished. Weary red lines crisscrossed the whites of his eyes, which were covered with a glassy sheen. I felt bad for consciously smelling for whiskey, but I did it anyway. There was none. The whole interior of the Scout smelled like stale cigarettes and nothing more. I guess I wasn't immune to rumors any more than anybody else, but I worried the stress of the job might be too much for Guy.

"I've been wonderin' how you were doing," Guy said.

"Same here," I answered.

"I'm sorry you had to see Nils like that."

"That's not your fault. We went looking for a missing girl. Finding her dead would have been difficult, too."

Guy agreed. "But still. I should have told you not to come with me."

"I didn't give you much of a choice."

A slight smile flashed across Guy's face. "Things would have been easier if we would have found Tina instead of Nils."

"For who?"

"Nobody, I guess. That was a silly thing to say."

Y'betcha, I thought, but didn't say. I sucked in a deep breath instead and said, "I called dispatch last night."

"I heard. George told me you thought you saw Tina Rinkerman.

By the time I was free to call you, I thought the hour was too late. Then things started in this morning as soon as the rooster crowed."

I was relieved. George Lardner had done his job. I was worried that the dispatcher had taken me for a foolish woman and hadn't told Guy about what I thought I'd seen. "Someone did call me. They called twice and hung up both times. I think someone dialed a wrong number."

"You're sure?" Guy pressed down on the accelerator, racing the engine of his truck to help the battery charge faster.

"As sure as I can be."

"If you notice anything odd, you call the station right away, okay?"

I'd noticed a lot of odd things since we'd found Nils's body, but I couldn't make sense of most of them. "I could have sworn I saw Tina Rinkerman in the backseat of that car, but I didn't really get a clear look. I've only seen her a few times, anyway."

"She's kinda hard to miss, if you know what I mean."

"I do. But George said she's probably not the only girl around like her. I guess I never put much thought into such a thing."

Guy stiffened and let up on the gas, allowing the Scout to settle back to a steady idle. "Girls like Tina are rare. From what I understand, most folks send them away to let other people take care of them."

"To the Grafton State School?" Anna had called the school a hospital for the feebleminded, which was the original name when the place was built. They changed names more than thirty years ago, but feebleminded stuck.

"That's where the Rinkermans kept Tina, but they brought her home recently."

"Do you know why?" The question slipped out of my mouth without my permission. I really didn't want to do that.

Guy shot me a look that I knew all too well. He couldn't say. Or he wasn't going to tell me. "Toren and his boys have all cooperated with the investigation."

I let Guy's words settle between us. His focus was still on the Jacobsen house. I wondered what he knew about them that I didn't.

"I'm sorry, I shouldn't have asked. I can't help myself sometimes. You know that," I said.

"I do," Guy said. "You've been a big help to me in the past, Marjorie. To be honest, I've wanted to talk to you more than once. But I don't want to involve you in something that might lead to trouble. And besides, I guess I really need to show everyone in the county that I can handle both of these investigations on my own."

"I'll help if I can, you know that."

Guy looked away from the house, back to me. "Have you heard anything that might be of help, Marjorie? You know, since you've been in town? Between you and me, I keep runnin' up against dead ends. I'm startin' to get worried the killer's trail is going cold, and if I don't come up with something soon, you know what's gonna hit the fan, especially if somebody else comes up hurt. That'd be the end of my job. So, you see, I really have to figure this out. Whoever did this to Nils is still out there."

"I need to organize my thoughts, but a few things *have* troubled me. Did you know Nils and Anna had an argument the night before he died?"

"She told me. So did Frank. They argued from time to time from what I understand. Makes sense to me. I got an inside track on how hard marriage is. People argue. That's the way livin' with someone is, you know that. Is there more to this than a bad spat?"

"I don't know Anna well enough for sure. To be honest, the only time I saw Nils and Anna together was at church, and, well, I haven't attended much in the past few years."

"No, I don't imagine you have."

I had more questions. Guy had asked, so I felt like I could let him know what I was thinking, what bothered me. "Do you know why they argued? You don't have to tell me. Honestly, I really don't want to know. But you should know. That way if there was more to the spat, something serious, you can work on that."

"Marital stuff from what I understand. Anna hasn't been too coherent or talkative. I figure she'll come around once the shock wears off. I plan on talking to her again if time allows. I hope I don't have to. I hope I find out who did this before then and lock them up where they belong."

"Frank told me there was tension at the store a few days before Nils died."

"Sounds right."

I took a deep breath, then said, "I'm hesitating to say anything about this, because I don't know that what I'm thinking is true. This is just a suspicion on my part, but Anna sure looks like she's pregnant to me. I've wondered all along if that's what the two of them argued about. They have a lot of mouths to feed, and Anna seemed at the end of her rope with everything she had to do. Maybe that was why they fought."

Guy shifted uncomfortably in his seat. "No one has said anything about that to me."

"I can't say this is true. Something seems off, though, and I always end up back at that. Darlys suspects that Anna is pregnant, too, but she doesn't know for sure. You might want to talk to her."

"Yeah, I should do that. See, that's why I like talkin' with you. I've come to trust your insight, Marjorie. You're one of the smartest people I know."

"Please don't say that."

"Why? It's the truth."

"Hilo used to say that."

"Oh." Guy shifted in his seat again, then said, "I'm going to go unhook the cables. Are you in a hurry?"

"I have to go by Jaeger Knudsen's to pick up Shep, and then go home to try and get some indexing work done. I have a little time, no worry." I didn't want to rush Guy along.

"Good. Stay right here. I have a favor to ask of you." Guy jumped out of the Scout and scurried over to the Studebaker, which nearly died once he took the jumper cables off the battery.

I wasn't left to wonder what the favor was for too long. Once Guy was sure the Studebaker was going to stay running, he came back to the Scout.

"That's a sturdy old workhorse you got there, Marjorie. But you might have that battery looked at."

"I'll talk to Jaeger." I stared at Guy expectantly. My curiosity was pushed to the limit of my restraint. *What's the favor, Guy?*

He looked at me, and I saw the same uncertainty in Guy's eyes I'd seen the first time we'd gone off on a search together. He was struggling to ask me something. "This is a big favor, Marjorie."

"Well, go on, ask. I'll say yes if I can."

"I said I needed to do this on my own, that I didn't want to pull you into this any more than I already had, but the thing is, I'm new at this. I mean, I was a deputy for a long time, and I thought I knew my way around the department. Then we lost Hilo as sheriff and Duke stepped in, and now Duke's out, and I'm in. Stark County is a small department, and there's people who favor Duke over me and some that favor me over Duke. But not so much me. I understand that people are uncertain of me. I've got a limp and two bad marriages in my wake. That doesn't say much about my ability to make things work out."

George Lardner came to mind. I could see the dispatcher taking Duke's side since he was dating Duke's sister, Theda. There was probably more inside stuff than that, but I'd heard the gossip, seen how people reacted to him. I knew what Guy was saying was true.

"Anyway," he went on, "I can't say this to anyone but you, but I'm not sure who I can trust. Not only in my department, but the state police are helping, and the US Marshal for this territory is on his way. There's a lot of people in and out of my office and on the phone that I don't know. I trust you, Marjorie. I hope that's all right."

"Of course it is," I said.

"This is a big favor."

"You said that already."

"At least the weather's cleared up," Guy said, looking to the sky.

I stared at him and didn't say a word.

Guy looked back at me. "You mentioned Grafton."

"I did."

"Well, I asked Grafton for their papers on Tina and a report about her. Who she associated with, why she left, any trouble with her running off, that kind of thing. I think Tina's life in Grafton is important to know about. Maybe she ran off to go back there. I don't know," Guy said, perplexed. "But I need to know everything about her that I can find out. If I wait for this report to come in the mail, it might be too late. They won't tell me much over the phone."

I furrowed my brow. My mind raced ahead of Guy's words. "I don't understand what the favor is."

"I'd like you to go to Grafton, Marjorie, and bring me back that report. But look around while you're there, too. Toren said they got a call to go get Tina, and that's all there was to her coming home. He might not be tellin' me everything, though I don't know why he wouldn't."

"You want me to drive up to Grafton?"

"I don't know who else to ask, Marjorie."

"That's a six-hour drive on a good day."

"The weather's clearing. The roads ought to be decent."

I sighed. "When?"

"Tomorrow, if you can. I don't know that the report will help me find Tina, but if I could get one of the investigations solved, then it sure would be a big help, not just to me but to Toren and his family. I'll call the school to tell them you're comin' in my place."

"I'm scheduled to help out with the Ladies Aid tomorrow, but I guess I could call Darlys and tell her something's come up."

"You need to keep this between us, Marjorie. Don't tell Darlys or anyone else that I asked for your help."

"I understand."

"I know you do," Guy said. "I know you do."

CHAPTER 22

Daylight slipped away, and the world before me turned blue. Without the clouds to trap the light and cold air, all I could see was the sky and its fading reflection off the snow. The sky looked as if the whole universe was nothing more than a glass bowl turned upside down. Blue was a sympathetic color, and the comforting sight was a relief from the long, blank white and gray evenings of the prior days. This sky was in a good mood, and it offered me a glimpse of a world capable of change at any moment. Beauty and peace were right around the corner—but I didn't believe that for a minute. Things were worse now than they were when the day had started. I wasn't sure that I could help Guy. Or that I should.

I couldn't tell him no.

The drive to Grafton worried me. But there was more to my discomfort than simple worry. I'd said yes to a sheriff once before when he came to me looking for help, and that hadn't turned out so well. The world had turned blood red then, and I still hadn't recovered.

Before I could fully digest the comforting color in the sky, the light faded away. Darkness fell in front of my eyes like a heavy iron curtain. My headlights cut into the suddenness of night like white-hot knives, allowing me to see the snow-covered road in front of me but not much farther.

Instead of driving to pick up Shep, I drove right on by the Knudsen farm until I was at home. I decided that I would call Jaeger once I got settled and ask him to keep Shep another day, until I got back from Grafton. I hated to be separated from the dog, but more than that I hated to be in the house by myself, alone, without another living creature nearby. I couldn't remember a time when that had happened in recent memory.

What'd you get yourself into now, Marjorie?

I had to punch the gas pedal to plow through the drifted driveway.

The first thing I did, after surveying the snow and property to make sure no one had visited the house while I was away, was plug in the block heater to the truck. Then I went inside and called Jaeger straight away. I didn't even take off my coat.

Jaeger said he'd be happy to keep Shep another day, and didn't pry, either, to ask where I was going or why. I was glad I didn't have to make something up and lie to him.

With those two things taken care of, I set about warming up the house by restocking the Franklin stove. I wanted out of my dress and boots, so I changed into some comfortable clothes, thick flannel pajamas, and put on three pairs of heavy socks. Then I started thinking about what I was going to eat for supper. To my surprise, my stomach was growling. I had worked up an appetite serving others. Darlys had predicted that would happen.

The thought of her made me realize that I was distracting myself from making one more necessary phone call. I had to call Darlys. I had to tell her I wasn't going to be at Anna's.

I picked up the phone, checked to make sure no one else was using the line, then dialed the number. The phone rang four times before someone answered.

A man said, "Hello. Oddsdatter residence."

I assumed the man was Darlys's husband. "Doctor Oddsdatter?"

"Speaking."

"Hello, this is Marjorie Trumaine. Is Darlys available?"

"Oh, hello, Marjorie. How are you?" Henrik Oddsdatter had a deep, soothing voice, which I was sure came in handy when he had to calm someone down in the dentist's chair.

"I'm well, thank you very much," I said. "Could I speak to Darlys, please?"

"Darlys isn't home," he said.

"I guess Darlys is still at Anna's?"

"I think she is, yes." The softness went out of Henrik's voice. I wasn't sure what I heard. Friction. Anger. Wind in the line?

"Could you have her give me a call when she gets in?" I said.

"Sure thing, Marjorie." Henrik hesitated, cleared his throat. "Can I ask you something?"

"Yes, sure, of course."

"You don't know anything about this business, do you?"

"What business is that?"

"This Jacobsen business. I'm accustomed to Darlys throwing herself into one thing or another. She's always been like that, but we're getting on in our life, you know, and she doesn't have children to keep her busy, so I think she feels the need to contribute in one way or another. But she seems more obsessed than normal. One minute she's at the Jacobsens', then out to South Heart to the Rinkermans'. Before that she was visiting you, organizing the next bazaar, and making sure the Ladies Aid was running like a fine-tuned machine. Honestly, I'm afraid she'll collapse. I'm never sure when she will walk in the door these days. I'm starting to worry."

I remembered Darlys whispering, "*That man*," in a frustrated voice when she walked away from him in Anna's front room. I almost felt like Henrik was looking for some information beyond what he was asking. Darlys had implied that Henrik was capable of being controlling, that she would pay a price for behavior that he didn't approve of. I didn't know what to say to him. I didn't want to get Darlys in trouble.

Darlys never talked to me about *why* she volunteered to so many causes. I never suspected that she was compensating for not having children. I should have recognized the behavior, since I was guilty of busying myself because I had little else to do with my time.

"No, Henrik," I finally said. "I don't know any more about this 'business' than anyone else. I think there's a lot happening, that's all. We all want to help."

"Of course you do. All right, I'll tell Darlys you called. Or do you want to leave her a message? I honestly don't know when she'll return home."

I hesitated. Leaving a message would give me an out. I wouldn't have to lie to Darlys directly if I didn't talk to her. "Yes, well, that's a good idea. Tell her I won't be at Anna's tomorrow. Something's come up that I absolutely must take care of. The funeral is set for Wednesday from what I understand. I'll be able to help Tuesday and that day, of course."

"Oh, I hope nothing is the matter," Henrik said.

"No, not at all." I didn't offer anything more.

"You do have your own set of demands. Darlys talks all the time about this editing that you do and the deadlines you have. Publishing sounds fascinating to me. I would like to know more about it."

"Indexing. I'm an indexer, not an editor," I said. People confused editing and indexing skills all the time.

"That's right. Indexing. Sorry about that. I've used a few indexes in my life, especially in school. A good index is invaluable. They are beautiful, too. The columns look like perfect teeth. Everything in its place. We are the same, you and I. We put things where they belong."

That was the second time Henrik had said that to me. "Thank you," I said. I appreciated being elevated to an equal standing with a professional. His deep voice was flattering. I could see how he had wooed Darlys and won her over.

"I'm fascinated by what you do," Henrik continued. "You'll have to come over for dinner after all this mess calms down, and we can talk all about books. I mean, if you want to."

"Yes, I'd like that."

"Good. I'll tell Darlys to make a date, and I'll tell her that you are busy tomorrow."

My stomach rolled a bit at the dishonesty, but I didn't say anything to the contrary. I couldn't. "I'll look forward to dinner, Doctor Oddsdatter, thank you."

"Okay, then. Goodbye."

"Goodbye," I said. As the line went dead, the feeling of dread in my stomach grew instead of fading away. Mother used to say, "Omission is a lie all unto itself," and she was right. I had already lied to two people according to those rules.

I felt a bit of anger flash toward Guy. But the anger fell away as quickly as it came. He had trusted me enough to ask for my help. I wasn't going to let him down.

I loved sitting at my desk, surrounded by books, stuffed in the warmest corner of the house. But I was uncomfortable with being rushed. I felt like I had to hurry through the page proofs, looking for index entries instead of digesting the text and allowing the entries to come to my mind naturally. Order took time. Pressure made a mess out of everything.

I had entered the species section of *The Central Flyway: Audubon's Journey Revisited* book. The pages before me concerned the American white pelican. The thought of a big white water bird helped to take my focus away from Anna's loss and my impending journey, though, as I read on, I had to consider the Chase Lake Wildlife Refuge where pelicans nested over the short summer months. My trip to Grafton would take me south of the lake, as I traveled east on I-94. There would be no pelicans there in January. They didn't show up until mid-April, visiting their annual nesting areas on two islands in the lake. Ice on the lake was probably a foot thick. The whole place was more a moonscape in winter than a potential habitat for pelicans to raise their broods.

I read on:

The American white pelican is one of the largest birds in North America, measuring six feet from beak to tail, with a wingspan of over nine feet. With a look of awkwardness on land, the pelican is an agile flyer, with the capability of soaring and then diving straight into the water after its prey: a bill full of fish.

Chase Lake, North Dakota, is one of the largest nesting colonies of American white pelicans along the flyway. After being nearly decimated at the turn of the twentieth century, a repopulation effort began in 1955 with an introduction of 36,000 chicks to the lake. In 1908, local settler H. H. McCumber wrote, "When I came here in 1905 there were probably five hundred pelicans that nested on the island. . . . [A]fter the number of pelicans was reduced to about 50 birds, President Roosevelt set it aside as a bird refuge in August, 1908." Proving that Theodore Roosevelt's conservation efforts have reached far into the future, the American white pelican continues to flourish and reproduce.

I sat back in my chair to consider what I had read. My mind filled with main entries, and I searched through the index cards I had already created. I quickly reached for the Rs in the shoebox and found the card I was looking for.

Roosevelt, Theodore, 1, 27, 36

President Roosevelt was a large figure in North Dakota's history. He came to the state in 1884 after the death of his mother and his first wife, Alice. Elkhorn Ranch became a place of healing for him, as the wonder of the land and wildlife convinced Roosevelt that there was reason to live. He left North Dakota with a new respect for the land, remarried, and started his second family.

I typed the page number on the card, then put it back in the shoebox. I felt a little despondent and disconnected. The spell of the book was broken by the thought of Roosevelt and his grief, so close to mine and to Anna's, though neither of us had the option of leaving our home and going to a wild and untamed country to start over. We could not, or would not, migrate. I could only speak for myself, though, not for Anna. I had no idea what direction she might move in the days to come.

I sat back in my chair, sighed, and thought about lighting a Salem to refocus myself. But I didn't move. I was distracted, once again, by grief, murder, and the mayhem that followed. I thought of Nils's face covered in frozen blood; a souvenir of my curiosity and need to be included in Guy's search for Tina Rinkerman. I was still numbed by what I had witnessed.

I pushed the page proofs aside and pulled out the index I'd made a few days earlier to clear my mind. A lot of the questions remained unanswered. But I had more information than I'd had before. I added what I thought would help:

B

black car, who owns one?

J

Jacobsen, Anna (widow)
Jacobsen, Nils (victim)

M

missing girl (Tina
   Rinkerman)
   who was the last person
     to see her?
motive
   who would want to kill
     Nils?
   is Tina still alive?
   why did Tina leave home?

R

relationships
   did Nils know Tina?
   murder and disappear-
     ance related?
Rinkerman, Adaline
   (mother)
Rinkerman, Tina (missing
   girl)
Rinkerman, Toren (father)
Rinkermans (three sons,
   find out names)

S

suspects
   could Anna be a
     suspect? Why?
   could be random, but
     doesn't make sense
   none right now
   Rinkerman men have
     been questioned

T

troubles
   is Anna pregnant?
   argued with Anna
     (Why?)
   did Nils have any
     problems?
   did the Rinkermans have
     any troubles?

V

victim, Nils Jacobsen

W

who saw Nils last? (I don't
   know)

I decided that I was going to take the index with me on my trip to Grafton. I knew my mind would wander as I drove that far. I got up from my desk, expecting to stumble over Shep, but he, of course, wasn't there.

I looked out the window over my desk, and the view was the same: white swirling snow had started to fall again, buffeting against the garage, spraying Hank's security light with hard, unrelenting flakes. Even the light wavered and struggled against the blackness all around its edge. I could see nothing past the light. Nothing but darkness; an infinite void of nothingness where no living creature dared to stir. But I knew there was an evil person out there somewhere. I could have been looking right at him.

CHAPTER 23

I nearly froze to death sleeping without a hairy border collie wedged between me and the back of the davenport. Life without Shep in the house had its consequences, and I didn't like them. I sat up stiff and didn't feel rested at all. Sleep had come in fits and starts. I didn't dream; I'd tossed and turned all night. I couldn't stop thinking about Anna or the book I was indexing or the trip I was about to take. I worried about that most of all.

As I had planned, I was up before the break of dawn. Darkness still reigned outside. The moon was in its new phase, unable, or unwilling, to cast any light onto the earth; I wasn't sure which. Stars twinkled like little frozen drops of mercury thrown into the air and glued to a black burlap background. The air was expectantly frigid—the temperature sat at ten below outside—as the wood burned away in the Franklin. I wasn't going to fully restock the stove; no sense in wasting wood on an empty house. According to the weather report on the radio, a visit from the sun later in the day promised to raise the comfort level to the mid-teens. A couple of storms threatened from both the south and the north, but they were out of range of my path. If there was a day to travel, then I couldn't have asked for a better forecast.

My intention was to be on the road to Grafton before sunup. Even on snow-covered roads and crossing from Mountain into Central time, I figured I could get to the State School a little after noon. There was more to my plan than my arrival time; I wanted to be through Dickinson before most of the town woke and headed out into their day.

I ignored the empty bedroom as I passed by. That room was a museum to my old life. Mornings used to be full, especially after Hank's accident. Once he'd come home from the hospital, his care had fallen mostly on my shoulders. Those days were busy. If I was lucky, I would never have that much to do or care about ever again. But I would trade places with myself if I could.

Hank urged me on, too, and somewhere deep in my mind, I could hear him telling me to go to Grafton, to help Guy as much as I could. *Somebody needs to find out what happened to Nils Jacobsen. He was a good man.* But I needed more than a whisper that I had to create on my own to drive six hours from home in January. I needed to prove to myself that this trip was worthy, necessary, and helpful.

What were you thinking, Marjorie? I said to myself, pushing Hank's made-up voice out of my head. *Of course I had to go.* But that didn't mean I was looking forward to the trip.

I hurried outside to start the truck. True to form, the Studebaker groaned like an old man waking up, acted like it was too cold to do anything, then fired to life, chugging and protesting, before the engine started to run smooth.

From there I scurried back and forth from the truck to the house, my mission as sure as a busy ant's. I loaded the passenger seat of the truck with my overnight bag; a few heavy blankets, a can of beans, a gallon of water, aluminum foil, and a fresh box of matches. I had more survival gear stuffed behind the seat, which included a small garden spade, extra tire chains, and a tarp. The glove box was stocked with candy bars, a couple of forgotten packs of stale Salems, and more maps than I could count. I knew the way to Grafton, but you never knew when you were going to need a map.

I was pretty sure that I hadn't forgotten anything as I made my way out the door, then stopped as I realized that I was wrong. I hadn't grabbed up the index I'd made concerning the investigations, so I went to my office for that, along with some blank paper, my red pen, and some of the page proofs for the *Central Flyway* book. I could work if I got stuck and had to wait for someone to find me. At least I wouldn't be wasting time.

I unloaded my haul, then hurried back inside the house and

grabbed one last thing: Hank's Revelation .22. If I got desperate I could hunt down a rabbit if I had to. That was assuming I got stranded for more than a day. Being stranded wasn't in my plan.

The county road north was vacant of any traffic as I skirted Dickinson. In any other season I would have taken the country roads over to Gladstone or Lefor and gotten on I-94 there, but the roads were icy, snow-covered, and their conditions unknown. Most folks were good about keeping their roads open, cooperating with the county, but there was only so much any of them could do.

I was pretty sure no one had seen me leave Dickinson. I had only passed three cars between home and Dickinson. Once I was on I-94 the roads were clear and navigable, thanks to the heavy use of salt and a wind that seemed tame and uninterested in stirring anything up.

The road looked like a gray ribbon fastened to a big white dress. All I had to do was drive for six or seven hours, depending on the road conditions. The concrete path would take me to Grafton. With some luck, I would be back home before the end of the day. A modern convenience if ever there was one.

As I drove, my mind danced around like I suspected it would.

I grieved for Nils Jacobsen and worried about Anna's future.

I obsessed over whether I really had seen Tina Rinkerman.

I watched for coyotes running across the road, unaware that the Studebaker meant them no harm but would kill them all the same.

I worried that Shep would think I would never return.

Ten miles ticked off the odometer before I saw another car on the interstate. And the farther I got from home, the more I started to think that this trip might not be such a good idea after all.

The radio kept me company. A clear blue sky and a little wind did nothing to interfere with the invisible signal that brought the world into the cab of the Studebaker. The Ag shows on KDIX had already played, and Peg Graham's "Women's Club on the Air" show wouldn't air until later in the day. The announcer on the air was Earl Mann, giving the news and weather report. He droned on with no emotion at all about a Soviet nuclear underground test that had created an instant radioactive lake in some place inside Russia called Chagan, Kazakhstan. I turned the dial, trailing downward, listening for a strong station, all the while keeping my eye on the road. I stopped when music replaced the dread and destruction of the news. The song was "Love Potion Number 9." I'd had enough death and fear in my life recently. I didn't need to fill my mind with images of atomic mushroom clouds and half the people on earth being incinerated.

At that thought, I quickly scanned the sky, searching for a lumbering B-52 out of Minot or Grand Forks, patrolling the northern border, promising a swift retaliation to a Soviet attack. A cataclysmic explosion would have made all of the everyday problems I'd accumulated seem small and inconsequential. Even if those problems were loss and murder.

CHAPTER 24

Tthere was little wildlife to see as I drove steadily east. I saw thin herds of antelope, a couple of soaring hawks, and one snowy owl, perched on a Burma-Shave billboard, watching the ground for any sign of movement. The owl looked like it had taken a dip in white cake frosting. Its eyes were bright yellow orbs, little suns beaming with life and intensity that I could see clearly from the road.

I was heartened at the sight of the owl. The snowy owl was a reminder that my preconceived notion of migration needed to be broadened. My initial thoughts about migration were rooted in the movement of spring, of birds coming north to feast on the abundance of insects and prey, taking advantage of plentiful nesting opportunities. But migration happened in winter, too. I was too focused on assumptions to see the topic clearly. That thought, thanks to the owl, would have to be a strong consideration once I returned to my indexing work. I knew I would search the page proofs frantically, looking to prove to myself that I was correct about the snowy owl. My brief encounter, driving by a billboard sitter at forty-five miles an hour, would make for a better index. But if that really was going to happen, I was going to have to open myself up and learn how to look at everything a little bit differently.

I arrived in Grafton six hours and fifty-six minutes after I had pulled away from my house. I was accustomed to sitting down for long periods of time, but my entire body was sore. The Studebaker was difficult to manage on the best of roads without power steering. If I wasn't careful, my arms were going to look like Popeye's muscles, all bulged up into a tiny anvil.

I didn't think finding the Grafton State School would be a problem. The address was on 6th St. West, and the school sat on a little under thirty-five hundred acres. I figured anybody in town could point me to the place if I couldn't find it on my own. I came into Grafton on Highway 81 North. The first major intersection was with 12th Street. The State School was six blocks away.

Grafton looked a lot like other North Dakota towns I'd been in, and the streets were named on the same kind of grid as Dickinson. I recognized a lot of the same stores, Coast to Coast Hardware, Dairy Queen, and, of course, they had a Red Owl too. I felt at home even though I didn't know where I was.

I decided to stop and get some lunch before heading to the school. Not knowing which café served the best food, I stopped at one called the Gamble Snack Shop. The café sat off 12th Street on Hill Avenue. Finding a parking spot was easy enough, and once I turned off the engine I sat in the Studebaker for a minute to get my bearings. I fluffed my hair, checked myself in the mirror, and gratefully put my feet on the icy ground.

Once inside, a waitress appeared at my table almost as soon as I sat down. She had dishwater blonde hair piled upward about three inches, bound by a colorful red, blue, and yellow bandana. Her uniform was a dingy white dotted with a splotch of mustard that unintentionally matched the color in the bandana. Her name tag said Barbara, and she looked to be in her early twenties.

"What can I get'cha?" she said, towering over me.

I hadn't had time to exhale, much less think about what I wanted. There was no menu to see. "Coffee would be nice," I said.

"Cream and sugar?" Barbara's eyes were uninterested in anything. "Black is fine."

"Our coffee is kind of strong."

"I could use some strong coffee about now."

"Okay." She didn't say "Suit yourself," but she might as well have. "Our special is the Gamble Burger and fries for a dollar twenty-five."

"That sounds fine," I said. Anything would have sounded appetizing after being on the road for seven hours. I was surprised by my hunger.

"You're sure you don't want to see a menu?"

"No, thanks."

"Okay." Barbara hurried off, winding her way through the tables, until she disappeared behind the counter and into the kitchen. "Order up," I heard her yell. "One special, straight on the bun."

I settled back into the orange vinyl chair, looked out the window, and started to relax.

Barbara returned with my cup of coffee in the blink of an eye. "Here you go, sweetie," she said, as she set the cup in front of me. "Your lunch ought to be ready soon. The big rush is over. Everybody has to be back to work."

I glanced up to the counter, and noticed some of the men wearing white orderly uniforms. They must work at the State School, or at a nearby hospital. "I'm in no hurry," I said.

"On your way somewhere?" Barbara lingered, and looked me over skeptically.

"I am."

"I thought you might be. I've never seen you in here before."

The coffee steamed in front of me. "I've only been to Grafton one other time, and that was a long time ago. I was only a girl."

"We get a lot of out-of-towners through here," Barbara said.

"Are they going to the State School?" I was making an assumption, but Barbara twisted her lip, then let the reaction fall away as quickly as she could. Judgment glared at me out of her dark blue eyes.

"That where you're headed?"

"Yes, to pick up some paperwork."

"Sure." Barbara leaned down to me, then said, "I wouldn't stay in that place long if I was you."

"Why's that?" The question popped out of my mouth before I could stop it.

"They do terrible things up there." Her voice dropped to a whisper. I leaned up to her. "Like what?"

Before Barbara could answer me, a bell rang. She stiffened, stood back up, and looked to the kitchen. "That's your lunch." She hurried off without answering my question, and I was left to wonder what kind of terrible things went on at the State School. I hadn't even considered such a thing.

CHAPTER 25

Aquick drive up Hill Street took me straight to my destination. Even on a bright, sunny day, the Grafton State School
was drab and foreboding. The building looked more like a prison than
a school to me, but I might've been influenced by Barbara the waitress
and her whisper that *terrible things* happened there.

The State School's main building had been built in 1903, sixty-
two years prior. I wondered why Grafton was chosen by the state government as the building site for the school. There was nothing much
around, the land empty and rolling but flat enough to see for miles.
The vistas were an empty sea that spawned an invisible and insatiable
wind that nothing could stop, not even man's considerable talents with
brick and mortar. They had called the place the State Institute for the
Feebleminded then. I had to wonder, too, who had come up with that
name, and what exactly feebleminded encompassed? What was the cri-
teria for admittance? I had little knowledge of such things. Sitting in
the truck, looking at the twin-towered façade, a mix of Prairie School,
Beaux Arts, and Classical Revival architecture, I was glad that I'd never
before had reason to know about or visit the State School. I knew what
I was looking at on the outside, but I knew nothing of the inside. I only
knew the place existed.

I took a deep breath, grabbed my purse, and pushed out the door
of the Studebaker. The wind instantly attacked my face, causing my
eyes to water up and my skin to tighten. I kept walking, seasoned to
the cold, to the discomfort of January, toward the entrance of the State
School. Thankfully, there was an iron rail erected on the right side of
the walk. I clung to it for dear life.

I stepped inside the building's tall vestibule and stopped to gather myself. I wiped the moisture from the front of my coat, smoothed my hair quickly, blinked my eyes to clear them, then headed inside the huge building. Guy hadn't given me any detailed instructions about what to do once I arrived. I assumed the report was already prepared and waiting for me.

My nose was met with a strong institutional smell as I walked in the door. The smell was a mix of cleanliness, sourness, and stagnation. I glanced upward to the two-story peaked ceiling, then allowed my eyes to take in the cavernous foyer. The lighting was dim, facilitated by sconces on the walnut-paneled walls and a small collection of hanging florescent bulbs scattered around the large foyer. Arched doors led off in each direction from an inlaid compass on the dull hardwood floor. Dusty gray curtains stood limply at the sides of each oversized window, open to the barren view. The only human being I saw, an older woman with brittle gray, hair, sat at a desk, staring at me without any civility.

I walked up to the woman and said, "Hello. I'm here to pick up a report for Sheriff Reinhardt of Stark County."

The woman's desk was littered with papers, a couple of faded green books that looked like ledgers of some kind, and a host of pens. Most of them had chew marks on the caps.

"I don't know any sheriff from Stark County." The woman eyed me like I was some kind of salesman trying to jip her out of her last quarter.

"This is the Grafton State School isn't it?" I said.

An incredulous look crossed the woman's thin bird face. "Of course, it is. Where are you from?"

"Outside Dickinson," I said.

"Never been there."

"I've never been here, either. The report's about a girl that's gone missing at home. She was here until recently."

The expression on the old woman's face changed instantly. Recognition replaced her previous attitude. "Oh," she said. "You'll need to go to admissions for that. I think they have what you're looking for. Ask for Anke Welton. If anyone knows about your report, it'll be her."

"Thank you." I hesitated, looked to my right, then to my left, searching for a sign to point me in the right direction. "And where's admissions?"

The woman, who had not offered her name, jerked her head backward. "Through the green door, down the hall, left at the first chance, then three doors down on the right."

"Sure, okay, thanks." This was one place I didn't want to get lost in.

"You betcha," she said.

I stood there for a second, staring at the woman. I wanted to ask her if she had known Tina Rinkerman, but I thought it best not to. There was a restrictive feeling inside the Grafton State School, like everything was all bound up on a need to know basis. Questions in places like this usually didn't go over too well.

"Is there something else?" the woman asked.

I couldn't help myself. I had a larger question to ask that wasn't exactly about Tina. "Where are the children?"

"The children are in the north wing, and some of the adults are in the south wing. The worst of them. The rest of them are scattered about on the compound, depending on their age and capabilities."

"Oh, adults live here, too?"

The woman sighed, and stared at me. "You really don't know? People show up here all of the time to dump children, then they never come back. This place was opened in 1903, and there are adults who have been here since they were babies. There are elderly adults, if you can imagine. Ernest Frantz is almost ninety. He's the oldest resident, I think. Came in when the doors opened, and he was twenty-something then. Dense as a board, but the nicest man you can imagine. Got the mind of a ten-year-old boy. Everything's a wonder."

"That's a good thing. There's adult women here, too?"

"Yes, of course."

"Doesn't that create problems?"

The woman looked past me to make sure we were still alone. I could have heard a mouse tiptoe to the door, so there was really no need.

"There used to be a law that let them take care of that," she said in a whisper. "But they did away with those procedures three years ago. There are pills for such a thing these days. The surgery was an awful thing to go through. Not that most of them would understand any of that anyway."

I didn't understand what the woman was talking about, but I wanted to learn as much as I could. Maybe it would help Guy find out what happened to Tina Rinkerman—or maybe he already knew all there was to know about this place. My confusion must have been plastered on my face.

The woman cleared her throat, then said, "They sterilized most of the women who came here. Or the girls who would grow into women. Some of the men, too. The law was meant to prevent criminals, rapists, defectives, idiots, and the like from procreating. Been a law almost as long as this place has been here. There's a surgery in the basement, and we have two doctors on staff all the time."

Defectives. I wondered if that's what they considered Tina. A defective mongoloid. "And the state does this?" I said.

"Did this. I said they stopped," the woman snipped.

"I'm sorry. I guess I never thought about such things."

"Well, most people don't. Even those that drop off their children. They try to forget that they ever existed. Life's easier that way, but something has to be done. You can't house all sorts of feebleminded people who still have human urges and not do anything about it, now can you?"

"I guess not." I stared past the woman toward the green door. I wanted to get Guy's report and get on the road home, be as far from the Grafton State School as I could. I didn't like being there. I didn't like it at all.

CHAPTER 26

The admissions office was easier to find than I thought it would be. I walked into a much smaller room than the overwhelming foyer. This room measured ten by ten at the most, with metal chairs lined up against the walls and another room, an office with the door closed, beyond that. Only one picture adorned the walls, and it was an old black-and-white print of the Grafton State School. The dull brass tag centered on the dusty frame still referred to the place as the Institute for the Feebleminded. No wonder the receptionist had used that word. It was still prevalent in peoples' minds; they were surrounded by feebleminded defectives. Did using words like that make them feel normal? Better than? Afraid? I didn't know for sure. I was uncomfortable, and I didn't like those kind of words. That's all I knew.

A gunmetal gray desk faced the wall, and I was greeted by another woman as I entered the room. She was younger than I was by about ten years. This woman, compared to the main receptionist, looked happier, a little warmer. She wore her thick brunette hair piled upward like the waitress at the café and had gentle blue eyes and a welcoming smile.

"May I help you?" The nameplate at the front of her desk said Mrs. Trudy Sawyer. A shiny silver wedding band on her left hand confirmed her marital status. She wore bright red fingernail polish that matched her lipstick and a heavy white Irish wool sweater with a ribbed turtleneck. I could smell her perfume, light and airy like a summer flower garden, as I approached her. The pleasant fragrance was a fresh reprieve from the institutional odor that was intent on making a permanent home in my nostrils.

"The receptionist said I should speak to an Anke Welton," I said.

Mrs. Sawyer looked past me as if she was looking for someone else, then back at me with a curious look on her face. "Do you have an admittance to make today, ma'am?"

"Oh, no. I'm Marjorie Trumaine. I'm here to pick up a report for the sheriff of Stark County."

"Well, that's good to know. I thought for a minute there you lost someone. Wouldn't a been the first time we had a wanderer, now would it? Anke's not in her office, but she should be back any minute. Off on an errand for one thing or another. You surprised me. We weren't expectin' a drop off today, but you never know. Folks have a habit of showing up without calling."

Mrs. Sawyer closed a magazine she'd been reading. She saw me glance at the cover and smiled. "I have to do something to pass the time, don't you know," she said.

I shrugged my shoulders. There was no window, no radio playing, nothing to distract her at all. "I imagine you get lonely sitting in here all day long," I said.

"I sure do." A look of relief flashed across her face. "Anke doesn't mind that I read these Hollywood rags. She encourages me to read some books we have in the library, but they put me to sleep. Besides, I love the movies. How about you?"

I looked at what she was reading. The magazine was a dime-store copy of *Movieland and TV Time* with a picture of Richard Burton and Elizabeth Taylor on the front cover. The two of them were all dressed up in fancy clothes, looking serious at something unseen in the distance. Big bold yellow letters on a sky-blue background screamed, "Are They Responsible For This? Even Liz and Burton are shocked by Lolita!" In the bottom right hand corner, there was a smaller headline, intended to get an eager reader to buy the magazine. The tease said: "Special. Will Jackie Leave America?"

Won't they leave that poor woman alone? I wondered silently. *Hadn't Jackie Kennedy been through enough?* I grieved with that woman, but I did not know her tragedy. I could imagine her pain. I tried to look away whenever I saw her face.

When I didn't answer straight away, Mrs. Sawyer asked me the same question again. "Do you like the movies?"

"Not so much, I guess." *How could I enjoy being inside a theater without Hank? I would only focus on what I didn't have.*

"That's too bad. I go every Saturday. And if the picture is good, I keep goin' back to the Strand to see it over and over again."

"That's nice," I said.

"Oh, well, okay then. Well, Anke won't be long."

"I can wait." All I had left to do was drive home. And that was going to happen as soon as I got the report in my hand. I wanted to have as much daylight to drive in as I could get.

Mrs. Sawyer smiled and shoved the movie magazine under a pile of papers. "Just in case the superintendent comes by. He doesn't like these things at all. Says they rot the mind. He might be right about that, but a girl has to dream, doesn't she?"

"Yes, of course." I looked over to the closest chair, then back to Mrs. Sawyer. "I'll have a seat to wait."

"I don't have anything to offer you. If Anke were here I'd go to the cafeteria and get you some coffee, but I'm not allowed to leave anyone alone. People don't tend to stay here long. They do their business and go."

I sat down in the closest chair. "Isn't it sad?"

"I try not to think about it," she said. "This place isn't so bad really. It's not what you think."

"I don't know what to think, actually. I really don't know much about any of this. I'm here on an errand."

"Todd, that's my husband, didn't want me to take this job at first. Any of us who grew up here have heard stories, ya know, about this place, but they're boogeyman stories that our parents told to keep us away from here, so we would stay on the straight and narrow. I have to tell you that I was a little nervous when I first came here, but it's been okay. Anke is real patient, and she sees this job as a service to people who need her. They don't know what to do with what's happened to them, and she tries to help them as much as she can. Most of the kids don't know any difference. And, then, well, Todd, he up and joined the service and now he's off to some place overseas called Vietnam. I don't understand what that's all about. I wish he'd stayed here and worked on the farm with his father, but he wanted to put on the uniform, serve his country like all the men in his family before him. I guess I understand that, but I sure do miss him."

Trudy Sawyer drew in a deep breath, and then she bit the tip of her tongue, trying to ward off a show of unwanted emotion—or a fresh set of tears. She missed her husband, and she really was lonely inside the windowless room. I was about to offer her a mint or a cigarette, but the door opened, taking our attention away from the sadness of missing our husbands.

A tall woman with blonde hair as yellow as October straw walked in the door. She wore an off-white wool blazer with a skirt to match. A butterfly brooch sat pinned over her heart, its wings dotted with a rainbow of tiny gems. Her blue eyes sparkled, and an easy smile sat on her face, making me comfortable as soon as I saw her. I assumed the woman was Anke Welton, Mrs. Sawyer's boss and mentor.

A short, overweight teenaged boy followed the woman into the room. I wasn't prepared for that. The boy was shorter than the woman by a head. He wore denim pants that were a few inches too short, and a blue-and-white striped sweater that looked like it had seen a lot of winters. He walked with a little bit of a shuffle, but the most disconcerting thing about the boy was his face. He had a moon face and slanted eyes, much like Tina Rinkerman's. If I didn't know that they shared a condition, I would have thought they were related.

The woman stopped a few feet short of Mrs. Sawyer's desk and looked at me curiously. The boy stopped behind the woman and mimicked her. "Hello," she said to me. Her voice was as calm as a gentle summer stream.

"This is Marjorie Trumaine," Mrs. Sawyer said. "She's the one the sheriff from Stark County called about."

I stood up and shook the woman's hand.

"I'm Anke Welton," the blonde woman said, releasing my hand. "I hope you haven't been waiting long."

"Oh, no, not long. Mrs. Sawyer has been good company. It's a pleasure to meet you." Both women smiled. "And who is this?" I said to the boy.

He smiled and stepped between me and Anke Welton. "I'm Joey," he said, then extended his stubby hand for me to shake. He sounded like he had marbles in his mouth, but I understood what he said.

I shook his hand, and offered him a smile. "It's very nice to meet you, Joey."

Joey let go of my hand, then shuffled up next to Anke. "Nice to meet you, too."

"Joey helps me in the office some days. I brought him up special today."

"I'm usually here on Tuesdays and Fridays. Today is Monday!" Joey said.

"It is." I still wore my smile. He seemed like a gentle boy. I wondered how old he was, how long he had lived at the school, what his chances for a normal life were, but I didn't dare ask any questions. I was afraid of being rude.

"You made a long drive," Anke said.

"Yes, and thankfully the weather cooperated," I said.

"That won't last long."

Mrs. Sawyer and Joey watched us both closely.

"No, I doubt that it will. Hopefully, I'll be home before the wind and snow pick back up."

"You're driving back today?"

"Yes. The sheriff needs to see all of this report as soon as possible. Me being a courier seemed the fastest solution."

"Well, I was certainly surprised that he sent a woman on the road this far."

I didn't think I could explain to her that Guy trusted me, and why, so I decided not to try. "Everyone in the department has their hands full."

"Yes, I gathered that. Still, you're not a police officer, though the sheriff vouched for you, said the reports would be safe in your hands.

These are state reports, you know. Normally only government officials have access."

"I'm only doing the sheriff a favor," I said.

"You must think a lot of him."

"I do. I'm happy to be able to help since the sheriff is short-staffed."

"I understand that. Well, hold on a second. The report's on my desk."

With that, Anke Welton swept away, disappearing into her office, leaving Joey behind. I stared at him for a quick second, then looked away to Trudy Sawyer. She seemed to understand my silent questions, but was not quick to say anything. A steam radiator in the corner clanked and crackled, diverting my attention. There had to be a boiler room somewhere, along with a cafeteria, dormitories, and the surgery the receptionist mentioned. The school was such a big place that I wondered how someone like Joey could make his way around without getting lost.

I looked at the boy again, and sighed. "What do you do when you're here on Tuesdays and Fridays, Joey?"

"I help Mrs. Sawyer welcome the new people," Joey said with a wide smile.

"He's very good at making people feel comfortable," Mrs. Sawyer said. "He's our little ambassador. Aren't you, Joey?"

"I make them not scared," he said.

"I bet you have a lot of friends," I said.

"Everybody's my friend," Joey said. Then, without warning, he walked over and wrapped his arms around me and gave me a soft hug. "I like you," he added.

I gasped out loud. I wasn't expecting the boy to hug me. "I like you, too, Joey."

"Oh good," he said, letting go and stepping away.

Mrs. Sawyer studied my face to see if I was pleased or appalled. She flashed me a smile, so I took it that she approved of my reaction.

"How long have you been here, Joey?" I said. Before he could answer, Anke Welton hurried out of her office carrying two large manila envelopes.

Joey sucked in a breath, then left his answer to my question unspoken.

"Well, here you are, Mrs. Trumaine." Anke offered me the envelopes, and I took them.

"Thank you. I'll be happy to have them," I said. "I hope they help."

"I'm not sure what the sheriff hopes to find, but there's everything in there that I thought was relevant and that he asked for."

Our tone had changed from conversational to serious. A confused look crossed Joey's face. "Is something wrong?"

"Oh, no, nothing for you to worry about. Grown-up stuff," Anke said.

"Are you sure?"

"Yes."

"Okay. But you know I don't believe you."

I smiled. "Nothing's wrong, Joey. I promise."

"Okay."

I took a deep breath, felt the weight of the envelopes, and knew there was only one thing for me to do. "Well," I said, "I should head back home. Daylight's burning."

"Home?" Joey said. "Where's home?"

"Dickinson."

"Oh, I know where that is on the map."

"You do," I said. "That's wonderful. I really like it there."

"I was born there!" Joey said, then he hurried another hug my way. I wasn't quite ready for this one, either. I think I gasped again.

Anke touched Joey's arm, and said, "Let go, Joey, Mrs. Trumaine has to leave now."

"That makes me sad. I like her."

"Maybe she'll come back again someday," Anke said.

He was still hugging me. He looked up with sweet brown eyes, and pleaded, "Will you come back and see me?"

"Well," I said. "Yes, the next time I'm over this way, I'll stop in and see you."

"Promise?"

"Yes, I promise."

"Good. You ask to see me. Joey. Joey Jacobsen. And I'll come running."

CHAPTER 27

Anke Welton walked me to the front door of the Grafton State School. Our footsteps echoed in unison up to the high, vaulted ceiling, then wafted away into silence. My shoes felt like they were filled with lead, each step marred with frustrated resistance. My mind screamed for me to stop and demand answers. I was numbed with revelation and fear, my heart broken for such a sweet, gentle, boy.

The vestibule offered privacy, one last chance for me to find out more information before I fled the school. Both Anke and I stopped and faced each other with dread.

"I know that name, Jacobsen," I finally said.

"I knew you would."

"Is he Nils Jacobsen's son?"

"Yes."

I looked away from Anke, away from the truth and sadness in her eyes, west, toward Dickinson, hundreds of miles away, another world so far removed from the one I stood in, but present somehow, in a way I could have never imagined.

"Why did you show me Joey?" I said. "I have spent the last two days at the Jacobsen house, tending to their grief. I had no idea that Nils had another child. Does the sheriff know about him?"

"It's in the report."

"He doesn't know?"

"We didn't talk about Joey directly, no."

"But you talked about Nils and the murder besides the information you shared with Sheriff Reinhardt about Tina?"

"Of course, I gave him all of the information I was allowed to over the phone," Anke said in her best administrator voice.

"Does he think the two incidents are related, Nils's murder and Tina's disappearance?"

"You'll have to ask him that."

"I will." I hesitated, still shocked by the revelation that Nils Jacobsen had a son that no one knew about. "You know nothing about me. I could go back to Dickinson and tell the whole town about Joey."

Anke Welton's face tightened, and for the first time I saw a hint of anger, of defiance in her eyes. She looked like a serious mother taking a hard stance against an unseen threat to one of her children. "Good. I hope you do. I wanted you to see Joey Jacobsen so someone from your town would know that he exists. I wanted you to see him so you would know that he will never have the chance to grieve for his own father. He will never know the day that his father died, or why."

"No one knows why," I whispered.

"They will. Your sheriff asks good questions. Your being here is proof of that. I believe they will find the person who killed Nils Jacobsen."

"So do I. But, the boy, what about the boy?"

"Joey Jacobsen will continue to exist with a happy heart and a warm smile for every stranger he meets. His well-being is not my worry; by grace and luck he is perpetually happy. My grudge is with the people who brought him into the world and refuse him the most basic right of all: To know that he matters, that he is a living being, that he has feelings, too, regardless of what nature did to him. It wasn't his fault that he turned out the way he did, less than perfect, but more perfect in ways than most 'normal' people can imagine. Love is unconditional for him. Joey would walk through fire if you asked him to. He doesn't deserve to be invisible. But he is. Or was. Until now. That's why I wanted you to see him. I want you to take back the sight of him and tell your sheriff that Joey Jacobsen is a sweet, innocent boy who never had the pleasure of looking into his own father's eyes. And he never will. Not now." She took a deep breath and wiped away the tears from her eyes. "Everything's in the report, Mrs. Trumaine. There's more there than the sheriff asked for, but everything I could find. Everything I know. I have no idea what happened to Nils Jacobsen, but I know this: you all have to find Tina Rinkerman. And when you do, you need to bring her back here to me. I will make sure she is safe and well cared for, for the rest of her life. Do you understand me? This place is not a dungeon or a trash bin for unwanted children. There are good people who work here. We take care of our own. You bring Tina back to me, you hear? You make sure she's okay. Can you do that?"

I had my own tears to wipe away, my own shock and confusion to deal with. "Yes, I'll do whatever I can."

I sat in the Studebaker, stunned by Anke Welton's words.

The engine clunked and groaned, with an attitude that I didn't care for. I had nearly seven hours to drive—again—twice in one day. I was testing the endurance of metal, oil, and rubber, along with my own mettle, my own desire to serve, to find Tina Rinkerman and the person responsible for Nils Jacobsen's death.

I could do nothing but sit and wait for all of the mechanical parts in the engine to join in a productive chorus and run smoothly. I glanced over at the two manila envelopes. They both wore red stamps that said Official Business, were sealed at the lip, and were doubly taped for added security. I knew what waited inside was for Guy's eyes only, but I couldn't help but speculate what Anke Welton had written in the report. I wondered if the paper was stained with tears of sadness or rage.

I needed to calm down. I needed something to take my mind off what I had experienced inside the school.

Next to the envelopes, my indexing pages had shifted during the long ride to Grafton. The top page drew my attention. I brought my mind back to my work, as far away from Joey Jacobsen as I could get.

Half of the page was blank, with instructions written across the top to insert an illustration into the book. Most of the time, pictures were already placed in the proofs, but if permissions had to be worked out, or the right image couldn't be found, then they were put into the book at the last minute. Unfortunately, that could affect the pagination, causing the page numbers in the index to be off, wrong, without any fault of my own. My editor usually held up the book from publishing so the changes could be made, but sometimes the error slipped through, and I would get a letter or a phone call, admonishing me not to make the mistake again. Mistakes like that were rare, but they happened. My defense was simple: The change was not my fault. Pagination changed after the pages left my hands.

The rest of the page from the *Central Flyway* book was about a bird that I was familiar with, the long-billed curlew.

But before I started to read in earnest, I closed my eyes, forcing my memory to the last time that I had made note of seeing a curlew. I wanted to be as far away from the Grafton State School as I could be.

It had been springtime, a few years before Hank's accident. We were walking the fields early in the day to see how things had faired over the winter, enjoying each other's company, taking pleasure in the vast world that was ours at every turn. We were optimistic, had the hope of a new season in our step.

Most shorebirds stopped in North Dakota to rest, then headed on north to feed on the prolific insects that swarmed and lived on the Arctic tundra. But some birds stayed on the plains, finding the food, shelter, and environment a perfect fit for their need to ensure another generation of migrants. I knew from prior experience and reading that these kind of birds mated and bred on my land, though the *Central Flyway* book did educate me further: There were twelve species of shorebirds that made my state their northern terminus.

I resisted the memory of being with Hank, because I struggled to see him clearly, strong and upright like he was at the time. Now, in the truck, outside the school, he was fading from me, and the more I tried to hold on to him, the weaker his image got, the softer his sweet voice became. I feared I was using up all the magic I had trying to hold onto him, to keep him with me wherever I went. But the truth was, I needed him to show me something. I needed to feel his presence no matter the cost, because my mind was swirling with questions, and I needed Hank to help figure out how to ask the right ones.

The fields had still been stubble, the memory of snow and cold recent, as we took our annual walk to the farthest reaches of our seven hundred and twenty acres. The mosquitoes had begun to hatch, bringing with them a sky full of migratory birds, ragged and hungry, in search of a mate and a place to settle down, no matter how briefly.

Not all of our land was tillable. There was an abundance of permanent and temporary wetlands, sloughs, a curve of river, and some shallow water that stood after the thaw or a decent rain. Long-billed curlews were wading birds, the largest sandpiper in North America. The elegant bird was twenty to twenty-six inches tall and, in maturity, thirty-five inches across the wing. The long, curved bill that gave the bird its name could extend almost nine inches and was used to probe deep in the mud for anything that lived there. This was not a small bird, with the female being larger than the male—which had a term, of course, that I'd indexed more than once: sexual dimorphism. And yet, on that day, out in the warm, spring sun with Hank, I nearly stepped on a nesting curlew.

Hank grabbed my arm, "Whoa, there, Marjorie." He stopped me dead in my tracks. "You almost stepped on that nest."

Sitting in the Studebaker in Grafton, I touched my arm in the same place that Hank had so long ago, trying to feel his presence. But I was cold and alone, and Hank was buried hundreds of miles away—yet, he was still with me, still guiding me, holding me back, showing me something important.

Curlews nested on the ground instead of in a tree or the eave of a house. They settled into a small hollow in a field, close to water, and lined the nest with available weeds and grasses. Once they took residence and laid eggs, the birds were almost invisible, camouflaged perfectly in hues of warm, earthy browns and whites. The chicks are precocial, which meant they left the nest as soon as they hatched. The parents looked after them, but the female abandoned the babies to the male after a few weeks and departed south.

"I'd have felt terrible if I'd stepped on her eggs," I said.

About that time, the male had flown in and started aggressively defending the nest, squawking, doing his best to drive us away. The female was upset, standing up in a dominant stance, wings out, head forward. I didn't want to get pecked. Not by that bill.

"Come on," Hank said, his hand still on my arm. "Let's leave them to their work and get on with ours."

We moved on, leaving four tiny eggs to be hatched by the curlews. Me and Hank had given up on building our own nest years before, though we had never tired of trying to have a family.

"I try to watch out for those birds with the tractor," Hank had said. "But I have to tell you, Marjorie, that I've run over a nest or two in my time. Such a thing can't be avoided, I guess, but I sure do feel bad when I kill a nest of innocent chicks."

I knew he did. I knew that Hank Trumaine hated taking any life when there was no reason to. His simple compassion was one of the many reasons why I had loved him so much. That was all he said. We walked on that day, with both of our eyes a little more focused on the ground, aware now that there were nests and working parents to look out for.

I sighed as the Studebaker started to run smooth and warm, comfortable air pushed out of the heater vent. I tried to keep Hank from disappearing, but in the blink of my mind's eye, he was gone, the field as empty as the seat next to me. I was alone, holding the *Central Flyway* page proof, my mind in the past but fully rooted in the present, considering the life of a curlew.

I hadn't realized that the female abandoned her chicks so early. The curlew's sole duty was to give birth and move on to live out the rest of her life without the bother of the children she'd brought into the world. I sat the page proof down, confronted by a more pressing question than I had considered before taking up the page about the curlew. One I was certain that I would have stumbled across sooner or later.

If Nils Jacobsen was Joey's father, then who was Joey's mother?

CHAPTER 28

I left the Grafton State School with more questions than I'd had when I first arrived. Questions that I had not considered, and I was sure Guy hadn't, either. Meeting Joey Jacobsen had changed everything. I had to reconsider all that I knew about Nils, which was, to say the least, not much. I only knew the basics of his life, one that seemed devoted to the Red Owl and his family. No secrets or scandals associated with Nils came immediately to mind.

I remembered a whisper of the conversation that I'd had recently with Anna in her gloomy bedroom about Nils. *"The sheriff knows things about people that no one else knows. Nils did, too. Did you know that?"* she'd said.

I had to wonder what else Nils knew about people other than the occasional shoplifting. I wondered what else Guy knew about Nils.

Hopefully whatever was in the two envelopes would help Guy solve Nils's murder and find Tina Rinkerman. For all I knew, he had already done that. My trip would be for naught if I arrived home and everything was solved. That would be okay with me. Everyone needed answers.

The afternoon sky was covered with a wafer-thin blanket of gray clouds that slightly obscured the sun. There was no threat of bad weather on the horizon that I could see. The forecast had called for a calm day, above-zero temperatures, little wind, and no snow. I wanted to get to I-94 before nightfall, giving me a straight drive home, not the turns and curves that I faced on the state highways as I headed south. Once the open country greeted me, I felt like I could almost breathe again.

My mind, of course, swirled with even more questions arising from the seeds that had been planted in Grafton.

Was Anna Joey's mother? came to mind quickly. But something about a yes answer to that question didn't add up to me. A quick answer felt wrong. A yes seemed impossible, somehow. Anna wasn't the kind of woman who would leave a child behind, abandon him to the state. She was frazzled with three normal children—and I hated to think of them that way, *normal,* but I couldn't think of her children any other way after meeting Joey. Even with that, Anna kept house, was diligent about the children's care, and may or may not have been pregnant again. She loved her children regardless of being overwhelmed by them. I didn't know, and could never know, how difficult life would be raising a child with a severe disability. Joey Jacobsen was never going to be normal.

What would I do if I gave birth to a child like Joey Jacobsen?

To be honest, I couldn't answer that question. How could anyone know how they would react until they faced a situation like that? Until you held that baby in your arms?

Could I hand a baby to a nurse knowing that I would never see him again?

I was pretty certain I knew my answer to that question. No. I would try to raise the baby regardless—but maybe Anna and Nils had faced the unthinkable at a young age and they'd decided that the best place for Joey was in Grafton.

Someone would have known.

Anna wouldn't have hid her pregnancy; she wouldn't have known about Joey's condition until he was born. I suppose they could have told everyone that the baby had died in childbirth, but I was sure I would have heard that story by now, and I hadn't. There'd been no mention from either of them about a lost baby or the existence of a less-than-normal one. Anna being Joey's mother didn't make sense to me. I couldn't make the story add up. My assumptions led me to answer that question with a near-definite no. Anna Jacobsen was not Joey's mother.

I drove on, focused on the road ahead of me. There was little traffic coming or going. I figured there would be more cars and trucks on the road once I hit I-94.

If I remembered correctly, Anna and Nils had been married for ten years, and that's where the real doubt settled in my mind. Joey looked like a teenager, maybe fourteen or fifteen years old. Nils was older than Anna, maybe by four or five years. I think she'd been out of high school when he'd met her in Stanley. Maybe she'd still been in high school for all I knew. That would have made Nils twenty-three or twenty-four at the time, and Anna around eighteen, plus some time for their courtship, so maybe nineteen when they'd married. I didn't know either one of them well enough to know exact dates in their lives, but I needed to find out, or put Guy onto this bit of information and questioning.

That was a good question. As an indexer, I included everything in an index that I thought the reader would look up. Everything in a book is connected in one way or another, by topic or association. Life and murder investigations were another matter altogether. But were they really? How could I know who and what was connected? Guy was looking for a killer. Did he know the motive for the murder? If Nils had betrayed someone, had stolen from someone, had lied to someone who was angry enough to seek revenge—or vengeance— that would be motive, point to the killer. Betrayal seemed unlikely from what I knew of Nils. But that was before I'd met Joey. Now I didn't know what to think.

What other secrets did Nils have?

Was it possible that he'd had a child with another woman? Another girl most likely, considering their ages? *Yes.* I answered my own question as I gripped the steering wheel a little tighter.

It was most definitely possible that Nils had had a relationship with someone else. But who?

As I drove south on the barren highway, the sky started to turn grayer—enough to cause me some concern. On top of that, my gas gauge tilted heavily toward empty. Between working my way through the questions that had spawned from my visit to the State School and keeping an eye on the road, I hadn't paid any attention to the level of fuel in my tank. I was in the middle of nowhere, surrounded by fallow fields and rolling prairie land. This was not a place to run out of gas.

I was still on Highway 45, a good ways from my turn onto I-94. Cooperstown was the next big town I'd come to. I had to turn west on Highway 200 there, then catch Highway 1 south to I-94. I knew there was more than one gas station in Cooperstown.

I turned on the radio but got nothing but static. I turned the knob, scanning the dial slowly, in search of a strong signal. I was in need of voices outside of the one inside my head—I really needed to revisit my personal index and write down my thoughts so I could see them clearly. But more than anything, I wanted to hear an updated weather report. The clouds had shifted from the west to the north. I had enough experience at reading the sky to know that there was snow and wind building up in the roiling gray puffballs pushing overhead. Something had changed.

I finally found a radio signal strong enough to settle on. The station played music all the way into Cooperstown. I pulled into the first gas station I came across, a small white building with a faded Richland Oil sign teetering over the door. I didn't care what brand of gas the place sold; I was relieved that I wasn't going to run out.

I crossed over a thick black air hose laid across the flat, packed down snow and ice and came to a stop next to the first of only two gas pumps. A bell, triggered by the hose, would alert the attendant to my presence.

A thin young man hurried out the door, putting on a red flannel coat as he came toward me. He didn't wear a hat but wore his hair over his ears like so many of the boys did these days. That mop head style would take some getting used to. He looked to be in his early twenties, about the same age as Nils Jacobsen before he married Anna.

I rolled down the window and said, "Fill her up, please."

The attendant yanked a gray toboggan cap out of his pocket and slipped it on his head. "Check your oil, ma'am?"

"Yes, you better go ahead. I've been on the road for a while."

The boy unscrewed the gas cap. "Regular or Ethyl?"

"Regular's fine," I said.

I looked away to the sky and watched the puffiness grow darker. I must have missed something in the weather report, or the forecasters had. That happened more often than not. The joke in North Dakota was if you didn't like the weather, wait ten minutes and it would change.

The boy came to the side of the truck with an expectant look on his face. "Yes?" I said, rolling down the window.

"Looks like you're about two quarts low on oil, and the front right tire is a little low."

"Good, thank you."

"Forty weight?"

"Yes."

He started to turn away to get on with my service, but I stopped him. "Excuse me," I said.

"Yes?"

"Have you heard a recent weather report? I thought we were going to have a calm day."

"Well, that's how it goes, aye. A clipper's bustin' down through the middle of the state. The temperatures are gonna drop twenty degrees, and that's before the wind gets ahold of it, then all bets are off, you know. Has more snow to drop, too. I hope you don't have far to drive."

"Dickinson," I said.

"Lordy, lady, you're a ways from home."

"I know."

"You might want to think of pullin' over, and ridin' this one out."

"There'll be something else tomorrow."

"You're right, but you might think about takin' a room at the hotel."

"I have to get home."

"You know best."

"I think I do."

The attendant went back to the engine to feed it some oil. I was tempted to reconsider his advice, especially when I saw the first snowflake strike the windshield.

CHAPTER 29

Before leaving Cooperstown, I decided to call Guy and tell him what I'd found out, that I had the reports in hand, and that I was heading home. Luckily there was a phone booth in the corner of the Richland Oil gas station lot, south of the building.

I pulled the Studebaker in front of the booth, gathered up my purse, then dashed to the phone as carefully as I could. The pavement was covered with snow and ice, hard as a rock, probably three inches thick. A fall would complicate my day even more.

Once I was inside the glass box, I dug into my purse, past my Salems and hairbrush, and found my little change purse. I only had a few quarters. The little worn pouch contained mostly nickels and pennies. The phone didn't take pennies. There were only three slots to deposit coins in: nickels, dimes, and quarters. I wasn't sure that I had enough money. I really didn't know how much money the call would cost, and I was sure the Sheriff's Department wouldn't accept a call if I reversed the charges.

I dialed zero for the operator, and waited.

"Operator. How may I help you?" A woman's nasally, no-nonsense voice asked.

"Long distance, please," I said, staring out of the phone booth. The snow was starting to fall more steadily, with small, hard flakes, almost as hard as pebbles, hitting the ground. The pebbles almost looked like sleet. I sighed with fear and regret. I was still a long way from home.

"Number, please," the operator said.

"701-555-0150." I had the phone number to the sheriff's office committed to memory. Another advantage of my indexer's brain. I usually retained information, especially phone numbers, if I used them more than once.

"That will be forty-five cents for two minutes."

I opened my change purse and inserted the money into the slots. My worry was for nothing. I had plenty of money to make the call. There was nothing but a hum in my ear as I went about the business of calling Dickinson.

"One moment please," the operator said, followed by two loud clicks. "Thank you for using Northwestern Bell."

Like I have a choice, I thought. With two more clicks the operator was gone, and the phone rang on the other side of the state. Technology never ceased to amaze me.

George Lardner answered the phone on the second ring. "Stark County Sheriff's Department. Dispatch desk. How may I direct your call?"

"Hello, George, this Marjorie Trumaine. Could I speak to Sheriff Reinhardt, please?"

"Oh, hey, there, Marjorie. Sheriff's out of the office. Can I take a message?"

The hum that was there when I was waiting for the operator to accept my money grew louder. "When do you think he'll be back?"

"I can't hear you, Marjorie."

I repeated my question, only I raised the volume of my voice.

"Can't rightly say," George said. "Where are you at, Marjorie? I'm still havin' a real hard time hearin' you. You sound like you fell down a well."

"I'm in Cooperstown. I'm coming back from the . . ." I stopped. George didn't know about my errand to Grafton. No one did. I'd almost let the cat out of the bag.

"Whatcha doin' in Cooperstown, Marjorie? There's a storm cuttin' down that side of the state. Didn't you check the weather before you took off?"

"I had some urgent business to take care of, George."

"Must be important."

"Can you tell the sheriff that I called and that I'll try back later?"

"You sure you don't wanna leave a message, Marjorie?"

A beep interrupted, and I sighed at the difficulty I was having talking to George. We were both yelling.

"No, that's fine, George. I better go. I'm in a phone booth. That beep you heard is telling me I have ten seconds before the operator comes back on and asks for more money."

"Okay, then. You drive careful out there. I'll tell the sheriff you called."

"Thanks, George. Goodbye."

"Goodbye."

We both rang off, and I hung up the black receiver, happy that I hadn't told George any more than I did. I'd try calling Guy again later, in hopes that he would be in the office so I could tell him about Joey Jacobsen. There were questions that the sheriff needed to ask, and the sooner they were asked the better.

The look of the sky worried me, but I knew I had to keep driving. There was no turning back now. I shook off the phone call, then stepped out of the phone booth. I had to wait for a car to pass as it pulled into the Richland station. The poor attendant hadn't had time to warm up from my purchase.

The road stretched out before me, covered with snow. I used the tracks of the cars and trucks that had gone on before me as a visible guide to stay out of the ditch. What little traffic there was had their headlights on, cutting through the gloomy afternoon with welcome brightness and presence. The back and forth movement of the windshield wipers made the road a little more difficult to see. The wipers squeaked with an annoying noise that I could hear over the radio.

A radio announcer interrupted the music, drawing my attention away from the road. "The National Weather Service is issuing a severe storm warning for the eastern part of the state. North to south, from Bottineau to Bowdon, until 10PM this evening. Be advised that the wind is rising up to sixty miles an hour and possibly higher due to the latest Alberta Clipper. Near-blizzard conditions are expected." The announcer, a calm man with an even baritone voice, took a breath, then continued on, "This storm is part of a larger system, and there is a strong possibility that the system could manifest into a rare panhandle hook as this short-wave system meets a longwave system making its way up from Texas and Oklahoma. The most memorable panhandle hook was responsible for the Armistice Day Blizzard in 1940. One hundred and forty-five people perished in that storm. The weather service does not know if this storm has the same potency as the Armistice Day Blizzard, but there is a serious-ness to the warning. Travel is not banned at this point, but discouraged. And now a word from our sponsor, Magnavox, with an introduction to their new Magna-Color television."

Great, I thought, *that's all I need. This couldn't be a normal blizzard.* If there was any consolation, I was west of the line the radio announcer had drawn for the warning. Not too far west, but far enough to miss the worst of the storm. At least, that's what I was counting on. *Maybe the storm would be a mild blizzard instead of a panhandle hook . . .*

The sky got darker as I continued to drive, and the snow started to fall in heavier bursts. For a while, as I drove on, there were no cars to be seen at all. I was alone, closed in a pocket of snow that blew directly at the windshield in waves. I wasn't sure how far I drove before I saw another car. At least fifty miles or so. This time the car was behind me.

The car—or truck, I couldn't tell which for sure—had the high beams on, four bright lights that cut through the snowy grayness with precision. I had to flip the rearview mirror to the night-side of the glass to take off the glare of the lights. That didn't concern me. What con-cerned me more than anything was the speed at which the car was trav-eling. There was nothing I could do, no lane to change to, no way to pull over and get out of the way. If I did, I'd end up in the ditch.

I dropped my latest cigarette into the ashtray and stiffened my grip on the steering wheel. Some old-timers drove fast no matter the weather. They knew their vehicle's capabilities, had tested their skills on the snow and ice, and weren't afraid of losing control like I was. They probably knew where they were, too—the lay of the land, how the pavement reacted to wind and salt on the road—and I didn't. The landscape all looked the same to me.

The high beams continued to draw closer. I looked up and down, to the rearview mirror, then out the windshield. There were no red taillights to be seen in front of me, and there was nothing behind me but two white-hot circles growing larger by the second. I let up on the accelerator and slowed down. I wanted this person to drive past me. I didn't want to be a deterrent to their byway.

When I looked in the rearview mirror again, the bright lights nearly blinded me. The glow filled the truck in an unwelcome way. Then they flashed, signaling me, I thought, to pull over, to get out of the way. I glanced back to the road before me. All I could see was two tire tracks ahead of me, indentations in the ice that were intended to get me home. I didn't know what would happen if I forced the truck tires out of the ruts.

A horn blared and the lights disappeared. I panicked when I looked behind me again. My heart raced faster each time the horn blew. *Honk! Honk! Honk!* I couldn't get out of the way, and, to make things worse, the reason the lights had dimmed inside the cab was because the car— and now I could tell that the vehicle was a car—had driven straight up behind me, was right on my bumper. I was scared. I didn't know what the person wanted me to do.

The car kept coming, and rammed into my rear bumper. The truck lurched to the right and jumped out of the rut. I fought back and popped the tires back in the tracks. My forearms burned, but I held onto the steering wheel for dear life. Bright light filled the cab again. Then the car dropped back. I couldn't tell the make or model. All I could see was white-hot light and a silver grill.

The car came at the rear bumper again, only this time at an angle. The driver was out of the tracks. They hit me again. The crash was loud, and I screamed, matching the pitch of metal against metal. I spun down the highway just like I had on Villard Street. Out of control, afraid that I was going to die.

I held onto the steering wheel, trying to keep sight of the tracks, of the road, but it was impossible. The wheel spun as if it had a mind of its own. My strength had failed. My fate was out of my control, in the hands of physics and nature. Before I could take another breath, I was off the road and into the ditch. All I could do was hang on and hope that I didn't end up on a lake covered with thin ice.

CHAPTER 30

Gray. White. Spinning. Panic. I was at the mercy of gravity, the pull of the moon, and the fury of the wind. Pages flew in the air around me like a flock of frightened, wingless birds. I was no different, trapped in the cab, unrestrained, not sure if I was going to live or die. Blood filled my mouth in between gasps. Then suddenly, the Studebaker came to a stop with a defiant thud. The front of the truck burrowed into a deep drift of snow, whipping my head back and forth. And then there was nothing, no motion at all. The world stopped spinning.

After I regained my bearings, I looked out the windshield and saw only snow. Dim light from the dashboard provided a slight glow, enough to see inside the cab. I realized two things right away: I was still alive and I wasn't badly hurt, other than a bang on the head and the bite on my tongue.

I was left to assess my situation. There was nothing to see beyond the snow on the hood of the truck. The view out the back window was pretty much the same. More snow on the ground. More snow falling from the sky. I was encased in a blustery, thick white sheet of frozen water particles, facing downward at a forty-five degree angle. Backing out of the drift would be impossible.

The engine was still running, which was a good thing, and I had plenty of gas in the tank, so I wasn't going to freeze to death anytime soon. I could stop and start the engine with the heater on full blast when I needed to warm up.

I was worried about the person who had run me off the road, what their intention was, where they were, if they were waiting for me to either climb out of the truck or try to get back on the road. What then?

Did I have a real reason to be worried? Or was I overreacting? My immediate thought was that caution was best taken in a situation like this. I didn't know who the driver was or if they truly meant me personal harm, but I didn't think that I had any choice but to believe that they did.

From there, I allowed my paranoia to manifest into a fighting stance. I had no choice but to defend myself, even if the effort and vigilance was against the unknown—or nothing at all. For all I knew the person who had ran me into the ditch was ten miles down the road by now, or stuck somewhere, too, as a result of the impact. Maybe they had crashed like I had. There was no way to know.

So if there was intent in running me off the road, I had to wonder who would want to stop me from getting home?

I didn't have to wonder very far.

The person who killed Nils Jacobsen, that's who. They must have followed me. Knew what I was up to. But how?

I had information that might help Guy Reinhardt figure out what had happened to Nils. Maybe the identity of the murderer was in the envelopes that I carried. I didn't know. How would anyone know that I had any information at all—unless I was followed to and from the State School, and the person had put two and two together about why I was there.

I glanced over to the passenger seat and saw that the two envelopes had fallen onto the floorboard. I looked around, then leaned over, picked them up, and set them on the seat next to me, where they would remain in my sight, close at hand. The next thing I did was reach behind me and pull the .22 rifle off the gun rack. I wasted no time chambering a round, then placed the rifle next to my leg, within quick reach. The touch of the metal barrel was the only comfort I could find.

Now that I had decided that I wasn't severely hurt—the bleeding in my mouth had slowed, and the throbbing in my head was subsiding, not requiring any headache pills—I really had to think about surviving. With a source of heat, I knew I had some time, but I couldn't last forever in the snowdrift. I had food, blankets, and other survival needs stored in the cab, and I had the knowledge and skills to use them. This wasn't the first time in my life that I had found myself stuck in a ditch in the middle of winter.

I tuned my ears to listen for anything out of the ordinary. All I heard was the scream of the wind and snow pelting the truck. Hank told me that if I ever got stuck to stay put. Someone would be out looking for me. *"Stay put."* He was emphatic and demanding even in death, even in my memory. Hank knew more about surviving a North Dakota winter than anyone I had ever met, so I listened to him, even now.

The problem was, no one knew where I was this time out. I was not on a trip into town. I was halfway across the state. Only Guy knew that I was on the road, that I was due back from Grafton in several hours. I had told George Lardner that I was in Cooperstown, but nothing else. If anything, I held onto the hope that Guy or George would notice my absence and send someone to look for me. I might have to get through the night, survive the drop in temperature and the growing storm. Maybe longer if the storm really did turn into a dreaded panhandle hook.

That thought spurred me to move, to reconsider staying put. I had to at least try and get out of the ditch, to get back on the road, on my way back to Dickinson. I couldn't sit there and wait for someone to find me. A killer or a rescuer. I had to try to free myself and get home. I missed Shep and the comforts of home more than I ever thought I would.

I rolled down the window in case the tailpipe was clogged, and revved the engine to test its strength. Every piston fired perfectly. The transmission was a standard three-speed column-shift. I rocked the truck by clutching and shifting from reverse to first, then back again. The Studebaker didn't move. The engine roared, determined to make the vehicle move. The tires spun, stuck in the snow, whirling at thirty miles an hour, going nowhere. Deep down I knew the attempt was pointless. My toes were already cold, and doubt crept around the edges of my confidence. I was scared, worried, but I couldn't let those emotions control me, get the best of me.

I rocked the Studebaker back and forth four times before I gave up. I was spinning my tires, going nowhere. I could smell the rubber warming up. I needed all the tire tread I had. There was nothing left for me to do but turn off the engine. I needed to face the fact that I was trapped.

I rolled the window back up, sighed, and put my head back against the gun rack. Closing my eyes was out of the question, too. I feared falling asleep. I feared freezing to death. I was going to have to keep myself awake for a while. For my health and for my safety, I had to stay vigilant and aware of every sound I heard outside the truck.

I couldn't let the truck run forever to keep warm. To make sure I wasn't going to die of carbon monoxide poisoning, I needed to go outside and make sure the truck's tailpipe wasn't clogged. I really didn't want to go outside, but if I was going to start the truck again, there was no avoiding the trek to the rear of the Studebaker. But that could wait now that I had turned off the engine.

I didn't want to alert the wrong person to my location. Time would tell if someone was looking for me. A bad someone. I shivered at the thought. I would wait before I made a move of any kind.

Beyond clearing the tailpipe and setting flares, the only other thing I needed to do was keep myself hydrated and warm. I had water and a can of beans, and I also had matches and candles. If I needed to melt snow for water, I could do that. But I wouldn't use the candles for light unless I had to, unless the batteries in my flashlight ran out of juice. I was prepared to be stranded. I wasn't prepared to wonder if someone was coming after me.

I started to tidy the passenger seat back up, organize my page proofs and the envelopes, along with my personal index, which I made sure was on top of the pile. I knew that I would have to organize my thoughts soon. There would be time to do that after I got everything settled.

With everything in its place, I felt like I could relax a little more. After getting a blanket settled across my lap and another one wrapped around my feet, I dug into my purse for my cigarettes. Before I lit one,

I rolled the window down about an inch to ventilate the cab. A quick peppering of snow blew inside through the crack. Winter was ambitious, determined to spread its cold, deadly touch to every inch of the world. I was going to have to ration my cigarettes as much as anything else. I gave up more heat to have a smoke. Being calm and focused was important, too.

I smoked the Salem as fast as I could, then rolled the window back up. Even in that short time, a thin layer of snow had collected on my lap. I was cold, could see my breath, but I put off starting the truck. I could endure the declining temperature for a while longer.

Snow had completely covered the windshield and the driver-side window. The passenger window was clear, cleaned off regularly by gusts of wind that wrapped around the truck, allowing me to see outside but not far. If I was going to pass time by reading or working, then I would need the flashlight. I hesitated to light the silver Stanley torch. That's what my father had called a flashlight, a torch. I smiled at his presence, even in words. He would have encouraged me to stay strong and brave in the situation I had found myself.

I knew I had to quit being afraid. I couldn't be scared to light the flashlight because a bad person might find me. I didn't know that the bad person really existed. What happened could have been an accident. Simple as that. And if there was a bad person out there? I had the rifle to fend them off.

If I was going to be stranded, then I was going to have to do something to pass the time or I was going to go mad. The first thing I needed to do was clear my mind. I lit the flashlight and white light immediately filled the cab. I angled the beam at my pile of books and papers. Then I went to work on my personal index. I had more questions to make sense of if I could.

B

black car, who owns one?

G

Grafton State School
did Anke Welton tell me
everything?
did Joey know Tina?
why did Tina leave?

E

enemies
did Nils have enemies?
did the Rinkermans have
enemies?

J

Jacobsen, Anna (widow)
Jacobsen, Joey (who knows
about him?)
Jacobsen, Nils (victim)

M

missing girl (Tina
Rinkerman)
who was the last person
to see her?
was it really her in the
black car?

motive
who would want to kill
Nils?
is Tina still alive?
why did Tina leave
home?

Q

questions
is Anna pregnant?
what color was the car
that hit me?
who is Joey's mother?
did Nils keep Joey a
secret?
did someone find out
about Joey?
did someone follow me?

R

relationships
did Nils know Tina?
murder and disappear-
ance related?
Rinkerman, Adaline
(mother)
Rinkerman, Tina (missing
girl)
Rinkerman, Toren (father)
Rinkermans (three sons)

S   T

suspects   troubles
    could Anna be a   did Nils have any money
    suspect? Why?   problems?
    an enemy?   did the Rinkermans
    none right now   have any troubles?
    a person who discovered
    Nils's secret?   V
    could be random, but
    doesn't make sense   victim, Nils Jacobsen
    Rinkerman men have
    been questioned   W

                                 who saw Nils last? (I don't
                                 know)

The additions helped me clear my mind but did nothing to get me closer to figuring out who had killed Nils Jacobsen. I had no motive, no suspect, and no theory about how or why the murder had happened in the first place.

I knew that Nils had a son that I hadn't known about, and I assumed no one else knew about him either. And I knew that a girl about the same age, who had spent time in the same place as the son, disappeared not long before Nils was murdered.

Murdered. Every time that word crossed my mind an image of Nils flashed in my memory. Not the happy, helpful Red Owl Nils, but the dead one, sitting in his car, shot in the head, the life drained out of him, the reasons for his harsh, sudden death unknown and unfathomable.

I shivered, sighed, and wished I had the answers we all needed to bring justice to Nils's killer, to honor Nils's life, if that were possible. Even if I did know who the murderer was, there was no one I could tell, sitting stuck in a snowdrift miles from home.

I sighed again, and looked over to the passenger seat at the two envelopes that I had retrieved from the State School. I was instantly angry and curious. Guy had sent me on a mission that had turned dangerous. I don't think he could have foreseen the surprise storm any more than I could have, but I had to wonder what he knew, if there was any hint that I could be in harm's way. I really didn't think that Guy would have sent me somewhere if he knew I was going to be in danger. He would have told me to be extra careful. Or sent someone who was better at protecting themselves. No, I finally surmised, Guy had no clue what was in the reports any more than I did. My guess was that he didn't know about Joey Jacobsen, either. At least not to the extent that I did. And that was where my curiosity overtook any anger I felt. I decided that Nils's murder, Joey Jacobsen's existence, and Tina's disappearance were all related. My theory was beginning to form. All I needed was more information.

My eyes had not left the envelopes. I knew they were for official business only. I knew I was only a courier. I also knew that I was stuck, short of freezing to death, with who-knew-what lurking in the blowing snow beyond the truck.

I picked up the sealed envelope and edged my fingernail under the tape just a bit to see if the adhesive would break free. I stopped. I knew I was about to violate a trust.

If I opened the envelope the rest of the way, would I be breaking the law?

If I froze to death before anyone found me, would my crime matter?

I wasn't immune to going places I wasn't allowed. When Calla Eltmore was murdered, I'd sneaked into her office and found a pile of letters that led me to a secret—one I would have never suspected—and ultimately to her murderer. That had turned out all right. What could be the harm of me knowing what was in the report?

I would tell Guy what I had done—if I survived.

I looked around, then I slowly peeled away the tape from the envelope.

CHAPTER 31

The wind pushed through every gap and crease in the Studebaker's steel body. Frigid air was an invisible snake that I couldn't see, but I sure could feel the bite of the nasty thing. I resisted the temptation to start the engine.

I sighed and looked back at the envelope in my hands. I hesitated to pull the first report out, still fearful that I was committing a crime, knowing that I was breaking the trust between Guy Reinhardt and myself.

I couldn't help myself. I had to know what was in the reports. But there was something beyond my need to know what the State School documents said, beyond the crime of the act. If I read them, committed them to memory, then no matter what happened, if they were destroyed or lost, I would be in possession of the information. I knew that argument was thin, but I felt like I could justify my actions if I ever had to. I had found myself in extraordinary circumstances, and I wanted to make sure I was able to deliver the information to Guy.

I looked around me for no real reason other than out of habit and fear, then pulled the papers out of the first manila envelope.

There was a collection of papers, four or five at first glance. The one on top was instantly identifiable in bold letters: "Admission Report." Tina Rinkerman's name was written on a thin line underneath the header in exact cursive script and dated 05/21/1952. The next lines were her birth date, 01/22/1951, her height, weight, and the color of her eyes. I tried to conjure an image of the girl, but the recent one was blurry, frozen on a dark, snowy night as she floated by in the backseat of an unknown car. Others were sightings in the Red Owl or Walgreens, but they were as vague as the first.

Tina's physical description was detailed in the report all the way down to the reason for her admission, which was noted as severe and irreversible retardation. The paper also said the child suffered from being a mongoloid at birth. *There is no known cure or treatment for the condition.* The form was signed by Toren Rinkerman, Tina's father, and countersigned by Anke Welton.

My hands shook as I read, and I *was* cold, but not all of the movement was caused by the weather. I realized what a horrible day that must have been for Toren, leaving his daughter that far away from home. I couldn't imagine such a thing. The thought of leaving a child behind made me sick to my stomach. Tina was almost a year and a half old when the Rinkermans gave her up. There was no mention on the form of Adaline, Tina's mother and Toren's wife. I guessed Toren's signature was sufficient because he was a man. *Did Adaline have a say? Did she agree to the admission?* I didn't know, and there was no way I would ever ask her.

There was more information on the form. Tina was discharged a year later in 1953, only to be readmitted three months later. The same again in 1960. Discharged in June and readmitted in October. The last date of discharge was 01/07/1965. There was no reason given for the discharges or re-admittances. I could only imagine that Toren and Adaline had tried to take Tina home to have a normal life. The last time she was discharged she went missing a few days later. I hoped more than anything that Guy had found her alive in my absence, but I had to wonder what would happen to Tina if that were the case? Would Toren send her back to Grafton? Anke Welton wouldn't have a problem with the girl's return.

Tina Rinkerman was fourteen years old and had spent most all of her life institutionalized at the Grafton State School. But that didn't mean she was forgotten. Or unwanted. I didn't know the Rinkermans well enough to be aware of their trials and tribulations with Tina, but they had tried their best to deal with the situation they'd found themselves in as far as I could tell. Maybe Hank knew more about their lives. He'd dealt with Toren for a lot of years, but he never said anything to me about the welder and his family life, nothing about Tina that I could remember. Still, there was no information in this report that gave me any clue why Tina had gone missing, or whether the murder of Nils Jacobsen had anything to do with Tina. Joey was the link between the two of them.

I put that paper back in the envelope and reached over to adjust the flashlight. The beam of light remained strong, but I had to strain to see every line of the report clearly.

The next paper was a mimeographed copy of Tina's birth certificate, confirming everything in the admission report. Nothing new there, either. Toren and Adaline were listed as her parents, and there was no mention of Tina's condition. The official document looked the same as everyone else's birth certificate.

The next paper looked newer and was titled "Procedure Completion Report." Tina's name was written on a line after the word "patient." The handwriting was different from the admissions report, and was dated 03/12/1961.

The procedure marked was "sterilization." I had to squint to make sure I'd read that correctly. I read on:

> In rules set forth by the North Dakota State Board of Control, and in accordance with the 1927 Sterilization Law, the board has deemed that Tina R. Rinkerman is a female of no mental capacity to understand or engage in acts related to procreation. Subject has been determined to be either mentally insufficient, insane, a confirmed criminal, a defective, rapist, or an idiot. All categories fall within the boundaries of the current law and the procedure is approved to be executed on this date, March 12, 1961, with authorization given by the county and state in which the Grafton State School resides.

Defective was underlined, given as the reason for sterilization. A man's signature, Horace A. Findley, was signed at the bottom, and a notary seal was pressed into the paper. I ran my gloved hand over the seal, then flipped the paper over. Everything was official, endorsed. There was a notes section on the back of the paper with the same handwriting that was on the front, stating that "the Subject" had experienced her first documented event of menstruation on 02/01/1961. The report went on to say: "Mongoloids develop early, and the board recommends that the procedure be completed as soon as possible."

I sighed and remembered my conversation with the unpleasant woman who'd staffed the reception desk. She had mentioned sterilization, that the surgery was once an approved procedure, but that now the state used other means of birth control, not eugenic sterilization. The law was changed in 1962. I wondered if the doctors and the powers-that-be knew that there was a deadline coming and had wanted to make sure that Tina was sterilized before the procedure wasn't allowed.

I had mixed emotions about what I had read. In the old way of thinking, sterilization made sense, but the categories seemed broad. *Idiots. Defectives.* Horrible words. Who was to decide what was what? The thought of a sterilization procedure made me uncomfortable. I didn't see what this report had to do with Tina's disappearance, but I had to assume that Guy had asked for all of the documentation the school had.

I couldn't help but wonder, *Did Tina understand what had happened to her, and why? Did she have a say in what happened to her own body?* I didn't think Tina had had any say at all about the procedure, and that made me sad and angry.

The next piece of paper was a copy of Tina's visitation record. This document had the most entries, the most information. There were at least sixty lines of small print, noting each visit and naming the person who visited. Over and over, the record stated that Tina was visited by her parents, Mr. and Mrs. Toren Rinkerman. There was no mention of any of her brothers, only Toren and his wife. I found that odd, and I was sad again.

I scanned the paper once more, found nothing, then picked up the last piece of paper that had come out of the envelope. The paper was fresh, bore the State School letterhead, and was handwritten by Anke Welton.

Dear Sheriff Reinhardt,

The enclosed reports contain all of the information that you asked for. I sincerely hope that they will assist you in your quest to find Tina. As to Tina's state of mind, up until a week before she left us this last time, Tina was well adjusted and had long ago accepted that the State School was her home. She had a special relationship with Joey Jacobsen (see separate report). They were friends for most of their lives. Tina became extremely agitated when we told her that Joey would be leaving for short periods of time on a trial basis to live outside of the school. Tina requested to go home, and everyone concerned thought that a separation from Joey would be for the best while we waited for the legal permissions to be completed for Joey's departure. That decision has turned out to be a terrible mistake. I pray that you find Tina alive and well. Please bring her back here so I can keep her safe.

Sincerely,
Anke Welton
Admissions Supervisor

I put the letter down and shivered deeply.

The cold had invaded my bones and my heart. Had I missed something? Joey was going to live outside of the school, at least part time, but where was he going to go? Anke hadn't said a word to me about that. Maybe Joey's trial basis leave had been canceled because of Tina's disappearance. The answer, I assumed, was in the other report.

I put everything from Tina's report back into the envelope and pressed the tape as hard as I could. There was no way I could hide the fact that I'd broken the seal.

I took a deep breath before opening the other envelope, then looked out the window. The snow still fell, still swirled around the truck in the wind. If the weather didn't settle down soon, the Studebaker was going to be buried. I was going to have to go outside before long and clear out the tailpipe so I could start the truck's engine.

I opened the other envelope as carefully as I had the first. As Anke's

letter had implied, this report was about Joey. She revealed his existence to Guy in the letter. That was a weight off my shoulders. And,
like me, she felt that Joey was related to Guy's inquiry, to the crime or
crimes that had taken place in Dickinson.

Joey's admission report was almost identical to Tina's. His birth-
date, 12/22/1950, and his admission date, 12/24/1950, were stated
exactly like her document. The form was signed by Nils Jacobsen and
Anke Welton. There was no mention of the mother.

I closed my eyes and imagined Nils as a young man driving on a
snowy day, on Christmas Eve, to deposit his defective son in the school.
Who was with him? The mother? His parents? Or was he alone? I doubted
that I would ever know. His day must have been as horrible as Toren's.

The papers in Joey's report were in the same order as Tina's. The
next record was a mimeographed copy of Joey's birth certificate. My
eyes scanned past the father and fell directly on the name of Joey's
mother. I gasped out loud and had to look at the name three times to
make sure I understood what I was seeing.

The name on the birth certificate was Darlys Gertrude Gustaffson.
"Darlys," I whispered. "Oh, Darlys."

The mimeographed document slipped out of my gloves.

I let the birth certificate drift to the floor as I laid my head against
the gun rack and closed my eyes. I didn't have to work too hard to
remember Darlys Gustaffson before she became Darlys Oddsdatter.
Tall, blonde, of Swedish descent, and related to most all of the Gustaffsons in Stark County, including Lloyd, the extension agent who had
introduced me to the USDA indexing course, and his nephew Lester,
who worked for Jaeger Knudsen.

As a child and teenager, Darlys had glowed brighter than the sun.
Everybody noticed her when she walked into a room. Not only men,
everybody, old and young. She was stunningly beautiful. She walked
like a timid doe, though, and there were times when Darlys was aloof,
unapproachable. We weren't girlfriends. Darlys was a town girl, a cheer-
leader–glee-club–student-council kind of girl. She was busy with a
packed social calendar even back then. I was a bookworm and a farm

girl. Our paths didn't cross much. I didn't know much about Darlys, didn't keep track of her love life, the boys she dated.

I worked my way through my memory of high school as slowly and methodically as I could to connect Nils and Darlys. There was nowhere in my memory where I ever saw them together, holding hands at school, on a date at the church ice cream social, nothing.

Was she with Nils when he gave up Joey? Did they drive to the State School together?

I wasn't sure that I would ever know, but my thoughts turned to Nils.

My memories of Nils were at the Red Owl when he was a sacker—a long way from manager—and on the basketball court, playing ball, even though he really didn't have the height for the game. Maybe, I thought, if I couldn't connect those two then Guy Reinhardt could. He had been the king of basketball in the county at that time. He hadn't gone to the same school as Nils, but I bet they knew each other. I bet they did.

Darlys, I whispered again. *Poor Darlys*. All of these years, I thought she couldn't have children. I thought we were in the same club, barren, on the outside of expectations to give the world a child. A woman was considered a failure if she couldn't have a child. We were joined by a social and physical inability to contribute, to share in the joy of watching our children become part of the community. At least I thought we were. Now I knew different. Darlys had given birth to a mongoloid boy, out of wedlock, with one of the most well-known and nicest boys in town. That must have been a hard secret to keep—for them both.

I suddenly remembered a conversation I'd had with Lene Harstaad. I asked her if there were any other girls in town like Tina Rinkerman, and Lene's face had flushed red. And then she'd said, *"Why would you ask me such a thing, Marjorie?"* Now I had to wonder if Lene knew about Joey.

Someone had to know. I was stunned by the discovery of Darlys's name, but somehow, as I let the information digest, I wasn't surprised.

Darlys wasn't the first girl in our town to get pregnant as a teenager, and she wasn't going to be the last. Maybe an out-of-wedlock child was a scandalous mark her family had a hard time bearing. I could see that, but people had sex. Young people who didn't understand the consequences let their desires get the best of them. I had. I wasn't a prude. I grew up on a farm and learned about sex and death at an early age. I understood that a moment of passion could change a person's life, like stepping in a gopher hole had changed Hank's life. Things happened. Bad things. Out of our control. The recipe for making Joey and Tina got all mixed up. No one was at fault, not everybody got a perfect child. I didn't blame God; I blamed nature.

Darlys had moved on with her life, married Henrik Oddsdatter, the local dentist, and had lived happily ever after. I'd thought so, anyway. Darlys lived in a beautiful house, wore fancy clothes from the best shops in Bismarck and Dickinson, and drove a pretty red car. I thought Darlys had everything a woman could want. Everything but a child. That's what I'd thought. But I was wrong. I didn't know anything about Darlys Oddsdatter at all. Not really. Not anymore than she knew about me.

Life, I thought, had moved on for Nils as well. He'd married Anna, become the manager at the Red Owl, had three healthy, happy children, and maybe another one on the way. He had something Darlys could not and would not ever have. Was there a motive for murder mixed up in their old relationship? And if there was, did that mean Darlys had killed Nils? Was she a suspect?

"Yes," I said aloud. "I think she might be."

CHAPTER 32

I couldn't take the cold any longer. I didn't care if someone was out there waiting for me or not. I bundled myself up, grabbed the flashlight and four flares from behind the seat, sucked in a deep breath, and shouldered my way out the door. I left the .22 behind. I only had so many hands, and they were full. If I didn't get warm soon I was going to die.

The wind and snow attacked me immediately, pummeling my face with small, frozen crystals, as hard and sharp as sewing needles. I looked away from the wind and pulled my hood over my head. I almost dropped the flares on the ground. They would have disappeared in the snow. I'd be lost for sure if that happened.

I hung onto the truck and edged my way to the rear end, fighting the wind. I felt vulnerable without the rifle, but I didn't let my fear stop me as I made my way to the tailpipe.

The exhaust was clogged. If I'd run the truck for a long time without the window down, I could have killed myself with the fumes. After clearing the snow from the tailpipe, I stood up with my back to the wind and lit the first flare. A steady red flame sputtered forth, bringing an eerie glow to the blanket of white in the darkness. Suddenly the entire world around me looked aglow with fire.

I threw the eight-inch candle-shaped flare as hard as I could, straight back from the tailgate. Then I turned to the right of the truck and threw another flare, followed by a throw of another one to the left side.

I edged myself back up to the driver-side door and threw another bright red flare straight out from the hood. I threw a flare in each direction in hopes that I'd hit the road, that someone would see one of them somewhere.

I slid back into the Studebaker and turned the ignition key, hoping that the engine would start. Thankfully the truck started. I could relax. All I had to do was wait for the engine to warm up and start blowing hot air out of the vents. My plan had worked. I didn't need the rifle. I locked the door anyway.

Satisfied that everything was going to be all right, I drank some water and ate a Hershey bar. I decided that I would turn on the radio and try to find a weather report, or at least a strong station. The weather would play sooner or later.

I found a radio station that only crackled a little bit. They were playing orchestra music. I didn't mind what they played and left the dial there. I wasn't alone. That was all that mattered.

I hadn't lost my train of thought about Darlys. She was all I could think about past my own survival, past making sure I was going to stay warm and safe. I was still confident that I could last two or three days in the truck if I had to. *"Just stay put, Marjorie,"* I heard Hank say again.

I hated to think of Darlys Oddsdatter as a murder suspect, but I had no choice. I needed to think back on the events surrounding Nils's murder that I knew. Could Darlys have killed him? I knew that there was a lot of information that I didn't have, couldn't have. Like where was Darlys the night Nils was murdered. I hadn't had any reason to think that she was involved in the crime until now. I figured she was at home, with her husband, where she belonged. But I didn't know that to be the truth.

What I didn't know frustrated me. I angled the flashlight so I could read again, then picked up the next piece of paper in Joey's report. Like the paper in Tina's report, this document was a "Procedure Completion Report." I expected to see Joey's name, since the document was in his file, but I was wrong. Darlys's name was on the report.

Darlys? I whispered again. Only this time I questioned what I saw. Why . . .? I had no choice but to read on. The form was exactly the same as Tina's, except this one was underlined in a different place:

Subject has been determined to be either <u>mentally insufficient</u>, insane, a confirmed criminal, a defective, rapist, or an idiot.

Tina was diagnosed as a defective, while Darlys was determined to be mentally insufficient. I trembled from the discovery, not from the cold.

The paper was signed by Darlys's father, Stefan Gustaffson.

The procedure was approved by her own father.

My heart raced as I let what I had found sink in.

Darlys couldn't have any children because she had been sterilized in 1951, not long after giving birth to Joey. All she would ever have was Joey.

I felt so sorry for her. I couldn't imagine such a thing. I was heart-broken for Darlys, and for Joey and Nils, too. They had carried a horrible secret all of their lives. Nils and Darlys were connected in a way that I could never have imagined.

I took a deep breath, noticed warm air hitting my face for the first time. The music on the radio played on. I was going to be all right, but honestly I wanted to cry. My loss of Hank seemed so easy, if that were possible. I had spent as much time with Hank as I could, and when he died, his passing was peaceful. Nils was brutally murdered, and Joey was left without a father.

I didn't know how or why Darlys came to be sterilized, but being mentally insufficient was a broad description. *Had her parents stood by that? Who decided?* Or had they insisted on the procedure after she gave birth to Joey, in his condition, without being married to Nils? Again, I couldn't know that. But Guy could find out.

I set the procedure completion report down and picked up the last piece of paper in Joey's report, a visitation record. Like Tina's there were a lot of lines with various writing styles. The visitor's name was the same over and over again: Darlys. She had come to see Joey at least every other month from 1953 on. My guess was that when she'd gotten her driver's license or had come of age she had started making the trip. I was comforted to know that Darlys and Joey had spent some regular time together. I felt better knowing they did have a relationship; they did have each other in their lives. And like any good indexer should when something on one page connects to another, I quickly went back to Anke Welton's letter in Tina's report and cross-referenced the information I'd discovered in Joey's visitation record.

Tina became extremely agitated when we told her that Joey would be leaving for short periods of time, on a trial basis, to live outside of the school.

I had to assume that Joey was going to go live with Darlys. But she hadn't said anything to me about a big change coming in her life. In all of her visits to my house for the Ladies Aid, Darlys did nothing to imply that she was getting ready to welcome a boy like Joey into her life, into her house, into her world. Maybe she had a plan. Darlys always had a plan. Maybe Joey was going to be one of her good works projects. Everyone would have believed that and never questioned her for one second. Everyone would have admired her. Everyone but Nils.

I sighed at the thought. I was getting close. I could feel the stitches pulling my thoughts together tighter. I needed to look at my personal index again. I needed to see if I had missed something, or if that something—or someone—was there all along, staring me in the face.

Darlys's was the only name on the report for year after year. Nils's name didn't appear once. Nor did Stefan Gustaffson's. The last time she had visited Joey was right before Christmas in 1964. She'd visited him on December 22, the day of his fourteenth birthday.

I looked closely at the end of the report and saw another name. One name, noted a single time on the last line of the report. A name that made no sense to me at first, then concerned me that he was alone, at the State School on his own, but maybe I could rationalize his presence. Maybe.

The visit was dated the day before Nils was murdered.

Maybe I was wrong about Darlys. Maybe she wasn't a suspect. Maybe she had set something in motion that had gotten out of hand, gone in a direction that she could have never dreamed. Sometimes good intentions weren't enough. Life took over. Bad things happened.

I stared at the name and I had to wonder: Had Henrik known about Joey all along, or did he only find out about him recently?

CHAPTER 33

*T*ap. Tap. Tap.

I nearly jumped out of my skin, rousing quickly from a shallow sleep. I had dozed off, which I'd tried to avoid, but the day had started early and I was beyond tired. Darkness and warmth had overtaken my senses. Lesser mistakes had killed people.

Tap. Tap. Tap.

The snow fell away from the driver's side window. I reached over and grabbed the .22.

"Anybody in there?" someone shouted.

Fear had frozen in my throat, then thawed quickly when I saw the image of a man come into view. He had his right hand cupped over his brow, focusing his vision into the cab of the truck. "Are you all right, lady?" he said. "I can get you out of here."

"Yes," I said as loud as I could. "Yes, I'm fine."

I opened the door, allowing a cold blast of air to rush inside. I still clung to the rifle, holding on for dear life. I believed the man could help me, but I wasn't going to trust him right off. Too much had happened.

"Boy, you sure got yourself in a heck of a mess, aye?" The man had a kind face, covered in a graying beard, peppered white from the snow. "I can winch you out of here with da rig, but I'm gonna need some luck to get ya out of here. Can you walk up to the truck and stay warm till I get things hooked up?" His deep North Dakota accent was a comfort to my ears and heart.

"Yes," I said.

The man peered inside the truck and his gentle face drew closer to mine. He looked me up and down, then at the .22. "Looks like you thought ahead. Got everything you need, aye."

"You never know what's going to happen out on these roads."

"Ain't that the truth." The man pulled back and looked up at the sky. "We better get you out of here. Storm's headin' east. Fargo's gettin' a brutal blast from da north, but west of here is dwindlin' down."

"That's good to hear. I need to get home." I started to gather up the reports, everything I wanted to take with me. I wasn't leaving those papers in the truck on their own, not even for a second.

"Name's Harald Crane, by the way. Where might home be?"

"Dickinson," I said, as I angled my body out of the truck.

"Aye, I came through there. Roads are clear about a hundred miles east of Bismarck."

I stood up with my purse in one hand and the reports in the other. I looked back inside at the rifle, and the man recognized my hesitation.

"No need for that rifle," he said, "unless you see some jackrabbits. I ain't gonna hurt ya, lady, I'm here to help."

Harald Crane had twinkling eyes even in the dark. I trusted him even though I didn't think I should. "My name's Marjorie. Marjorie Trumaine. My husband told me if I got stuck to stay put. Someone would come find me. All I could do was set those flares and wait. I really appreciate you stopping on my account."

"Your husband's a wise man."

"Yes, he was. He really was."

The rig was a big Kenworth with a long semi-trailer hooked to the tractor. Harald was hauling motor blocks to Detroit. The oversized truck wore a winch on the front of its long pointed nose. The hardy man connected a heavy cable to the rear of the Studebaker with ease. Then he ambled back to the rig and climbed in without a groan or complaint. Harald Crane was at least thirty years older than me and spry as a young goat. He told me he'd been driving a truck ever since he came back from fighting in the Pacific Theater in World War II, and had seen more of this country than he'd imagined possible.

"Gonna have to ask you to go back to your truck, Marjorie. I can yank you out, but you're gonna have to give the engine some gas."

"I've done this before."

"I imagine you have. You ready now, aye?"

"Yes." I walked back to the Studebaker with the reports and my purse in hand. The white carpet of snow crunched underneath my feet. The wind slapped at the back of my head, but I ignored the cold. I knew I had won my battle. The weather wasn't going to beat me this time.

Harald Crane and I managed to pull the Studebaker up the embankment with some concerted effort. Our years of experience driving in the snow paid off in spades. We said our mutual goodbyes and went our separate ways. But not before I told him to give me a call the next time he came through Dickinson. I promised to buy him a cup of coffee for his trouble.

Harald Crane was right about the condition of the roads. They were still icy and snow covered as I headed south, but once I finally made the turn onto I-94 the falling snow started to dwindle and the plows were able to keep up. I stopped for gas, then found a phone booth at the corner of the lot. I dialed the operator and made a long-distance call to the Stark County Sheriff's Department.

"Stark County Sheriff's Department. Dispatch desk. How may I direct your call?" George Lardner said. He was still working.

"George, this is Marjorie. Marjorie Trumaine."

"Good to hear from you, Mrs. Trumaine. Sheriff's been worried about you. He's had me callin' all over the state tryin' to find out where you were."

"Tell him I'm fine. I got stuck outside of Cooperstown. Someone ran me off the road."

"On purpose?"

"I don't know, George. Maybe. Maybe not. The weather was bad. If I was run off the road on purpose that person is long gone. I'm lucky that there's no major damage to my truck."

"Good thing that storm turned east of you."

"I got lucky. Look, George, can I speak to the sheriff?"

"He's not here right now. Be back later is what he said. The sheriff's been followin' one lead after the other."

"I planned on being back by now. Do you know if they've found Tina? Or solved the murder? I know you've been instructed not to tell anyone, George, but I really need to know."

The line went silent except for some static.

"No," George finally said. "There hasn't been a crack in either case. Sheriff said he feels like he's chasin' his tail, but that's between you and me."

"All right, George, you have to do me a favor. Tell Guy to go check on Darlys Oddsdatter and make sure she's all right. Tell him to ask her about Joey and if there are any problems because of that. Tell him to ask her who knows about the boy. Ask her about Henrik. I'm worried about her, George. Tell him to be careful."

"Who's Joey?" George said.

"That really doesn't matter, George. Darlys will know what this is about. You tell the sheriff exactly what I told you, and I'll head straight to the police station as soon as I get back to Dickinson. Tell the sheriff I have some information that he needs. This is really important, George."

"If you say so, Mrs. Trumaine."

"Do as I ask, George. I'm worried about Darlys." Henrik's name was on Joey's visitation report. If Henrik had known about Joey before then, wouldn't he have gone to Grafton with Darlys sooner? I thought so. The timing and the lone signature made my stomach churn. *Why was he there only once? So he could see what Darlys had brought into this world?*

"Okay," George said. "You be careful on the way back, Mrs. Trumaine. If I don't see you in a couple of hours, I 'spect the sheriff'll have the National Guard out lookin' for you."

"I don't think that'll be necessary, George." The line beeped, and I knew the operator was coming back on the line to ask for more money in ten seconds. "Goodbye," I said, and hung up. I didn't wait for him to saying anything. I didn't have time. I had to get back to Dickinson as soon as I could.

CHAPTER 34

I tried not to panic every time a pair of headlights appeared in my rearview mirror. The last thing I wanted to happen was to end up in a ditch again—or to feel like I was being tracked down and hunted. I couldn't take that chance. I had to stay vigilant and aware. I had the window cracked so cold air would hit my face and a Salem in between my fingers to give me something to do to keep myself awake.

Night had completely fallen hours ago. An impenetrable black sky surrounded me as a salt shaker of snow shook down in front of my headlights. The precipitation was light, a distraction my eyes were accustomed to. I could see the road and tire tracks clearly in front of me. Once I turned on I-94 I'd felt a sense of relief. The road would take me straight home.

I looked in the rearview only to see darkness behind me. Ahead, there was a distant pair of taillights, offering me a hint of pale red embers to follow.

I glanced over at my pile of papers and reports, feeling a tinge of pressure. Deadline pressure. I knew I'd lost a day indexing the *Central Flyway* book by driving to Grafton, but the day had turned out to be much longer than I had anticipated. Once I got home and got settled, I was going to have to focus entirely on the index and leave the Ladies Aid duties to the other women. After Nils's funeral, of course. I wasn't going to ignore Anna in her time of need. I sighed out loud, torn between the life I had built as an indexer and the life I was living after Hank's death.

I looked over at the papers again. My personal index sat on top of the pile. Driving didn't allow me to re-read its contents, but as I drove straight toward Dickinson I thought of something that I hadn't considered. Indexes weren't linear documents. On the surface, they looked like they had a start and finish, from A to Z, but that was only a matter of form. A reader with a question accessed the index at the point that they needed to find the information. No one would read an index from beginning to end if they were trying to find something that concerned pelicans. They would start with *P*. Another reader might look in the *W*s for waterbirds first. No one used an index the same way. As an indexer, I had to answer all of the questions a reader might look up. And that was my own revelation now. I was looking at Nils's murder as though all of the events were linear. A person's life, like an index, did not follow a straight line. We made decisions based on events or emotions that had occurred in the past. People carried references to their history with them everywhere they went, acted and reacted to them every second of the day. Bad experiences ruled people's daily lives in ways none of us could ever know.

Now that I had more information about Nils's life, I had a fuller picture of who he really was. Maybe now I could ask the right question: What had set the killer off? What had made him or her angry enough to commit murder?

I was sure that the murder was an act of passion of some kind. Betrayal. Hatred. Rage. Nils had one big secret as far as I could tell. I think, for a man like him, that was enough. I was sure Guy hadn't turned up any business dealings gone bad. This was a murder about passion, about emotions that got out of hand. I would stake everything on that assumption.

I thought I knew what had set the killer off. A boy none of us had known existed was at the heart of all of this. All I had to do was make my way to the Sheriff's Department and see if Guy agreed.

The snow-covered, green Welcome to Dickinson sign was a sight for sore eyes. Midnight had come and gone. The veil of darkness had followed me home and touched all of the storefronts along Villard Street. Snow spit out of the sky with reluctance, and the wind had tamed to a breeze. Other than the streetlights, there was no sign of life, no activity at all.

The lower section of the courthouse was all lit up. The parking lot was scattered with cars, most of them covered with a couple of inches of fresh snow. I found a spot up front, got out of the Studebaker, and plugged in the block heater. Then I headed back to the cab to get the reports to take to Guy. I nearly slipped on the ice as I stepped up into the truck. I had been sitting for so long that my legs felt rubbery and weak. I ached all over and my eyes burned like I had read a thousand pages instead of driving five hundred miles. My forearms were sore from fighting the manual steering all day, and I felt like I needed a long, hot bath and a good night's sleep. But all of that would have to wait.

I was surprised to see George Lardner sitting at the dispatcher's desk as I hurried inside. "What are you doing here, George?" I said, as I set the manila envelopes and a few other papers down on the counter.

"I should ask you the same thing, Mrs. Trumaine, but I know better. Sheriff's on pins and needles waitin' for you to arrive." George looked like he hadn't slept for days. Dark circles accented his already bulbous, bloodshot eyes, and his wiry hair was more a mess than usual, in need of a comb.

"He's here, then?" I said.

"In his office. He said for you to go on back."

"No change?"

"Nope, not since I talked to you last."

"I was hoping for something else," I said.

"We all are." The phone rang, and George looked away from me, then picked up the receiver. "Stark County Sheriff's Department. Dispatch desk. How may I direct your call?"

I didn't move, even though I should have.

"Oh, hey there, Theda . . ." he said after a second. George noticed that I was still standing there and waved me back toward Guy's office. I heard him say, "Nope, I'm workin' a double shift. Sheriff's got everybody out lookin' or catchin' some sleep . . ."

I left George, pushed through the nearest door, and headed down a long, well-lit hallway. Guy's office was at the very end of the hall. He must have heard me coming. I was halfway down the hall when he appeared in the doorway. I smiled at the sight of him.

"Boy, am I glad to see you, Marjorie," Guy said, as he ushered me into his office. "I was startin' to think sending you to Grafton was a big mistake."

I offered him the envelopes. "You'll need these," I said. "Did you find Darlys?"

"Oh, heck no. After George talked to you, I sent Duke on over to the Oddsdatters." Guy sat down behind his desk. The top of the desk was a rat's nest of books, maps, and papers. He looked haggard and frazzled, too. Even more so than George. This case was really weighing on him. "No one was home, so I sent him over to the office. Everything was locked up tighter than a drum."

"That concerns me." I stayed standing.

"Oh, I don't think there's a thing to worry about, Marjorie. I called Doris Keating, his receptionist, you know, and she told me that Doctor Oddsdatter called her and told her to take a few days off. He and the missus were going out of town for a few days."

Even though I was warm and comfortable in the office, a cold chill ran down my spine. "I think there is something to worry about, Guy. Darlys wouldn't leave town; not now, not with everything going on. She was bouncing back and forth between Anna's house and the Rinkermans' like a tennis ball."

"Doris said the dentist takes his wife to Arizona a couple of times each winter. The only thing she thought was unusual was the suddenness of the decision to go, but she wasn't real concerned."

"I don't like the sound of that, all things considered."

"Why, what'd you find out, Marjorie?" Guy stiffened in the chair, sat up straight at the sound of my tone. I was sure the look on my face was one of concern.

I told Guy everything that I'd read in the reports and that Anke Welton had told me about Tina, then about Joey. But I stopped after that, hesitated and looked away.

"So Nils and Darlys had a son like Tina Rinkerman?"

"Yes."

"Boy, I woulda never thought that in a million years."

"Me either." I was talking to the wall. I couldn't look Guy in the eye.

"What's the matter, Marjorie?"

"I was stuck in the snow for a while, Guy. I wasn't sure that I was going to survive."

"George told me about that. I feel real bad that happened, Marjorie."

"I did something I shouldn't have done, Guy. I'm sorry, but I looked at the reports. I was afraid something might happen to them, to me. I wanted more than anything to help you out. I'm sorry. I know I'm not a policeman, that they were for official business. I only wanted to help."

Guy sighed. "I don't think there's anything in there to help us."

"You sound like you've given up."

"No. I can't . . ."

I grabbed Joey's envelope and pulled out the sheets of paper. I handed him the last report, the visitation report. "Look, I'm not sure that Henrik Oddsdatter knew about Joey before Christmas, but somehow he found out. He went to the State School one day, and then Nils was murdered the next. I'm not sure that all of this means anything, either, but you need to question him, see why he was there, and we need to find Darlys. She might be in danger. She might be in danger like Tina Rinkerman is in danger. We have to find them, Guy. You can't give up. If I'm right, something might happen to them that you'll regret for a long time to come."

"You really think Henrik Oddsdatter killed Nils?"

"I do," I said. "Yes, I really do."

CHAPTER 35

I stood staring at Guy, tempted to put my hands on my hips so he could see that I was serious, but I knew that really wasn't necessary. I had driven to Grafton and back, skirting a major blizzard. Nothing stopped me. Here I stood. If my presence didn't convince him that I was serious, nothing would.

"So," Guy said, "you think that Henrik found out about Joey and that sent him over the edge? Everybody's got a past, Marjorie. The dentist sure doesn't seem the type to go off the deep end to me."

"I don't agree. Darlys told me he was the jealous type. Controlling is what she called it. And I talked to him on the phone. He wanted to know if I knew anything about all of this. He was asking me about Darlys and her whereabouts. He was checking up on her."

"I can see that. Darlys Oddsdatter is a looker."

"She's a good woman, Guy."

"I didn't say that she wasn't. Just that men notice her, that's all."

He was right. I had seen it myself. George Lardner had looked Darlys up and down in a way that had made me uncomfortable. Henrik had probably seen that a million times since they'd been married. I was sure something like that could wear on a man. Especially if that man was predisposed to jealously.

"I think there's more to the story than just the jealousy, Guy. After Darlys gave birth to Joey and gave him up, she was sterilized. The paper said she was mentally insufficient, but we both know that Darlys Oddsdatter has never been insufficient at anything. I think her parents were horrified by Joey's birth, his condition, and made sure something like that couldn't happen again. I don't know that for sure. I don't know anything for sure. But she could never have another child. After that, she changed, got her life back together, kept herself busy with different kinds of causes, and married the town's most successful dentist. Darlys became the socialite she was destined to be from the beginning. I wonder if that put her back in good graces with her parents? That must have taken some effort and skill. She coordinated the Ladies Aid, among other things, and was friends with Anna Jacobsen.

"Now, I don't know what happened between Nils and Darlys, but they didn't seem to carry on their relationship after Joey was born. My guess is they went their separate ways. She saw Nils go on to have a productive married life, have three children of his own. Normal children. Darlys had Joey, who, if you look at the reports, she never gave up on. She visited the boy as often as she could." I took a breath and stared at Guy. His face was stoic, taking in everything I said. "Remember," I continued, "I speculated that Anna was pregnant? You didn't know. When I said something to Darlys, she said, 'That would be a tragedy, wouldn't it?' Maybe that was the straw that broke the camel's back. Nils having another child. Another reminder of something Darlys couldn't have."

"But what's that got to do with her husband?" Guy said.

"Maybe she finally broke down and told Henrik about Joey. Maybe she said she wanted to bring Joey home. No one would have to know Joey was her son. He could be one of her projects. We all would have believed that. We know Darlys. Or we thought we did. She would do something like that. She would take in a boy like Joey Jacobsen out of the goodness of her heart."

"I still don't see what you're gettin' at, Marjorie. I still don't think that would cause Henrik to snap. I think he would welcome the boy into his house. I think he would give Darlys whatever she wanted. He always has. A new car, a nice house, fashionable clothes, trips to Arizona in the winter. Darlys Oddsdatter didn't do without anything."

I stared at Guy. He was right. Henrik had given Darlys everything she ever wanted. "What if," I said cautiously, "Darlys had to have Nils's permission to bring Joey home, and Nils refused to give her his approval? Anke Welton's letter says that's all they were waiting on for

Joey to leave the school. Legal permissions." I stopped and dug through the pile of papers, found the letter, and handed it to Guy so he could see for himself.

Then I kept on talking. "What if the only way to bring Joey home was to get Nils out of the way so Darlys could have what she wanted? What if Nils said no to bringing the boy home. Do you think Henrik might kill him then? Wait for him in a hunting stand and ambush him? Nobody would know, and in the end Darlys could bring Joey home because she was the only surviving parent, his only legal guardian."

Guy sat back in his chair. The springs squeaked as he sighed. "Why would Nils go out there?"

"Nils and Anna got into a fight the night before he was murdered. I thought the argument was because Anna was pregnant again. Now I think they fought because of Joey. Nils told Anna about Joey because he had no choice, and they got into a fight. This was a bad fight, bad enough for Nils to stay the night in the Red Owl, away from his pregnant wife. He'd done that before, so she wasn't too worried at first. Maybe Nils called Darlys to clear things up, to tell her once and for all that he wasn't giving her his permission for her to have custody of Joey, I'm not sure. Henrik must have intervened, set up a meeting between the two of them. Henrik assured Nils they could solve the problem, come to terms of some kind. Why wouldn't Nils go? Henrik was a respected businessman, a respected member of society. Everybody's reputation was at stake. You know how this town is. Nils and Darlys had gone to great lengths to keep Joey a secret. Maybe he wanted to keep Joey a secret forever."

Guy sighed again. "This is all speculation, Marjorie."

"I don't have any proof that Henrik killed Nils. But my theory speaks to motive, and maybe opportunity if everything checks out, if Henrik can't account for his time, if he doesn't have an alibi. So, to answer your question, yes, I think Henrik killed Nils."

I stopped talking and stood there and stared at Guy while he considered everything I had said. As he did, I started to run through everything I knew about Henrik Oddsdatter to make sure I hadn't missed anything important. Henrik became a main entry in my personal index:

Oddsdatter, Henrik
  controlling
  jealous
  local dentist
  married to Darlys
  no children
  obsessed with perfection

"I don't know, Marjorie. I don't think a man would kill another man so his wife could have what she wanted," Guy said.

I took a deep breath and had to consider that he might be right. I was going down the wrong track. "Darlys told me I was going to be good at being a member of the Ladies Aid. I think you're going to be a really good sheriff, Guy."

"Why's that?"

"You ask the right questions, and you stand your ground when your gut tells you something's not right. You've got good instincts," I said.

Guy smiled. He had perfect white teeth.

"Wait," I said, recalling my conversations with Henrik. "What if Henrik was appalled when he found out about Joey?"

Guy put Anke Welton's letter on top of the pile, and sat forward in his chair. "Go on," he said.

"He went to see Joey for himself, to see if he could deal with it. Darlys could have been with him. He could have made her wait in the car. And he couldn't deal with what he saw. Maybe I was wrong about the permission. Maybe Nils *was* willing to give Darlys custody of Joey. Maybe Nils was tired of carrying a secret with him everywhere he went. Maybe he wanted to do the right thing, no matter the cost."

"That would mean Darlys could bring Joey home," Guy said.

"Yes, and Henrik's perfect wife wouldn't be so perfect anymore. Word would get out that Joey was Nils and Darlys's son. Henrik would have to share that story, have to share Darlys with a boy that was truly hers and not his. There would be a division between them. Maybe he couldn't handle it. Maybe he would be embarrassed by Joey. He said he and I were alike because we liked to put everything in its place, that we both pursued perfection in our careers. Maybe Henrik saw Joey as a defective, a feebleminded boy. Most people would. That's one of the reasons why the State School exists, so people don't have to see the flaws of the human race."

"So if he killed Nils, then the boy would have to stay in Grafton, out of sight."

"Yes, he knew he could control Darlys. He could refuse to give her his permission to bring Joey home. And," I said, "he wouldn't have to deal with seeing the man who had slept with his wife so long ago every time he went into the Red Owl. Maybe he couldn't bear the thought of Nils and Darlys together at any point in their life. Maybe he thought he was the only man in her life."

Guy sat back in his chair, sighed, and nodded. "I can see that, Marjorie. Especially if Henrik was as controlling as you say."

"Darlys said it herself."

Guy nodded. "I've seen how jealousy can destroy a marriage."

I didn't know what he was referring to. Guy had never talked to me about his marriages or why they didn't work, but I had to assume that he was talking out of personal experience. I wasn't going to pry. "There's something else," I said.

"What's that?"

"Henrik was at the Jacobsens' house after the murder. He was talking with Pastor when I came in and went over to say hello. He said something to me that I thought was odd at first. He said it was terrible that Anna would have to raise four children on her own, or something like that. I corrected him and told him that Nils and Anna only had three children. He cleared it up by saying that he couldn't keep up with all of the families that came to his office. What if he was testing me to see if I knew about Joey? What if he was there to find out who knew about the boy?"

"It's not exactly the killer revisiting the scene of the crime," Guy said.

"No, it's worse. It's arrogant and psychopathic."

"Or he's innocent, and he was at the Jacobsens' paying his respects."

"Don't you think you need proof of that?"

Guy sighed and nodded at the same time. "Okay, the motive makes sense to me. More sense than anything anyone of us has come up with since this whole thing started. But I have one more question."

"Sure," I said, "what's that?"

"Does your theory have anything to do with Tina Rinkerman?"

"Yes, of course. If Darlys felt like Tina was in danger, then she would have done anything to protect her. Darlys knew Tina. She visited Joey too often not to. Joey and Tina had a close relationship. They were friends. There's no way Darlys couldn't have had a decent relationship with Tina. There's a link there, a reference that's connected. If Darlys loved Joey, maybe she loved Tina, too. No matter what anybody did to Darlys, they couldn't sterilize the mothering instinct out of her. She took care of everything, of everyone. She would protect Tina if she thought she was in danger."

"Who would want to do Tina harm?" Guy said.

"There's only one other person in Dickinson who knows about Joey Jacobsen."

"Tina Rinkerman, as far as we know," Guy said. "She knows about Joey."

"She was in danger from Henrik, Guy. He was looking for anyone who knew about Joey. Darlys knew she had to protect Tina or he would kill her, too. If we find Darlys, I think we'll find Tina."

"What about Anna?" Guy asked. "Wouldn't she know?"

"I don't think she does. She never mentioned any indiscretion that Nils committed. As raw as she is, and as honest as she's been with me, I think she would have at least insinuated something about Joey, and she didn't."

"Okay, I can buy that. I hate to keeping playing devil's advocate, but Henrik and Darlys are in Arizona."

"Maybe that's a ruse. Maybe Henrik thought you were getting close to figuring out what had happened, and he felt like he needed to disappear."

"Or he thought you were going to put all of the pieces together, Marjorie. Maybe he was the one that ran you off the road."

"I thought that, too, at first, but he never came back. Wouldn't he have tried to kill me? Still, it might be the truth, but, Lord, I hope not. Henrik might be right here in Dickinson," I said. "I think you should check the house and his office again. Go inside instead of knocking on the door."

"I'll have to convince the judge of probable cause."

"You can do this, Guy. At the worst, I'm wrong, and they are in Arizona."

"And I'll have one angry judge on my hands for waking him up in the middle of the night."

"Or," I continued, ignoring the negative tone in Guy's voice, "we're right. Henrik is the killer, and Darlys and Tina are in big trouble."

He picked up the phone, and said, "I'm going to have to get a search warrant for the house and the office."

I stirred awake two hours later when Guy came back into his office. He had tried to convince me to go home, but I wasn't leaving. I'd told him that I would wait, that I needed to know if Darlys and Tina were all right.

Guy tried to be as quiet as he could. I was exhausted from the day, but my ears were tuned to hear any sound, even in what seemed like a sound sleep. I'd had plenty of training listening for Hank to have trouble breathing, or for him to call for me while I slept. Sleeping light was a skill I had acquired out of necessity, not desire.

I was huddled in an orange vinyl chair with my coat thrown over me for a cover. "Did you get the warrant?"

Guy stopped. He looked like a hungry boy sneaking to the Frigidaire in the middle of the night. "I'm sorry, I didn't mean to wake you, Marjorie."

I sat up, noticed the papers in his hand. "Is Duke going with you?"

"He's working an accident on I-94. Semi jackknifed. Three more cars slid off the road trying to miss the wreck. He'll be there a while working cleanup."

Harald Crane was heading toward Fargo and not Montana. I didn't have to worry that it was him in the accident.

"You're not going by yourself," I said. I regretted the words as soon as I said them. The innocent boy turned into an angry sheriff unaccustomed to being told what to do.

Guy froze, stiffened. "I can't call in reinforcements at this late hour based on your theory, Marjorie."

"I'm sorry. I didn't mean to say that." I took a deep breath. "I'll go with you, if that's all right."

"Marjorie, this is police business."

"I've been with you on police business before, Guy."

"You have . . ." Guy exhaled, relaxed a bit, stared at me like Hank used to when he knew he was in the middle of a losing argument. "If you're right, this could be dangerous."

"You're going to need backup. I'm all you have unless you want to trust George Lardner with a gun."

A smile flickered across Guy's face. "He couldn't hit the broad side of a barn."

"I can."

"I know you can."

"Backup, Guy. That's all. I promise. I'll do exactly as you tell me."

"If this was anybody but you, Marjorie, I'd send them packing."

"I'm not just anybody," I said.

"No, you're not." Guy hesitated, then reached down and strapped on his gun belt. "I'm assuming you have that peashooter of Hank's in the truck?"

"The .22?"

"Yeah, his Revelation. My dad bought me one from Western Auto when I was a boy."

"I wasn't going to leave home without protection."

"Too bad you don't have his shotgun with you."

"I haven't touched that gun since the day . . ."

Guy's face flushed red. He obviously felt like a fool for saying something about Hank's death. He was going to have to get over that.

"I'm sorry, Marjorie," Guy said.

"Don't be. I'll get the .22 out of the truck."

CHAPTER 36

The house was dark inside and out. The porch light was off, as well as the security light mounted on the single-car garage at the side of the house. Only the streetlight offered a view of the Odds-datters' neat little house.

Bare-limbed shadows danced across the brick exterior; spindly arms reached out of the darkness, touching nothing. Tall, snow-covered bushes sat at each corner, perfectly shaped in the fall to serve as Christmas trees.

The house was a two-story brick affair with the gable end facing the street. The place was modest, not a rich man's palace by any means, a perfect example of the Franco-Germanic architecture that was common in town. Henrik Oddsdatter maintained a dental clientele made up of humble, hardworking people. Anything fancy would have put people off. Darlys, everyone thought, was Henrik's pride and joy, but even she drove a Plymouth, not a Cadillac or a Lincoln Continental.

Guy turned off the engine, and the inside of the police car went dark. "I think you should stay here," he said, looking at me with a determined look on his chiseled, Gary Cooper face.

I forced a smile. "I've been stuck inside a vehicle for more hours today than I can count. I'll stay behind you. I'll only come to help if you call, if you find Darlys or Tina, if that's all right with you?" I wasn't going to overstep my boundaries again.

The police radio hissed with static, drawing Guy's attention. He picked up the mic and said he was, "10-23," which I knew was police talk for "Arrived at the Scene." George answered back with a tepid "10-4."

Guy set the mic back down and looked at me again. He reached over and gently touched my gloved hand with his. I didn't pull away.

"I don't want anything to happen to you, Marjorie. I couldn't live with myself if you got hurt because of being with me," he said.

Guy's tone and the seriousness in his eyes forced me to believe him. "I don't want anything to happen to you, either, Guy. That's why I think you should let me go with you. You might not have an hour to wait for Duke."

"Okay, you're probably right. I know you can handle yourself." He didn't pull his hand away; he let his touch linger. His deep blue eyes softened, changed in a way that made me uncomfortable. I looked away, then reached for the door handle, breaking contact. I couldn't breathe, and I didn't like how I felt, how the atmosphere inside the car had changed. For a brief second, I was somewhere sultry, tropical. A surprise in the darkness of a snowy night.

Cold air rushed against my face as I stepped outside, washing away anything but the reality of our presence at the Oddsdatters'.

I waited for Guy to get out of the Scout, then followed him up to the front door. He had his weapon out, a Police-Special .38 caliber, and I carried the .22, with a round set in the chamber. The safety was off. I only had one shot.

Guy peered into the triangle window, then tried to open the door. I was surprised that he didn't knock on the door and present the warrant to Henrik—if he was home. Guy motioned for me to follow him as he made his way to the side of the house. He edged along the cold brick like a burglar might, shuffling through half a foot of virgin snow all the way to the garage, trying not to be seen. I followed in his tracks and came to a stop next to him. He grabbed a flashlight off his belt with his free hand, then shined the familiar beam inside the garage window.

"What kind of car does Darlys drive?" Guy whispered.

"A red Plymouth Fury."

"There's a black Pontiac in there. Now I know what to look for if we have to leave."

A black car. I guess the make might have been a Pontiac. I didn't say anything, but I would when the time was right, if I had to remind Guy that I thought I'd seen Tina in the back of a black car driving down Villard Street.

Guy turned off the flashlight, then headed to the back door, which was a couple of healthy steps from the garage. He stepped up on the stoop, opened the screen door, and knocked as loud as he could. "Doctor Oddsdatter, this is the sheriff. If you're home, please come to the door." Then he knocked again, cocked his ear, and listened for a sound of any kind.

I couldn't hear anything, didn't see a light come on. A dog barked a few houses down, and my attention was drawn away from Guy for a second. I wished Shep was with me, keeping a lookout.

Guy knocked again, even louder this time. He waited a second, then knocked again.

Nothing.

Without any warning, Guy reached for the doorknob. The door opened at the first turn. He wore a quizzical look on his face. "Everybody's locking their doors these days," he said in a soft voice.

"Maybe Henrik doesn't have anything to be afraid of."

"I'm going in. You stay here. If anything happens, you go back to the Scout and radio George and tell him you need help ASAP."

I watched Guy edge inside the house uninvited. He turned on the kitchen light, announced himself again, and walked out of sight, making plenty of noise as he went, hoping, I was sure, that Darlys and Henrik were sound sleepers, up in their bedroom, completely unaware of what was going on. I hoped so, too.

After Guy searched the entire house and found nothing out of place, we drove straight to Henrik's office, which sat a block off Villard in a sixty-year-old building that had originally belonged to a deed and title company. Henrik's dental practice was on the second floor. All of the floors were marble, the ceilings tin, and the walls paneled in burled walnut. The office was old luxury made modern with a waiting room, a television, and the latest, most comfortable chairs and most up-to-date equipment.

Guy parked across the street from the front entrance with an ear turned to the police radio. There was no sign of Darlys's red Fury.

Duke radioed that he was on his way.

"We're going to wait until he gets here," Guy said.

"What if I'm wrong? What if Henrik and Darlys *are* in Arizona?"

"That would be a good thing, right?" Guy said.

"Yes, of course, but then you wouldn't be any closer to figuring out who killed Nils or where Tina is."

"I'm not going to give up until I solve this crime, Marjorie. I don't care how long the investigation takes, or if the whole town gives up on me. I don't care. This happened on my watch. I've known these people most all of my adult life. None of us should live in fear of losing our child or find a good man like Nils Jacobsen dead like we did. I'm sorry you're here at all, Marjorie. I wish you were home asleep like the rest of the town." He looked over at me, stared me in the eyes, and said, "How did you figure this all out? I know you read the reports, but I'm not sure I would have been able to put all of that together."

"I don't know, parsing information is what I do, I guess. I'm an indexer. I organize ideas and words so they make sense to readers, to strangers. But everything has to make sense to me first, I guess."

"I'm sure glad you got a brain in that pretty head of yours."

I blushed and looked out the window. There was nothing I could say to that. I felt relieved, assured. There was nowhere else I would have rather been. But I didn't say that. I couldn't.

A pair of headlights cut through the darkness and headed toward us. Duke Parsons pulled up alongside Guy's Scout, leaned over, and rolled down his window. Guy followed suit.

Duke craned his neck and looked at me with surprise and disdain all rolled into one. "What's she doing here?" he snapped.

Guy looked at me, then back to Duke. "We wouldn't be here if Marjorie hadn't figured this out."

"Great, another wild goose chase," Duke said.

"Deputy, if you don't mind showing some manners and respect, Mrs. Trumaine is here because she brought me some information that I asked her to retrieve. We both feel there's a good possibility that our suspect is holed up somewhere close."

"You have a suspect now? Since when?" I could see Duke roll his eyes even in the darkness. I wasn't the least bit surprised by his reaction to my presence.

"I do have a suspect, and we're going to go search Doctor Oddsdatter's office."

I sat there with my mouth shut. I was staying out of this.

"Can't this wait? Doctor Oddsdatter, really, Guy?" Duke said.

"No, this can't wait," Guy said. "I don't have time to explain all of my reasons to you."

"Well, she's not going with us," Duke said.

Guy looked toward me with stern eyes and squared his shoulders. "Yes, she is. I'm not leaving her out here by herself."

The office door was locked. There was no way in other than to break the door glass that bore Henrik's name and announced his profession as a dentist.

"The janitor's closet's in the basement," Duke said. "The key to the office is in there."

"We'll all go. Marjorie, you stay between us."

Only the light from the exit signs lit our way. Duke led, and Guy followed, but in the darkness I could still read anger brewing on Duke's neck, just under his skin. He had never liked me, and I was certain, from this point forward, that he would hate me.

The marble floors echoed all around us. There were no other sounds as we descended into the building's basement. The basement wasn't like the cellar under my house, full of spiders and unseen creatures, but was made of cement bricks, with walls, storage rooms, and hallways shooting off in every direction. Guy used his flashlight to light our way to the janitor's closet, aiming the beam at the floor so we wouldn't announce our presence to anyone.

There were no sounds to be heard in the basement other than a constant drip of water coming from an unseen faucet somewhere close. The basement smelled musty, old, with an undercurrent of decay to the odor.

Duke led us to the janitor's closet. He grabbed the doorknob and shouldered his way inside as quietly as he could. I had no idea how he knew where the closet was or how to open the door, but he did. He quickly returned with a key in his hand.

As Duke handed the key to Guy, I thought I heard a sound, a whimper. Duke froze. The keys dangled a few inches from Guy's hand, who looked toward the sound, toward the whimper. I was sure I had heard a whimper.

CHAPTER 37

Guy flipped the flashlight off. He stood there and let his eyes adjust to the darkness. The whimper seemed distant, coming from somewhere at the end of the hall we stood in. The sound could have been anything in that old building—a rat, a joist creaking under the weight of the snow on the roof, anything.

Guy motioned for us to follow him. All three of us edged along the wall, our individual weapons at the ready. I didn't like where I was, what I was doing, and I was starting to rethink my decision to come along when I heard the sound again. Someone was crying.

Nothing could have stopped me, then. If Darlys or Tina were hurt, I'd be the first one to help.

The cry echoed down the hall and was quickly followed by a muffled voice, a male voice. Angry, intent on admonishing or quieting whoever was crying. Then silence.

I could feel Duke's hot breath on the back of my neck. Guy was nothing more than a silhouette leading the way. I was inches from him.

We finally arrived at the end of the hallway, which, to my surprise, turned left and went deeper into the bowels of the building. A sliver of dim light reached out from under a door about thirty feet down the hall.

Guy stopped and mouthed, "Stay here."

I didn't argue or ask him to repeat himself. I knew what he meant, and why: *You're in danger. Let us do our job.*

No words were needed for Duke to understand, either. He pushed past and rubbed against me to let me know he was there. The move was done in a bullying kind of way, to show who had power and who didn't.

He smelled of sweat and discomfort, like he hadn't had a bath after three days of baling hay. I plastered myself against the wall and kept my eyes on the moving shadows. My breath was caught in my lungs. I really didn't like that man at all.

Guy and Duke took up their positions on each side of the door. The light didn't flicker or move as it would if there were someone moving inside the room.

Then the whimper came again. The sound reminded me of a first-year doe that I'd hit with the truck driving back from town. The cry of its pain had been too much to bear. I'd had no choice but to put the poor thing out of its misery. There was still hope for a rescue here.

The whimper was followed by the voice. Even from where I stood, I recognized Henrik Oddsdatter's voice. So did Guy.

He didn't hesitate to pound on the door with his fist. "This is the sheriff, Doctor Oddsdatter. There's no way out. If you come out peaceably, I'm sure we can talk this over." Guy was demanding, firm, but not threatening.

A female scream came right behind Guy's words. I couldn't tell if the scream had come from a grown woman or a girl. Then the sound vanished. Like someone had put a hand over someone else's mouth.

Seconds seemed long and strained. Finally, Henrik said, "This is a family matter, sheriff. You need to go on about your business."

"I have a warrant."

"This is a family matter," Henrik said again. The light vanished, and darkness overtook the hallway. Any detail I could see on Guy or Duke's face disappeared.

I heard rustling inside the room, followed by a groan or a moan, I couldn't tell which.

Guy flipped on his flashlight and motioned for Duke to go low. He was going in high. Then Guy looked to me and mouthed words I knew all too well. *Stay put.*

Without any warning or further requests, Guy set the flashlight on the cold floor, then stood up and kicked in the door. "Everybody put your hands up! Everybody put your hands up!"

Duke's flashlight clicked on, and I could see that he was kneeling at the edge of the door, his .38 Police Special aimed inside, exactly like Guy's.

Henrik didn't obey. I heard a loud explosion, a gunshot in a small room, a bright flash of orange, then a thud, and a yell from Duke as he tumbled backward. His gun fell from his grip and spun out of the light, into the darkness, out of reach. Bright red blood sprayed from his shoulder, and he crumpled to the floor on his side, eyes wide open, hurt, stunned, but not mortally wounded.

Henrik must have seen what I saw. He fired again, hitting Duke below the first wound.

Guy pulled back. I think he was uncertain where to shoot, afraid he might hit Darlys or Tina if they were close by. I didn't blame him for not taking a shot.

"Looks like we have a problem, sheriff," Henrik said. "If your deputy moves a muscle, I'll shoot again. Only this time, I won't be so kind. I can see his head clearly. Now, you need to drop your weapon, stand back, and let us leave. Then we can all pretend this never happened. You can tell everyone that this was a routine check and a vagrant shot your deputy. I am in Arizona."

Guy was still as a statue. "I can't let you do that, Doctor Oddsdatter," he said.

"You have no choice. You have Deputy Parsons's life in your hands."

Guy looked down at Duke. The deputy's eyes were wide with fear and pain. Blood pooled on the floor.

"Then you'll have two murders to answer for," Guy said.

"You don't know anything."

"I know that you killed Nils Jacobsen. You wouldn't be doing this if you weren't guilty."

"Guilty is an ugly word. We couldn't reach an agreement, much like we can't here. We're at an impasse," Henrik said. "I couldn't let him bring that boy here. Not now, not ever."

"You ambushed him."

"Put your weapon down, sheriff. I am not asking again."

"I can't do that." I could tell Guy was searching the darkness for a place to shoot, but he wasn't confident.

Henrik was as good as his word. Only he didn't shoot Duke, he shot Guy, hitting him in the forearm and sending the .38 flying into the air. I heard the steel bounce off the cement floor. Guy was smart enough to jump out of the way, leaping away into the darkness, out of Henrik's sight, but Duke was still at risk. The next shot would surely be at Duke's head.

I couldn't breathe, and my whole body was numb. I blinked and tried to regulate my breathing. I had to do something; I couldn't stand there one more second.

"Hold steady, Marjorie. Aim for the heart. That poor coyote's got distemper. Shoot to kill. Don't make the creature suffer." Hank's voice had come to calm me, to direct me. My father had taught me how to handle a rifle when I was a ten-year-old girl. I was the son he never had. I'd had no choice but to learn how to shoot on the farm. Reasons to fire a weapon didn't come along very often, but when they came I had to be ready. Hank had made sure I put into practice what I knew. We both took life and death seriously. There was no place for a soft heart on a farm like ours.

Henrik didn't know I was there. He would either shoot Duke, or he would go looking for Guy. I was betting on the latter.

I aimed Hank's Revelation .22 midway up the door. I breathed in, exhaled, put my finger on the trigger, and sighted the scope, which had come attached to the rifle when Hank's father bought the gun at the Western Auto store in 1935. I had to imagine that I was on the farm, stopping a rabid animal from doing any more harm.

The flashlight was still on the floor. I saw Henrik's shadow first.

"Never point a gun at anyone unless you mean to kill them," my father said, early on. I had both of them at my shoulder, urging me on.

I had no choice. Henrik had killed Nils. He would kill Duke and Guy to get away. He would kill Darlys and Tina to silence them.

And then he stepped into the doorway and stopped.

"Breathe in, pull the trigger back. Exhale, and release."

I fired the .22 directly at Henrik's heart. I couldn't miss. A small caliber rifle like the Revelation was difficult to kill a man with.

I hit my target right on.

Henrik took a step back with an odd look on his face. He turned to me, surprised at my presence. He pressed one hand against his chest, a pistol dangling from his other hand.

Blood began leaking through the fingers of the hand over his chest. He gasped, then staggered backward into the storage room. I heard him collapse a second later. I didn't follow; I didn't try to get another shot off.

Guy appeared in the beam of light with his weapon in his hand again. He rushed inside the room, yelling, "Drop the weapon! Everybody down!" But there was no answer this time.

Somehow, I made my way to the door as Guy flipped on the lights inside the storage room.

Henrik lay on his back, staring upward. He was dead. I had killed him.

I had killed a man.

Darlys and Tina Rinkerman were hunkered down in the corner, almost hidden in a pile of cardboard boxes, both of them very much alive. Frightened, but alive.

They held onto each other for dear life. They were shaken and afraid. Tears rolled down Tina's chubby cheeks. She understood what was going on, what had happened. I could see intelligence in her eyes. The same narrow eyes I had glimpsed on a dark, snowy night, floating by me on Villard Street. I wondered who had been driving, Darlys or Henrik, where they were coming from? I think I knew where they'd been going. Here, to the basement. To hide? Or to be safe? I would know soon enough, once the dust settled. All that mattered was that they were alive. The Rinkermans and Anke Welton would be relieved, but Darlys, oh, Darlys. She had joined the same club as Anna and me. The widow's club. At my hand. I had killed her husband.

I could find no joy in finding out that I was right about who had killed Nils Jacobsen or why.

CHAPTER 38

A few weeks later, the three women from the Ladies Aid showed up at my house right on schedule. I had bowed out, all things considered. Pastor John Mark still visited weekly, as well, and encouraged me to get out more, to get on with living, but winter still had hold of the land, all covered in a blank white sheet, and I had plenty of indexing work to keep me busy until spring. The farm would have plenty of demands once the thaw came. I would have little time for the business of town life then. My seven hundred and twenty acres, and my indexing work, would be demanding enough. Besides, I wasn't ready to face the world, to listen to the whispers. *She killed a man.* I wasn't sure that I would ever be ready for that.

Shep didn't get nearly as excited as he used to when the Ladies Aid came for a visit. Darlys had given up her directorship and had chosen her own seclusion. No one had seen her since the funeral.

Theda Parsons had taken Darlys's place, and I got the distinct feeling that Theda, like Lene and Anna, felt that the inside of the house was no place for a dog. Shep, ever keen with his sense of people, only roused a bit when the three women made their way inside the house. The dog lay by the Franklin stove the whole visit.

February's weather could be as bad as January's, but on this day there was no fresh snow on the ground, and the wind was only a slight breeze.

"Nice and warm in here, Marjorie," Anna said, as she kicked the snow off her boots on the mat inside the door. Once she took off her coat, I could tell her stomach had grown a bit since I'd seen her last. She was a little under three months along.

Anna handed me her bowl of Jell-O salad, then gave me a hug. "It's so good to see you," she said.

I smiled. "You, too."

Anna had picked herself back up after the funeral and decided to keep herself busy with the Ladies Aid for as long as she could. Everything would change once the baby came.

"Did I tell you that my mother's moving down from Stanley?" Anna said.

I followed her over to the table, leaving Theda and Lene to themselves for the moment. The seed catalogs were gone from the table, replaced by a big manila envelope that held the index to the *Central Flyway* book. I was done with that project and on to the next one, a book about growing and processing tea in China.

I sat the salad down. "That's good news," I said.

"Mother will be a big help," Anna answered, as Lene walked up to me and gave me a hug, too. Theda Parsons held back, her coat off, eyeing Shep nervously.

"I'm out of strawberry jam, so I didn't bring any sandkakes. I know they're your favorites," Lene said. She'd brought an apple kuchen, a German cake. I could smell cinnamon and cloves.

"That's okay. I'm just happy to see all of you."

After our hellos, we sat down and ate our treats, drank our coffee, and smoked our cigarettes. Anna was trying to quit, but she sneaked a puff of Lene's cigarette when I was in the kitchen.

"Duke says to tell you hello," Theda said.

"How's he doing?" I shifted uncomfortably on the davenport.

"Okay. The healing's comin' along slow. The doctors thought he might lose his arm at first, but that's not going to happen, thank goodness."

"What about his job?" I said, before I thought.

Theda didn't seem to mind. "Sheriff said Duke would always have a job, even if that meant tradin' places with George Lardner, don't ya know."

I smiled. "I bet George might have something to say about that."

"George will do as he's told." Theda stiffened, then took a drink from her coffee cup. "The sheriff's wound was minor, you know. He was back at work the next day."

I sat there stone-faced. Guy and I had only spoken once since the night in the basement, and that was when I'd made a formal statement at the station. The killing was ruled as self-defense. I wasn't going to face any charges.

Anna cleared her throat. "Come spring, I'm going up to Grafton, Marjorie. Me and Darlys are going to go see Joey and Tina. You're more than welcome to come with us."

I didn't know what to say. Darlys and I had little to say to each other. Time, I hoped, would take the sting out of seeing of me. I'd learned at Nils's funeral that Tina had gone back to the State School, and that Joey was going to stay for the time being, maybe for a long time to come, until Darlys got herself back together.

"Well, we'll have to see, won't we," I said. I hesitated. I had a question but couldn't bring myself to ask her. Anna knew me well enough to know something was bothering me.

"What's the matter, Marjorie?" she said, putting her hand on mine.

There's something I don't understand."

"What?"

"About Tina, but I don't want to talk about something that will bother you."

"I'm okay, really. I'm not over this, not by any means," Anna said, "but I know that Nils didn't do anything wrong. He was a good man. He made a mistake as a boy, and in a way he paid for his mistake all his life. Maybe he could have handled the situation differently, but we all keep a lot of things to ourselves, don't we? Nils loved me and the children. I know that."

"Good," I said. "But what I don't know is how Darlys ended up being with Tina?"

"I can answer that," Theda said. "Duke told me. Darlys knew Tina from her visits with that boy. Once Henrik found out about Joey, Darlys got worried about his state of mind. He was madder than she'd

ever seen him. She was afraid for Tina, so she called out to the Rinkermans, something she did regularly to keep in touch with Tina. Tina
answered the phone. Toren and Adaline didn't know Tina had spoken
to Darlys; they were out in the shop. Darlys figured she could hide Tina
for a few days until things cooled down, but they never did. Things got
worse. Darlys didn't mean to cause the Rinkermans any sufferin', she
was worried about Tina. That's why she put her in the basement."

"I thought maybe that was what happened, but I wasn't sure. Toren
and his wife must be relieved," I said.

"I think they are," Theda said. "They're not going to make any
trouble for Darlys. They figure she's been through enough."

We talked about the spring bazaar, the weather, anything we could
until the ladies decided to leave.

We all stood, and I said, "Can you wait a moment?" I went to the
bedroom without waiting for their approval and headed straight for
the closet. I stared at the box of clothes for a long second.

"Marjorie," Anna said, soft as a mouse, "can I come in?"

She'd startled me. I looked up to find Anna at the door, hanging
onto the jamb for fear of falling. Her face was ashen and her eyes
pleading. She had let me into her bedroom in her darkest hour. I saw
no reason not to let her into mine.

"Sure, is something the matter?" I said.

Anna stopped inches from me and spoke in a voice meant only for
me to hear. "There's more to this if you want to know."

"You don't have to tell me anything," I said.

"I do. This was all my fault. I knew about Darlys and Nils, you see,
but I didn't let on like I did. The past was the past. But I was jealous
of her. She was so beautiful, how could I blame Nils for wanting to be
with her? I didn't know about Joey, though, not until Christmas. I was
starting to have morning sickness, and I confided in Darlys that I was
afraid I was pregnant again. I shouldn't have done that. I wouldn't of
told her had I known everything."

"You can't blame yourself for what you didn't know," I said,
reaching and putting my hand on her shoulder.

Anna touched her belly. "I can. That was only the start of things. I set Darlys off. She hadn't told Henrik about the boy. I don't know how she kept her trips to Grafton a secret all those years."

I'd wondered about that, too. "Darlys kept herself busy. I don't think he ever knew where she was or what she was doing. She did that on purpose so she could breathe, have something of her own. Henrik was a jealous, controlling man. Her deceit took some effort, but Darlys could have probably driven to Grafton and back in one day, and explained her absence in one way or another. Henrik told me he rarely ever knew where she was."

"Once we all knew, Darlys wanted to bring Joey home for good," Anna said.

"I know that."

Anna's lip trembled. "But I said no. I didn't want to deal with that. A new baby was on the way. We would have four children. And him. A boy who would never grow up. I couldn't handle the thought of that boy being here. I told Nils and Darlys no. Nils wanted to be done with all of the secrets and finally get everything out in the open. He wanted Darlys to have the boy at home if that's what she wanted. And I said no." Anna burst into tears. I pulled her to me, into as tight a hug as I could muster. "This was my fault," she continued. "I told them no, even after Tina disappeared. Darlys stopped in the store on the way out here after Tina went missing. Of course, she knew where Tina was, but she pleaded with Nils to convince me to let Joey come home. She wouldn't say anything to me with Lene in the car, and I made sure I was never alone with her. Nils said he would talk to me again. I was afraid that Tina's disappearance had something do with Joey. I said no again after I got home from visiting you, then Nils and me argued. He stormed out and must have called Henrik, or Henrik called him to try and work the disagreement out, or not. I don't know. I was scared having that boy here would change everything. Make things worse than they already were. What would people think? Nils the father of a retarded boy? He could have lost his job. We could have lost everything . . ."

"This wasn't your fault, Anna. There was a better solution to this than murder."

Anna couldn't talk anymore. I let her cry. I wondered if she'd told Guy all of this? I hoped so. I didn't know what else to do other than sing her the lullaby that I'd sung to her in her bedroom,

> "Rock me a little, mama mine,
> And you shall have ribbons on your shirt.
> Do you want yellow? Do you want blue?
> Do you want shiny ones? I'll give them to you,
> On your shirt,
> Mama mine."

The song calmed her down. Once Anna caught her breath, she looked up at me, and cleared her eyes. "It wasn't your fault, Marjorie. I wanted you to know that. I wanted you to know that more than anything. It was my fault that you had to shoot Henrik. I would have come around. I would have said yes to Nils. If I would have been a better person, none of this would have ever happened. It was all too much. I'd just found out I was pregnant again. Now I'm left to wonder what would have happened to us all if I had said yes. I'll never know. That's the only reason why I came out here today, to tell you to blame me."

"Don't you worry about me. I'll be fine. I'm not going to blame anyone." I wasn't so sure of that, but I wasn't going to share my guilt and grief with Anna about what happened in that basement. Not right then. If ever. *I killed a man.* I really didn't know how I was ever going to be able to live with myself. "Come on, dry those tears. I think the ladies might be getting impatient. Lene was looking at her watch before I came in here."

Anna stood up, then said, "I'm sorry."

"It's okay, really." I picked up the box of clothes and walked out into the front room and handed it to Lene without any hesitation. "Here," I said. "Here's that box of Hank's clothes I've been promising you."

Lene took the box gingerly. She glanced at Anna, then back at me, and said, "Are you sure?"

"You know, Hank Trumaine's with me every second of every day. I didn't lose all of him. He still comforts me when I'm scared and encourages me when I need encouraging. I miss him more than I can tell you, but I can't keep hanging onto his things forever. Somebody else needs those shirts more than I do." I glanced over at Anna, who'd followed me. She still looked stricken.

"If you're sure?" Lene repeated.

"I am. I've never been more sure about anything in my life."

We walked outside, and Anna stopped to give me a hug. She started to say she was sorry again, but I stopped her. "We have to walk forward together," I said. She got in the car with the other two women, and they drove off, leaving Shep and me to ourselves.

Evening was in full swing, the ground white, the sky gray, and Hank's security light on the garage burned bright.

"Come on, boy, I've got some work to do. Let's go see how they make tea in China. Doesn't that sound like fun?"

Shep barked, spun around in a circle, and ran back inside the house. I followed him, closed the door, and locked it.

AUTHOR'S NOTE

The Dickinson, North Dakota, portrayed in *See Also Proof* is a fictional Dickinson. For the purposes of storytelling, the author has taken liberties with the history, map, and organizations that appear on these pages. For more information about the town, please visit the Dickinson Museum Center, 188 East Museum Drive, Dickinson, North Dakota, 58601, or visit online at dmc.omeka.net.

The book Marjorie indexes in this book, *The Central Flyway: Audubon's Journey Revisited* by Jacob T. Allsworth, is a product of the author's imagination. Information concerning birds that migrate, breed, and live in the central flyway may be found at http://www.audubon.org/central-flyway. Also, *The Life of John James Audubon, The Naturalist* (G. P. Putnam's Sons, 1868), edited by Lucy Green Bakewell Audubon, can be found online at https://archive.org/details/lifejohnjamesaud00auduiala, or in your local library.

Information concerning indexing and careers in indexing may be found at the American Society for Indexing's (ASI) website (https://www.asindexing.org/). The USDA correspondence course that Marjorie took to learn indexing is no longer in effect. ASI currently facilitates a training course that offers certification as an indexer.

The North Dakota Institution for the Feebleminded was established in 1901. The name was changed to the Grafton State School in 1933, and it is now known as the State Development Center. The Sterilization Law was passed in North Dakota in 1913 and was law until 1962. There were 1,049 victims of forced sterilization during this period. This novel is by no means a criticism of the Grafton State School and is not meant to take away from the good work that the Development Center does on a daily basis. Words such as defectives, idiots, insane, and retarded were commonly used in this era, including in the law itself. Such words in our modern world are considered hurtful and pejorative. Please note that the author has meant no harm or offense by using these words. The author has only sought to portray the realities of the time in history and the consequences that the law and practice of forced sterilization inflicted on society. The first instance of the use of the term Down Syndrome was found in an issue of the journal *Lancet* in 1964. The term would not have been in full use during the period portrayed in this story. For more information concerning Down Syndrome, please visit the website of the Global Down Syndrome Foundation (http://www.globaldownsyndrome.org).

ACKNOWLEDGMENTS

A special thanks goes to Dan Mayer, Steven Mitchell, Jon Kurtz, Jill Maxick, and to the publicity, marketing, and art departments at Seventh Street Books. All of your efforts to bring the Marjorie Trumaine mysteries to readers is greatly appreciated.

I am grateful to Norman Campbell, Matthew Clemens, Stephen King (we've never met, but his book *On Writing* is a continuing source of inspiration and advice), Cheryl Lenser, Erika Millen, Cathleen Snyder Small, and Brenda Stewart for their help and encouragement. This book would be less without their research contributions and suggestions. Any mistakes are my own.

Thanks also to Cherry Weiner, my longtime agent, who has been a champion of my work from the beginning. Thanks for everything that you've done, and continue to do, so I can carry on with my dream of telling stories. I couldn't do what I do without you.

And, finally, thanks to my wife, Rose. These stories have given us a life that we could have never imagined. I can't thank you enough for the belief, encouragement, love, and conviction you've shown me, and the world, over the years. Thank you seems so little for so much.

ABOUT THE AUTHOR

L arry D. Sweazy (www.larrydsweazy.com) has been a freelance indexer for nineteen years. In that time, he has written over nine hundred back-of-the-book indexes for major trade publishers and university presses such as Addison-Wesley, Berghahn Books, Cengage, American University at Cairo Press, Cisco Press, Pearson Education, Pearson Technology, University of Nebraska Press, Wayne State Press, Weldon Owen, and many more. He continues to work in the indexing field on a daily basis.

As a writer, Larry is the author of fourteen novels, thirty-one short stories, and forty nonfiction articles and book reviews. He is a two-time WWA (Western Writers of America) Spur award winner, a two-time, back-to-back, winner of the Will Rogers Medallion Award, a Best Books of Indiana award winner, and the inaugural winner of the 2013 Elmer Kelton Book Award. Larry also continues to speak and teach writing courses based on his twenty years of experience working full-time in the publishing industry. He has served on the faculties of the Midwest Writers Workshop and the Indiana Writers Center. He also conducts writing workshops at libraries and other locations throughout the Midwest. He currently lives in Noblesville, Indiana, with his wife, Rose.